MISTRESS OF BIRDS

MYSTERIOUS POWERS
BOOK SEVEN

CELIA LAKE

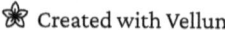

About Mistress of Birds

Thalia wants to make an impact.

Thalia's life is full of artists, authors, and other creative minds, but she's barely keeping herself together. After yet another rejection of her writing, she's willing to keep an eye out on a remote home on the edge of Dartmoor while her reclusive great-aunt takes a rest cure.

Reggie hasn't been the same since the Great War.

Adam's family have long since run out of tolerance for his continuing shell shock. His uncle's broken leg is the perfect excuse to get Reggie out of the house - at least he can make himself useful fetching and carrying. Adam's not at all sure he can be any sort of help to anyone. When he visits his uncle's apple orchard, he's even more confused by what he finds - and no one else seems to find the late-ripening apples at all unusual.

The house has its own secrets.

At first, the house seems a pleasant enough retreat for Thalia. The housekeeper and maid are competent, if distant. The food is wonderful, and she didn't have to buy or cook it herself. But there's the odd noise from the attic, the locked rooms, the ageless photographs. When she meets Adam, they can, at least, both agree that something is odd. The question is, can they discover the secret and change their futures?

Mistress of Birds is the seventh book of the Mysterious Powers series, exploring the institutions of Albion during and after the Great War. All of Celia Lake's Albion books exploring the magical community of the British Isles can be read in any order.

It is full of gothic mystery, feeling out of place, apples, birds, and how to move forward into a new stage of life. Enjoy this charming romantic fantasy set in 1927 with a happily ever after ending!

ALSO BY CELIA LAKE

Learn more about the world of Albion and future books at my website, celialake.com. Additional information linking characters, places, and timelines is available at bit.ly/celia-lake-wiki

Sign up for my newsletter to be the first to hear about future books and learn about fascinating bits of research. Happy reading!

CHAPTER 1

SEPTEMBER 9TH 1927, IN AN ARTIST'S STUDIO IN LONDON

"What are you working on now, then?" It was the inevitable question, and Thalia tried not to wince, taking a moment to figure out what to say. The party swirled around them, three dozen artists and writers and theatre people milling about and drinking someone else's drinks and eating someone else's food. Martha meant well, she really did. But the line between enthusiastic interest in other people's art and pressing on all the bruised and raw spots could be a very fine one. Martha didn't want anyone's art to be forgotten or lost, and she had reason for that, but that didn't make it any easier for Thalia.

Thalia was not precisely working on anything. She'd had another rejection in the post that afternoon. It had been the sparse 'does not meet our needs at this time.' Nothing but the barren signature.

Once upon a time, last year, the year before, she'd at least got a little personal note of encouragement, asking her to send the next thing along. This curt form letter felt like several steps back. Worse, she was neither young enough

1

nor new enough to be interesting to most people, especially not editors.

Selling that story would not have put food in the larder, or paid her rent, but it would have been a reason to keep trying. As it was, she was down to bread and cheese and a few tinned things. And whatever she could snag at a party like this one. She'd spent too much on books again this month.

To be fair, the food was rather good here. They were up in the long attic with clusters of old chairs, easels, bits of sculpture, and who knew what else. Anna and Una were eccentric, even for artists, with a giant wolfhound, three cats, and rumours of a parrot. But they also knew how to feed artists with more inspiration than sense. Lashings of tea, a reasonable amount of alcohol, heaps of sandwiches, and there were still some of those salmon pasty cup things that Thalia particularly loved.

Thalia had found a space in the corner she preferred, where she could look out at the lights and the people, but have a wall behind her. Not the cluster on the other end, that was mostly men who needed the wall behind them, who couldn't be surprised because it was horrible for them. They'd collected a lot of their usual set, the ones in their thirties who were constantly trying new things. Someone to her left struck up a bit of declamation, and Thalia turned to one side, trying to get her bearings again.

The illusionist who'd been performing across the room was quite good, actually, and there was someone doing intricate little designs in light and colour charms in the near corner. Another corner had a cluster of people tumbled over chairs, earnestly talking about stage costuming. And that knot there, nearer the door, seemed still deeply in the throes of a conversation about painting. Eston looked engaged, there on the sofa, and he was even chatting with someone rather than his usual distant observation of the frailties of humankind. Mercia, at the piano, looked like she was wrapping the music around her like a comforting shawl, a wall between her and the world, not realising it was getting a titch loud.

None of this answered the question and Thalia realised she'd been quiet far too long. "Honestly, town's so draining this time of year, isn't it? All the humidity." Weather was always a safe topic. The post had brought something else. She remembered she'd wanted to see what her friends thought. "Actually, that's the oddest thing. I had a letter from my parents today."

"Surely not terribly odd? You actually get on with them well enough, right?" Martha settled back, sprawling a bit in an oversized armchair. She didn't get on with her parents at all, and honestly, given her parents, that was probably better for everyone. They were rigid polemicists of the first order, refusing to recognise that Martha really did have a fair bit of talent as an artist.

"Well enough." Thalia considered. Well, they got on better when they were most of an island apart, to be fair, but that wasn't that unusual. Even if it was a smaller island than some. "Actually, it was about my great-aunt."

"Who's she when she's at home?" Peter leaned in over Martha's shoulder to grab a roll from the side table. He had washed up before coming along to the party, but not terribly well, and he had a large smudge of charcoal behind his ear. He must have had a long session in the studio again, and forgotten to eat. Possibly for a day or two, he did that. Once he had more food, he perched on the arm of Martha's chair.

"That's the point. She never leaves home. Large house

3

on the edge of Dartmoor, the land goes back near enough to the Normans, looks more like a castle than a house should, crenellations and everything." Thalia waved a hand and asked, "Could someone snag some of the salmon things and another sandwich, I don't care which?" She heard a noise behind her of amiable agreement.

"You are dawdling in your story, love." Hilaria shifted to prop one of her feet up on the chair Thalia had claimed. She was grinning, the sort of grin that meant she would come home from the party and be up all night sketching. She had the flat next to Thalia's. They had been friends for ages, and best friends since Hilaria had moved in five years ago.

They were not quite of an age - Hilaria was thirty to Thalia's thirty-three. Hilaria was stylishly dramatic, with gleaming black hair, pale skin, and a fine touch with cosmetics. Beside her, Thalia often felt a bit washed out, especially when they made a fuss for a night out. Medium brown hair, medium brown eyes, pleasant complexion. None of it made much impression. Like, apparently, her writing. She yanked herself away from those thoughts to continue.

"There is a certain amount of obligatory dawdling. See, Mother and Father have been trying to get her to go for a cure in the south of France for years now. And she's kept refusing, but now her health is actually worse. There's a housekeeper and all that, but Great-Aunt Avis won't go unless someone from the family can come stay at the house. For months, through the winter, most likely. And of course Mother and Father won't, and my sister is horrified anyone would ask her to give up the social season, and you can fill in the rest."

"Will she feed you?" Hilaria gestured at the plate someone was holding over her shoulder.

Thalia looked up, grinned at Oswald, and put the plate in her lap. "Ta, appreciated." She then waved at it. "Food is a considerable incentive. Yes, she would. But I've got the flat, and…"

That was the trick. You gave up a good flat, you'd never find one when you needed a place again. Not that it was a particularly excellent flat. She thought about moving at least one week out of four, and more like four out of four when the fogs were bad. But it was up above the worst of the fog and the smell of London. The light was quite good when the weather obliged, and it was hers.

All right, and it was also tiny, draughty, and she shared the loo and bath with the entire floor. She had only a small gas cooker, enough for tea and soup, but not much else. A writing desk, her bookshelves, double and triple stacked with books, and her bed. But still it was hers, earned by the work of her own hands. Mostly her fingers, to be fair, since she did secretarial work to pay her bills.

What was good about it, though, was the location. The building itself was full of her friends and artists and writers. All magical, so no one had to watch their tongue in the house, but with plenty of others to talk to in the nearby cafes and parks and theatres.

There was always someone to talk to, even when she really should be writing. And it was only minutes from the British Museum and its enormous library, and from any number of used bookshops. And new bookshops, but her funds rarely stretched that far. Anyway, she didn't want to give it up and risk never being able to come back.

Hilaria tilted her head. "Would you be up for letting it out? Tammy has a sister who's got a job working on a show that's likely running through the winter. I mean, if you had to come back early, she could sort something out, but she really didn't want to share."

"But the books..."

"There's space in the boxroom. And yes, even for the number of books you have. Remember, Bruce finally moved all of his sculpture wire out of the corner? We could stack them very neatly. You know it won't flood, and I think Polly has plenty of cedar blocks to keep out moths."

"Cedar's for clothes, not books." Thalia said idly. But the idea was beginning to grow on her.

"Would your aunt object if we came round for a bit of a hol?" Martha leaned forward. She could see what Martha and Lily and Michael would make of it now, wanting noise and bustle and picnic outings on the moor, declaiming over darling quaint village ceramics or wood carvings, all the things done the old ways. "You can't be all off on your own, darling, it's not remotely good for you." Martha wanted the bustle, she wanted to know where everyone was. Thalia found it a tad overbearing, now.

"It's not near anything." Thalia said immediately. "And great-aunt, and she probably would."

Hilaria snorted. "Might do you good. Some peace and quiet and a different library and climate. And you still haven't really got over your cough from last winter."

Thalia hadn't. Thalia kept trying not to think about that. To be honest, it wasn't like there was anything to do. She'd talked to the Healers after her mother had taken her to lunch and been very alarmed. It wasn't TB; it wasn't anything in particular, just the smog. Everyone coughed in London. Admittedly, some more than others.

"Might." Thalia let out a breath, then added to Martha. "Maybe she'd be all right with a few people? I can ask. But it's a long way from everywhere. It's not so bad getting to

Newton Abbott, but then there's a smaller line up to Bovey Tracey, and then it's, I don't know. Four miles? Six? From there. Long winding road, I remember that, and a pony cart. No public portal anywhere near."

"When's the last time you were there?" Hilaria leaned back, kicking her feet up.

"I was seven. No, maybe I was eight. Most of the summer, that was when my great-uncle was dying? Father's uncle. But the house has been in Great-Aunt Avis's family for yonks. There's no one around closer than the village except for the house and maybe a gardener's cottage or something? I vaguely remember a gardener whose grandson was about my age." She hadn't thought of him in decades. The chances he'd made it through the War, well, she couldn't think about that, not now. There was a crash behind her, then, that made half the room including her flinch and jump, and another three glasses went over in the aftermath. Someone gesturing too broadly, probably, not that knowing the cause actually helped with the panic.

Once everything settled again, Hilaria picked up without commenting on the interruption. None of them ever did. They just went on, as if there hadn't been a pause of a minute or three or five for everyone to get themselves back together. "So. On one hand, no distractions, except maybe whatever the library has. Pleasant environs, if a little full of moors, and free food. On the other hand, you've been hating the current secretarial work, you can let your flat to Tammy's *sister*, and we'd miss you terribly, but perhaps come and visit. Paint and sketch and opine about the desolate moors. People have built writing careers out of far less."

Hilaria gestured broadly with her hand. She nearly knocked over three wine glasses, and one of her rings collided with a fourth, ringing out a pure and clear sound.

Someone grabbed it to keep the glass from toppling over and the sound cut off suddenly, allowing the whole room to breathe again.

Thalia shook her head. "Are you that interested in being rid of me?"

"No, darling, never. Just - you know you're stuck. And you'll be in a foul mood all winter until something unsticks you. One couldn't possibly." She had a knack for voices, and this one was pure cut glass.

Like Thalia, Hilaria also came from money. The sort of money that would grudgingly pick you up if you got really desperate, and would send urgently needed pound notes on the obligatory festive occasions. Often a nicely large one. It was part of why they got on so well. Both of them would have turned into brittle society wives if they'd done as their parents wanted, and that was a particular kind of hell, or so Thalia thought.

She lifted her glass. "Well. I'll think about it. Write my parents and see how long they think I'd be wanted. And to Great-Aunt Avis about what exactly needs someone there."

After that, the party turned to other topics. A bit of satirical poetry first, that was always a favourite among their set. It went faster and faster, a frenetic desire to outdo each other in cleverness and wit. Thalia managed to win the awful limerick context with a well-turned phrase about a recent political cartoon Oswald had done. It made him blush in a way that meant she walked out with Hilaria an hour later, arm in arm. She didn't want Oswald to offer to walk her home. He wasn't a bad sort, but she was sure he was more interested in her, in ways other than artistically, than she was in him.

Hilaria had drunk a bit more than was probably good for her, but there were potions for that, and they even had some. Thalia wondered, suddenly, if she could get Great-Aunt Avis to run as far as a stipend, since she wouldn't be working. Or maybe her parents. Guilt could be a powerful incentive, and then she could put a bit of money away.

"You should go." They were coming down their street now, but Hilaria stopped, deeply earnest. "No, really, you should. I can feel it. Something important."

Hilaria got these moods. Thalia didn't really believe in messages from beyond, or whatever you wanted to call them. She wanted nothing to do with them, in fact. Not since her mother had fallen in with a whole nest of spiritualists after her brother had been killed in 1917. Most of them were predators, and the exceptions weren't much help to anyone, as far as Thalia could see.

On the other hand, one of the principles of their lot was letting people do their thing and see where it led. So long as it wasn't actually hurting anyone.

"I'll write, I promise. Tomorrow, though." If she wrote tonight, Father would disapprove of her handwriting. Which, of the things about her life he could disapprove of, was actually one of the better options, but still tedious.

Hilaria patted her hand. "Do. I'll miss you. I can come visit. Not a whole mess of people, just me. Though I think Martha's mostly worried about Adrian, he's been having a bad time, something about his lungs again." She took a couple of steps, then stopped again. "Didn't you have another letter in your cubby?"

Thalia sighed. "A rejection from *The Second Pan*."

"Oh, Thal." Hilaria turned and flung her arms around her shoulders. "No wonder. You should definitely go. You have such good things in here." Hilaria tapped her head. "You need to let them out. Figure out how to open the door. A bit of country would do you good."

"You really will come visit if I'm there for ages?"

"Couldn't keep me away with a stick. And I'll write in the journal, we all will. Send you packages, even. Come on. I have some cocoa and some milk left. We'll curl up and talk. Oh, I heard the best story from Una. I simply have to tell you."

That would, at least, be an agreeable end to the evening, up till all hours, until they fell asleep. Whenever that was.

CHAPTER 2
SEPTEMBER 16TH

A week later, Thalia found herself staring at the house. It had been a rather tedious train journey. She'd had to make three changes and there'd been a stopped engine on one line. Finally she was here, and it was still only mid-afternoon. Getting on for dusk, but not remotely there yet. It seemed like everything had rolled to a stop, and the last effort of getting up the hill had been too much for the world to keep turning.

The housekeeper, Mrs Harley, had arranged for a man with a cart to meet her at the train station. He had been a man of very few words, it turned out, other than grunting "Miss Morgan?" at her. But he'd loaded her trunk and suit-cases into the cart with ease, and now he was taking them into the house. She'd kept the case with her typewriter, of course, though now it felt like an anchor weighing her down.

It was almost exactly the same as she remembered, the house itself the same blue-grey that seemed never to age or change or weather. The trees nearest the house were ever-greens, a deep dusty green, whatever the season. The plants nearest the house were unexceptional groundcover, except for the rows of rose bushes climbing the stone walls between the driveway and the garden. That, too, was mostly heavily manicured grass, shaped shrubs, and a fountain. Very tidy, and rather sterile.

You couldn't even tell properly what season it was. The road leading up here had been properly autumnal, but everything here was a green that might be spring or might be summer or might be evergreens.

Sterile. Also as she remembered it, honestly. That wasn't right, it couldn't be right. So much had changed, in the world, in the family. There had been a war. Pierus had died. How had this place escaped all the awfulness? It still seemed entirely untouched.

Her better memories of her childhood visits here had always involved the woods. Further out from the house, certainly. She half-remembered the paths she'd liked. That would be her treat once she was properly settled, exploring the woods again. Woods changed, it was part of how they were.

She wasn't sure how long she'd been standing there, she'd lost track of time. Davis, the man with the trunk, was long gone. Thalia was still stuck, not sure where to go, when the large front door opened. A woman stepped out, wearing a severely cut navy blue dress, her hair up in a bun and a small cap. Thalia walked over briskly enough, her trousers catching the breeze and pulling back against her legs. The pace that had seemed so natural in London, her usual stride, felt wrong here. It was out of proper time, rude and noisy somehow. Unacceptable, and yet another way she was failing to do as she ought.

Thalia suspected this was not the sort of place women wore trousers as soon as she saw the housekeeper's expression. Best to start off as well as she could, then. "Mrs Harley? Thank you for having Davis meet me. Very efficient. I'm Thalia Morgan, of course. We've been corresponding."

Mrs Harley, up close, looked to be well past the age where she should have been pensioned off to a comfortable cottage. She must have been seventy if she was a day, and she had lines on her face that might have been severity or might have been some ongoing pain. It wasn't the sort of thing one could ask about on first acquaintance. Or probably ever. Thalia was sure she had her own expectations of how matters went between the housekeeper and a family guest.

"Of course, miss." There it was. She was unmarried, of course, and thus, to a certain sort of person, would never be ma'am. Formally, properly, she should be 'Mistress'. She should get the courtesy title for anyone who'd done a proper magical apprenticeship, regardless of her age or station or role in the family, but she wasn't going to fuss about it. Then Mrs Harley coughed. "Mistress, pardon."

"I hope it hasn't been too much of a bother? This all seems to have happened quite quickly. I really am very easy-going, I promise." Thalia remembered Mrs Harley being exceedingly stern when she'd been here as a child. "And I no longer steal biscuits from the cooling rack, though I do remember yours were excellent." There, a bit of a compliment might not hurt. Thalia was decent at this sort of social chit chat.

Most of the time, apparently, not this time. Mrs Harley merely gave her a brief nod. "We've a room prepared, and a desk. We'll see to your things." Thalia suspected that included judging the state of the darns in her underthings, but there was no help for that. Mrs Harley went on. "We're a simple household, for all Mistress Morgan likes nice things." There was an emphasis on that, as if pointing out that Great-Aunt Avis wouldn't tolerate darning.

Thalia nodded. Really, it was the only thing to do, even if she was now halfway certain this woman could read minds. That was ridiculous. Even if such a thing were possible, and Thalia was reasonably sure it wasn't, using it on her would be unfathomable. She had a mind, a quite good one, actually, but it wasn't as if she were thinking anything particularly interesting right now.

"I gather Davis was bringing my trunk and cases up. I tried to tip him, but he just looked at me. What's the done thing? I don't want to be insulting, of course."

Mrs Harley blinked at her, slowly, as if she were some unusual bit of wildlife who had wandered into the courtyard. "You're not in the city now, mistress. We do things a bit different here. Come through, if you please?" That wasn't a request, it was near enough an order, and they both knew it.

Thalia nodded. "Of course, you have your way of doing things. But I packed rather a lot of books, you see, I didn't know what Great-Aunt Avis had here in her library, and I'm a writer."

"You mentioned, mistress. We've plenty of space for that sort of thing." Mrs Harley's tone was simultaneously quelling and reassuring.

"I know you must have your own customs and traditions. And I'm not Great-Aunt Avis, who could be, but I don't want to be a bother for you. And I'm really very easy going about meals and things."

"Not one of those city women who only eats cress sandwiches and weak tea, mistress?"

That could almost have been a joke, but when Thalia glanced over, she didn't dare assume it might have been.

"No, not like that. And I expect I'll be out rambling some of the time, if the weather holds. Something light in the morning, toast and jam and perhaps an egg. A sandwich or soup or something like that for lunch, and a country tea, the way you would, nothing fancy. Substantial food, in moderate amounts." Never mind that it would be rather better than she had been eating for a while.

"Yes, mistress." That got a nod. "The mistress takes her meals upstairs, in her rooms, but we set up this room here for you. The late master used it as his study."

It had clearly been ignored for some years, other than for the dusting. There were empty bookshelves along one wall, but a pleasant table looking out a large window. A clock stood on the mantelpiece, ticking away evenly; it looked like it had been wound a few days ago. She would dine in solitary splendour, then. "Whatever is easiest for you and - there is some other staff, yes?" She put that little inquiring lift in her voice.

"There's a girl from the orphanage, Bessy. She's sixteen and a good worker, but very quiet. We've our rooms in the farmhouse, behind the house, mistress, so you won't hear us at night."

Thalia frowned. "And if my great-aunt needed something?"

"Oh, one of us could sleep in, if she were poorly. But she rarely has been until recently."

Again, Thalia wasn't sure how to read the tone. There might have been a note of concern there, there might have been distance, there might have been disapproval for Thalia not visiting much earlier. It was impossible to be sure. "I gathered this was unusual, the way Father was talking about it. This will be fine, thank you, though if it's easier for me to have a tray in my room, honestly, that's fine."

"Do you rise early, mistress?" Again, that note that might be a reasonable question or might be the sound of someone who thought rising with the larks was only proper.

"Ah, um. Rarely." Thalia coughed. "Would a breakfast tray at nine be a bother, and a keep-warm charm on the teapot? Some nights I end up awake at all hours writing."

"Of course that's fine, mistress." Then the housekeeper tilted her head. "We've no electric light, so it's candles or charmlights."

"I can manage my own charmlights." Her flat in London had gas, but she was always a tad dubious about it, especially given the more obvious flaws in the flat. And the electric light bulbs could be terribly unreliable sometimes. Also, she'd rather spend her pay on paper and ink or ribbons for the typewriter. And books. Always books.

Upon consideration, she added, "Though if you've a good lantern, I'd appreciate that. Rather easier, really."

"Of course." Mrs Harley turned, gesturing. "The sitting room, here." That was a room full of girlish lavenders and hints of pinks, decked out like a spring flowerbed. Thalia caught a glance of the windows looking out toward the garden. She could explore that later.

She was sure there was a radio somewhere on the property, but possibly not anywhere in the public rooms of the house. Their family house, not quite so remote, did well with the crystal radio.

"I gather Great-Aunt Avis rarely had visitors?" Thalia had to take bigger strides than she expected to keep up.

"Very few, mistress. The doctor stopped by every two months, like clockwork, just to chat and check in. And the parson's wife from time to time. They're new here, mind, only been here a few years." And somewhere like this village, that would be no time at all. "Tradesmen and such, but I deal with all that. A few people working on the grounds, but nowhere near the house as a rule."

"Of course. My great-aunt is very fortunate to have you." Thalia happened to glance over again as she spoke, as Mrs Harley was leaning against a door inclined to stick, and she saw a fleeting complexity, some emotion quickly repressed. It might have been wariness, or protectiveness, like a dog who'd assigned herself guard duty. The tail of it, though, seemed more like a moment of weary courage, like she was going into battle one more time. That made Thalia think of Pierus, and she immediately asked something, just to fill the silence. "What's this room?"

"This was the dining room, once upon a time, but it's been the library since the late master died. Mistress Morgan does like her light." It was off on the end of the building, three walls nearly made of windows, with a staircase up against the wall. It was actually a rather lousy room for a library, seeing as how there were very few places to put bookshelves. But the room did have an enormous fireplace and lovely light. "That must be quite cosy in the winter if the draughts aren't bad."

"Yes, Mistress." Thalia had the strong sense now that Mrs Harley had gathered something around herself, protectively. It might just be force of will, it might be some magic. She was sure she was doing something wrong here, but for the life of her, she couldn't figure out what. She might not live with servants anymore, not more than the porter for the building or the woman who did the heavy cleaning, but surely she hadn't forgotten everything.

"And it's not a bother if I'm in here? Even late? I do like the light."

Mrs Harley shook her head. "Of course not, Mistress.

Just don't go up the stairs. It's locked, of course. Those are Mistress Morgan's rooms."

"Of course not." Thalia was glad to agree to that. Father had suggested she could have a poke around, see what his aunt had been so focused on. He'd rather implied that since she was a writer, she had no sense of discretion about other people's lives. That, mind, might have been him subtly making it clear he'd read one of the stories she'd actually got published. It had featured a man not unlike him, in a difficult situation.

It wasn't her fault Father was such an easily defined type, differentiated from his peers only by tiny details of dress and manner. Or that any description of Mother might fit dozens of other women of her age and class. If they saw themselves uncomfortably portrayed by anyone's art, never mind hers, it was their own fault and they could do something about it if they wanted.

"Back out in the main hall, these stairs will take you to your rooms. Bedroom and sitting room, with your own bath. Mistress Morgan's had that redone some years ago. Quite comfortable."

Thalia nodded. The stairs were unremarkable, though they did not have the range of family portraits that Thalia would have expected. Great-Aunt Avis had never had children. Thalia wasn't sure why. It certainly wasn't something her mother would have told her about in any detail. Sometimes people didn't. And Thalia wasn't married, so she didn't get told that sort of confidence. Not like her sister, who got swept into the arms of all the other mothers and grandmothers at whatever social event they were all at.

Mrs Harley turned the corner to the right. "Here we are. If there's anything you find lacking, you can ring there, or come down. It will ring through to our cottage at night. No guests in my kitchen, please."

"Of course not." Thalia replied. "That is your space. Do I knock, if I'm downstairs?"

"There is a proper bell pull in each room, of course, mistress. If you knock on the kitchen door and no one answers, you can leave a note in the box on the hall table. I rarely go out other than the shopping or the kitchen garden, though."

"That should be fine." Thalia took a step into the room, finally. It was rather white and pastel for her tastes, but it wasn't a bad room. Pale greens and blues, mostly, colours she found decidedly restful. The sitting room had what looked like a comfortable sofa, and an easy chair, as well as a fireplace, and good light. The desk here might do quite well for writing space, honestly. It looked out toward the drive up to the house.

Thalia wandered along through the door, into the bedroom, which was decidedly, well, a bedroom. Sizeable bed, not the narrower one she was used to. Fluffed up pillows and such, and a wardrobe for her clothes. Her trunk and cases were already here. She'd want the books from the trunk out on a shelf somewhere, but she could sort that out later.

When she looked back, Mrs Harley was waiting by the door, so quietly that she might have been invisible. "Would you like Bessy to come help you unpack, mistress?"

Thalia shook her head. If she was awkward with Mrs Harley, she couldn't imagine what it would be like with an orphan maid who'd rarely dealt with guests in the house. "Oh, no, I can manage quite well. I didn't pack anything fussy, of course. A nice frock or two, just in case." She could hear her mother's voice echoing in her head. "But mostly sturdy things."

"If you let me know when there's laundry, we do that Mondays and Tuesdays. We send a few things out, too. Bulky wash." Mrs Harley nodded. "Tea at half-five, in your dining room, mistress. If you need anything else, ring and someone will be up momentarily."

Thalia could tell a dismissal when she heard one. She nodded. "Please thank Davis again for me, however he'd appreciate."

Mrs Harley nodded, and disappeared, leaving Thalia to wonder just how long she was going to be here. Isolation was supposed to be good for writing. At least it made it far harder to procrastinate about putting words on the page. There was, however, taking a good thing too far.

CHAPTER 3
SATURDAY

Adam stretched out his hands, peering at them. The tremor wasn't too bad today, in the left. Better than it had been yesterday, anyway. He'd nearly dropped a glass twice, and that would have been no good at all. Neither for the glass nor his ability to clean it up. He always dropped things at the worst possible moment, too.

His uncle was still napping, snoring gently where he lay propped up on the sofa, his bad leg well padded by several pillows. It was something of a test, Adam being here. It had been a week, and he'd only begun to get his bearings in the last day or two.

Uncle Benjamin had broken his leg, badly, three weeks ago. The first Adam had heard of it had been his mother coming up and knocking on the door of his room, and asking if he'd come downstairs. He had, though he felt like a ten-year-old about to be scolded for scrumping apples, rather than a grown man in his thirties.

On the other hand, he was bloody useless these days, and they all knew it. Whatever they wanted to call it, it came out the same in the maths. Among posh circles, officers, like he'd been, they used the word neurasthenia, as if Greek roots to the word made everything better. It was a more sophisticated-sounding word, expressing a delicate, elegant condition. In other words, a lie.

Adam preferred the harsher, briefer "shell shock" that offended most people, even though it was no longer actually censored. And of course, there were plenty who just called it cowardice. Whatever name they called it by, he had it. He had since 1917, and as far as he could tell, he always would.

His hand twitched, and he sighed, taking a breath as he'd been taught. It was one of the things that sometimes helped, that's why he kept doing it. This time, however, not so much as he wanted.

Which made him wonder again exactly who thought this was a good idea. His mother had proposed - ordered - that he go and stay with his uncle while his leg mended. Make sure he didn't overdo. Or if he couldn't manage that, and Adam was very clear his uncle wouldn't, Adam could fetch and carry and help oversee the orchard harvest. Not do the heavy work. Uncle Benjamin hired out for that. She made it clear he'd have to be sociable, not hide in his room with a book.

Adam thought that was a poor judgement on her part. Uncle Benjamin at home was just as taciturn as Adam was these days. When he was awake, he was likely to be reading when he wasn't working. The newspaper, a book, a magazine, or in a pinch, the labels on whatever tins and packaging the housekeeper left lying out in the kitchen.

And if his uncle couldn't go about his usual work, designing and laying out gardens, well, it was heading into the season where he spent most of his time at his drafting table, anyway. Not quite yet. He couldn't manage the bad leg well enough for that. But Mrs Whitmore's husband was making up a stool to rest it on that would fit under the table. Adam wasn't going to win any arguments about Uncle Benjamin getting more rest, so he wasn't even going to try.

None of this made Adam feel any more competent or useful or anything else good. He was now taking up space on the edge of Dartmoor, which was at least a change of scenery from his parents' current home near Bath. Honestly, the rather desolate effect of the moor suited his mood. Or it would, if he trusted himself to go that far afield and get back to the house safely. He honestly didn't trust himself to go down the lane and get help if his uncle went poorly, but his mother insisted he'd manage just fine.

Adam just hoped nothing would happen. It was a test he knew he'd fail. He hated the way it lurked there, knowingly. And he didn't want his uncle hurt. But everyone else in his life had insisted this was a grand thing all round, and shipped him off again. Like he'd been shipped off to Craiglockhart, and then home. Then a quiet rest home, back to his mother and father, and then the third place, he didn't even remember the name. And then home. And finally to the Gospatricks, who'd actually helped a bit. As much as anyone could. And home.

And then three jobs, no, four, that he'd tried and failed at. Messily. Repeatedly. In ways there was absolutely no hope he'd recover from. At least here, so long as Uncle Benjamin didn't have some crisis, he probably couldn't do too much harm. And his room was at the far end of the hall, so he probably wasn't waking his uncle up too much with nightmares.

Though this had been a rather long nap. He didn't even know how to ask about it, if he was being a bother. He could manage, these days, more or less well enough when he was awake. When he could keep busy, as they'd taught him. It was the middle of the night that was the worst. Sometimes he just curled up and read the same passage over and over again. Sometimes he stared at the ceiling, seeing things replay there in his memory. Either way, it left him groggy and cranky and uncivilised.

Uncle Benjamin, bless him, didn't apparently mind that. He just shoved coffee over when Adam finally appeared in the morning, and something to eat, all provided by his live-out housekeeper. They read the paper, or at least stared at it, until well into the morning.

His uncle coughed and stirred. "Adam?"

"Yes? Need some water?"

"Please. Actually, a pot of tea, could you?" Uncle Benjamin's voice was creaky, and Adam diagnosed that he was refusing to ask for a pain potion.

Adam considered the variables. Hot water, but he could bring over a tray with handles. That usually went better. "Sure. Give me a tick." He went off to the kitchen, the next room over, and took his time, leaning heavily on the counter while the kettle came to a boil again. Mrs Whitmore had gone home to her husband and children an hour ago, leaving their tea warming in the oven. There was a definite chill in the air, a coming autumn.

Five minutes later, he'd managed all the tea things without dropping anything, and without splashing boiling water on himself. That was a definite victory, if a tiny one. If his mother was right about the moor air being good for him, he'd be both put out and pleased, all at once. That seemed far more emotion than he was fit to handle.

He'd thought about adding a vial of the pain potion, but that had gone badly last time, too. His uncle wasn't the sort to take kindly to cosseting. Adam didn't need another argument, done through implication and eyebrows, comparing properly masculine responses to pain to whatever it was Adam was doing with himself.

"You go out?" His uncle cupped his hands around the tea, taking a long drink.

"Didn't want to leave you on your own. Mrs Whitmore was just finishing up when I was done reading."

"Huh." It came out more as a grunt than anything else. "Need you to check the orchards. I'll write a list. See how they're getting on."

Adam wasn't at all sure he could manage going along to the orchards. Some piece of it must have showed on his face, because there was another grunt. "Take a walking stick. There's a spare, there." Uncle Benjamin gestured at an umbrella stand that held one solitary umbrella and three sturdy sticks, tall as Adam's six feet. "Not the green handle. That's mine."

"Sure." Adam let out a breath. "And I've the map."

"You don't remember it?" Uncle Benjamin tilted his head.

"There's a fair bit I don't remember." Adam pointed out. Whatever had gone wrong for him had rattled his memories as well as his body. Not that he had forgotten everything, but it came bubbling back to the surface oddly. Unreliably.

It was part of why he read so much. When it was words on a page that brought something new boiling over, he could take his time to make sense of it. If you did that in conversation, people found you exceedingly odd. "And it's been, what? Twenty years? I was eight. Twenty-five."

Uncle Benjamin snorted. "Fair enough. Down the lane, follow it a mile or so. Sketch or take notes or something."

He didn't glance at Adam's hands, and Adam was grateful for that small courtesy. He'd do his best, and so long as he could read the resulting notes, he supposed they could manage.

"How far along should they be? When I came through on the train, getting here, there were bushels of apples at market day."

"Oh, they ripen late, up along toward the hall. Always have." Uncle Benjamin shrugged. "And they're going into cider, anyway. Can't drink it for a while yet."

Adam tilted his head. That tickled something in his memory he couldn't begin to pin down now. "Normal for them, then?"

"Mmhmm. You know what I say, every field is different." It was, in fact, the centrepiece of Uncle Benjamin's design work, finding what suited that particular land. He had a gift for it, one Adam envied, the ability to see what could grow given time and care and nurture. It required seeing into the future in steps. Adam had always been better at noticing what was going on now, like the places where some blight was just beginning to take hold.

Not that he could make a living at that. He wasn't fit for office work; he hadn't been even before the War. Less now, when a book being dropped or someone speaking sharply or too loudly could set him off again. And the kind of work Uncle Benjamin did, that required an excellent reputation. Adam's was in shards. People whispered about him at home, and in all the circles that Mother and Father travelled in. All the professionals of their circle, the lawyers and businessmen and skilled crafters.

He might have made a decent life for himself as a gentleman farmer. Honestly, he'd be rather good at it. He'd done well at Snap. He'd come out at the top of his class.

He'd made a good show of apprenticing to another uncle, who'd run a flourishing farm in Cumbria. But his uncle had remarried, his new wife had several sons too young for the War, and they were doing well with the place. It had left Adam rootless.

His parents didn't precisely approve of the farming. Selling the results of the farming, that was how they'd made their money in groceries. But the actual farmers weren't their sort, his mother said. Uncle Benjamin was a skilled professional. That was different.

Adam suspected this might be a test to see if Uncle Benjamin would take him on as an assistant, then as a partner. He honestly didn't know what he'd say. He liked what he'd read of the work, while he was keeping an ear out, but that wasn't the same as being able to do it. Or even assist properly, beyond the fetching and carrying any apprentice of eighteen could do. And which any boy of sixteen could do far better than Adam could when it came down to it.

"Pass me another scone?" His uncle had at least got a fair bit of his appetite back. "How's the flock?"

"Very well. Mrs Whitmore says the red queen laid an egg. She's stopped worrying about her." There was a healthy kitchen garden out back, and chickens in the pasture beyond. Between the two, they were currently showered in harvest still. "Oh, and there should be pickles ready tomorrow. She said you'd been looking forward to them."

"I have." Uncle Benjamin let out a contented sound. "Right. Hand me the paper? I want to read until supper."

CHAPTER 4
SUNDAY

It took the better part of the morning for Adam to work himself up to leaving the house. He had to read about the apples. His uncle had dozens of books, but had left out a field guide for him to refresh his memory. He had a sudden urge to tidy the top of his dresser, and put everything in precise rows that would only last until the next time he touched them. Then something was rubbing in his sock. Even he could admit he was putting it off.

Mrs Whitmore was very patient with him, but she eventually knocked on the door of the sitting room while his uncle was napping. "Himself said you were off to the orchard. I've made up a lunch. I could do some cleaning while you're out." Which meant he had to go out, really.

He didn't want to be a bother, and Adam suspected she wanted to do some sort of loud cleaning. Beating rugs or something. His uncle would sleep through it, but it would make Adam jump every time, and it would take him hours to settle after.

He had sighed, but got up, found his boots, and tested both walking sticks, finally choosing the one bound with an oxblood red leather. It fit satisfyingly in his hand, and it was the sturdier of the two, which seemed necessary today.

When he finally got out the door, it was at least a pleasant day. There was sun to go with a pleasant autumn breeze. Not too chilly, though Mrs Whitmore had pressed a cloak on him, to give him something to sit on if he needed it.

He'd grabbed his satchel with a notebook and the guide and something to read, as well as a lunch. It was the same one he'd used since his school days. It was battered and beaten up, but it had not gone to War with him. He found it a comfort to have one thing in his life that hadn't changed.

The orchard was a steady mile's walk, not too hilly. He followed the road down, then the lane, and then the Reddaford Water, ending up in a valley that was tucked away along the stream. He could feel some sort of charm as he went past the fence line. A keep away charm, perhaps, or something else? He couldn't tell from here, and it was rude to rummage in other people's magic.

There were customs there, very strong ones, about the agricultural land. He didn't know all the local ones, and he wasn't entirely sure Uncle Benjamin did, either. Normally, he was away much of the spring and summer, well into the autumn. Mrs Whitmore probably knew who to ask, but that would mean talking to strangers, and that was no good. She might know herself, but she'd seemed far more a woman of kitchens and their gardens than the fields.

The orchard itself, when he got well into it, seemed healthy enough. But it also seemed wrong, in some indefinable way. It felt a hair warmer than it should, this far into the autumn, for one thing. And he heard birds, but couldn't place them. Something indefinable in the air, certainly, like he'd crossed some hidden boundary without warning.

He made a long slow circuit around the orchard, first, to get the sense of things and find the Old Man. He stopped, halfway around his circuit, to look across the space, and found the immensely old tree, maybe more than a century, arching over a fair swath of the orchard. The other trees were younger, but all were full grown. Every single one was still full of apples, and only a few of the apples were near ripe. Far more full and far less ripe than they should be, even allowing for this being sheltered in the valley.

Adam frowned, but he knew his duty here. He went over to the Old Man, levering himself down to kneel on one knee, and pour out a little splash of cider at the roots, before he stood. "Old Man, my uncle sends me to see how the apple trees do." It seemed both ridiculous to say, to think that it made any difference, but also necessary.

That said, he continued his circuit. He certainly didn't recognise every apple in England, and he especially wasn't up to date on everything in this part of the country. But he could spot three or four varieties, at least. A couple of wildlings, where seeds had sprouted, rather than the apples being grafted. He remembered what that felt like, under his hands, what seemed like centuries ago. He'd had something of a knack for it, back when he could still trust his fingers with a knife.

He finally found a spot to settle, where he could see most of the different trees. After unpacking his lunch, he ate it slowly. Cheddar and apple sandwich. One of the earlier varieties, according to his book, as he rummaged through it. Having the reference in his hand made him peer up at the trees.

That one, there, he thought it must be a Beauty of Bath. A good eating apple. He'd had it over the two summers when he'd stayed at school for the summer work. But it should have been ripe and harvested weeks ago, by the middle of August. It was now well into September.

And that, there, that was Court of Wick, and it should be harvested now, but it was some time off that. It had been a long time since he'd been in an orchard properly, but he guessed it was a month or more from ripe, by the size and the colour.

It was baffling, honestly. And his uncle had seemed not at all bothered by it. There was certainly variation based on how sheltered the trees were, how much light they got, what the soil was like. All that sort of thing mattered, and much more. But this was, well. This was unusual.

The whole thing was exhausting, and within minutes, his head was aching. He leaned back on the cloak, slipping his hands under his head. It was at least quiet here, and no one was likely to disturb him. It did not seem like rain, and he could hear bees...

No, wait. The bees sounded slightly wrong. He knew bees better than he did apples. His parents had hives when he was growing up. They should have been slowing down for the winter, the sound thinning out. The ones he could hear, there must be a hive fairly near, they sounded like the height of summer, when the world was full of pollinating plants.

He also didn't hear much in the way of birds, which might be why he was hearing the bees more clearly. There were some, certainly, he could see a couple in the trees nearer the road, but there was an unnatural silence closer to the fields and the hill.

The whole thing felt off. Which was one problem. The worse problem was he didn't know if he could trust his senses, never mind explain it to anyone else. Uncle Benjamin had brushed it off last night, after all.

It could just be that Adam was out of sync with the world again. Still. Continuously. And he wasn't supposed to be the one fussing about the details. Just come out and keep an eye on things when the harvest got going.

None of it made sense. He gave up, after a few minutes, and lay back down, staring up into the branches. It did not improve anything in terms of reason and logic. On the other hand, the branches were forming lovely patterns, and the sky was blue, and it was neither raining nor muddy at the moment.

Adam did not fall asleep - it was far too exposed a space for it. But he did find that drifting and transient peace that he treasured. It slipped away as soon as he paid too much attention to it, like a snowflake melting on your hand as you noticed it. But that instant before, it was real enough to him.

By the time his pocket-watch said it was coming up on three, Adam thought he ought to get back. The return took a lot longer, it felt like. He'd turn and there would be another long stretch of road or path reaching out before him. He thought several times he was nearly back, it wasn't as if the village was that big. But the church tower didn't get closer, not until he'd made the sixth or seventh turn. Finally, he could see the cottage, and Mrs Whitmore was bustling about the kitchen, finishing up. "It's near five, my, you were out a long time. Himself is about due to wake up, I'll bring in your tea."

Adam blinked, but the clock agreed with Mrs Whitmore. His watch must be running slow, or he'd taken far longer to walk the mile and a half than he'd expected. Both, perhaps. It wasn't as if he could explain how queer it had felt, coming back. He was sure she would think he was even more batty than she already did.

The oncoming tea meant Adam could collapse in the easy chair and catch his breath. The stick had been a help, but he'd got tired enough on the way back that he'd gone wobbly again with the effort of walking. His uncle woke up twenty minutes later, and then, of course, it took time to parcel out the tea and make sure he was settled.

"How's the orchard, then?" Uncle Benjamin seemed to be doing better today. Adam envied that, honestly. Both the getting better in general, and the steady rate of progress. It seemed a vastly simpler matter than the insides of Adam's head, or the rest of him, for that matter. He took his bone-setting potion, took a pain draught here or there. If he avoided banging it up, he could expect to be fully healed up in two months. And that was with a quite bad break.

"Uncle." Adam swallowed and tried again. "Uncle, how late do things ripen?"

"Oh, fairly late. There are notes somewhere around. I think one of the higher shelves. Later than the surrounding. They always have, as long as I've been here."

"And that's what. Forty years?"

"Nearer fifty." His uncle seemed in a talkative mood, at least. "And there's no one terribly near. We're on the edge of the village as it is. Half a mile down the road, you get the core of it, farmhouses a few places, cottages, what have you."

"And the big house?" Adam had caught sight of it once or twice, well up in the rolling meadows.

"Ah, don't be bothering the lady." Uncle Benjamin shook his head. "Keeps to herself. Has a housekeeper, you'll see her from time to time in the village. She brings a pony cart around for the shopping. There's a maid, an orphan girl, I think. A few of the men help with the grounds every so often. Not much to do, near the house. Roses and grass and boxwood just needs a bit of trimming. Nothing interesting."

Of course, his uncle would think something that sparse would be boring. Adam couldn't quite blame him. "Just the three of them?"

"Aye." Uncle Benjamin shrugged.

It was at that point that Mrs Whitmore stuck her head in. "Just going, sir. But pardon, there's someone else up there now, I gather. The old lady's taking a seaside cure, something like. Someone of her family, staying, I think."

"That doesn't change much about the garden." Uncle Benjamin wagged a finger at Adam. "Don't you be bothering whoever it is. They're not for the likes of us, and they make that very clear."

Adam drew back, curling an arm around himself, tucking his hand in under the other elbow. "Of course not." His parents had been clear about that. Uncle Benjamin had been clear about it. His aunts. They were proper folk, with plenty of money these days, but that wasn't the same as being someone who owned a house like that. Or gardens like that. He hesitated, then asked, "The apples?"

"What about the apples, lad?"

"They're very late. Is that a Beauty of Bath?"

His uncle nodded. "Aye."

"And a Court of Wick?"

"That too." Uncle Benjamin shrugged. "What of it?"

"It's coming up on the end of September. They should have been harvested a month ago. And what happens when we get a proper frost? Does that ruin the rest?"

"Never been a problem, all the years I've been living here. They take their time ripening, but we won't see a frost there until at least December. Sometimes well into January." Uncle Benjamin shrugged. "Mind, I'm better at gardens than orchards. It's the cider I care about. Goes to the presses, sells well, makes a tidy sum, and that's no bad thing. Puts a fair bit of money into the village, too, at a time they could use it."

"Which means a late harvest is better for them." Adam could make sense of that, at least. Staggering harvest was key, he'd learned in school, if you could. That, though, made a thought catch in the back of his memory. It was like a book tucked away on a dusty, spiderwebby shelf. You might vaguely know where it was, but you didn't really want to rummage for it, you didn't know what else you'd turn over.

On the other hand, something just felt off about that whole thing. No frost until midwinter? It must be a very sheltered little grove. He tried to think about what he'd learned about landscape and growing things in school. Even if he'd paid more attention in school, it would have fallen out of his head by now, though.

"Entirely sensible, really. It works well." Don't interfere, in other words. Adam could get that message, loud and clear. Not that he could do anything much about the weather. He hadn't gone to Forvie, for one thing. Snap's teaching sensibly tended toward not mucking with powerful forces like the weather.

"Of course, Uncle. So what's my next step?"

That got them into a safer and far less touchy discussion about what Adam could do to help get things ready. It would be another few weeks, likely, but he could walk down to the orchard every day, or at least every day it didn't bucket rain. Adam was quite sure that would leave him staggering, but they could deal with that when it came to it, he supposed. It might prove a point.

CHAPTER 5
SUNDAY MORNING

The first day in the house, Thalia woke about when she expected, well into mid-morning. There was a tray waiting outside her rooms, and the teapot was still steaming hot. She ran a bath, and then had a leisurely meal, nibbling at the toast and jam and drinking milky tea.

It was frankly both a relief to have a solid meal, and a delight not to be the one to do the cooking and the washing up. Those were the things that most tempted her sometimes to make amends with her family and slip back into the life they thought best for her.

Though, of course, then she'd be not eating for other reasons. She'd be watching her figure and needing to fit into fashionable frocks that showed every curve. She wasn't at all sure how her sister lived like that. Mother had it easier, but Thalia would be expected to catch a husband if she could. She felt like a stranger with them, as if everything about how they worked was different, somehow unfamiliar even if she'd grown up surrounded by it. It was like a bird, laying its eggs in different nests, trusting the world that they'd hatch up, black or grey or some other colour against the bright shared colours of their nest mates.

Once she was done eating, she set the tray outside the door again to bring down later, and got dressed. That had been a challenge, figuring out what to pack, especially as it was going into autumn. Her tweeds were horribly dated, and she never wore them in town, anyway. It wasn't like anyone would be seeing her here, either, so perhaps the amount of thought she had put into it was wasted.

She had brought most of her sturdier wool skirts and comfortable blouses, and a range of jumpers and cardigans that she generally never let anyone but Hilaria see. They were warm and cosy, but did not suit her image of a literary writer. All of them seemed to wear smart jackets and billowing trousers and pristine blouses, with a cigarette holder and cigarette always at the ready.

And she did have a pair of sturdy boots. For the moment she put on ordinary shoes, hearing them clump a little on the old floorboards by the cupboard, before she stepped onto the carpet. Everything was actually less faded than she'd have thought, for a house that had barely had anyone living in it for decades.

Finally, she felt as fortified as she would get to go have a proper look at the place and get her bearings. First stop, the library. For one thing, a library told you a lot about a place and about the people who lived there. For another, she wanted to know what books she might want to send for. Hilaria had promised to post things if she needed them. Or there was probably a lending library in the village, something of the kind.

There was no portal remotely near, though. They were on the wrong end of the moor for that, apparently. It would have made both the post and getting here in the first place much easier. Instead, the train had been the better course, especially with luggage. She had gathered the Newton Abbot portal was a good mile's trudge from the train, which was not something she wanted to do with her bags.

Ridiculous, in this day and age, not to have them line up better. Or more portals, though she remembered someone telling her they were terribly difficult to establish. Of course, you didn't have one everywhere like Tube stops or buses. It was terribly awkward, though. And Thalia hadn't really given much thought to exactly how isolated the house was.

Perhaps there was a bicycle she could borrow, even a pony. She hadn't been on a horse in ages, though they had more self-preservation, at least. But also more of their own opinions. Besides, she didn't think she'd seen anything like a proper stables.

That was getting her nowhere quickly, so instead she made her way down the stairs, listening halfway down to see if she could hear anyone in the house. When she heard nothing, she went along to the library, inhaling the scent of books. There was a small fire in the hearth, and the curtains had been opened, letting the light shine in directly. That was bad for the books, Thalia knew that, but it made the place more cheery. Rather spring-like and hopeful, somehow.

She took her time browsing the shelves. An entire wall of them, four sets of standing shelves, held books about birds and folklore. They stood a good two feet taller than Thalia could reach. Or possibly they only had folklore about birds. She couldn't entirely be sure without reading through some of them. They weren't just in English, either. Some of the texts were Latin, some in German or French.

Curious, she hadn't thought Great-Aunt Avis had a

particularly scholarly bent. And that seemed like a tremendous number of books about any one subject. She pulled one down, a muted green, and flicked through the pages. It seemed to be stories about different birds, the folklore associated with them. The cuckoo, the nightingale, the owl, the wren, a dozen others. She set that aside. The writing was decent, it might make pleasant evening reading.

Of course, it had been ages since she'd been here, and it wasn't as if she'd had a good sense of what Great-Aunt Avis had been interested in. She remembered Great-Aunt Avis as rather little and fluttery. A good head and a half shorter than Mother, about Thalia's own height at the time, but terribly fine boned. Elegant, flitting from place to place, person to person.

Other people's elderly relatives had, Thalia thought, more of a tendency to stay put. Great-Aunt Avis didn't leave her home, but within her home, she was constantly moving or circling or - well. Hopping. Mother thought it very undignified, and she'd said as much.

She'd always seemed quite young, too. Her hair had been blonde. Mother had always assumed she'd dyed it, but Thalia remembered it having a depth of colour that didn't usually come from a bottle or a charm. Not childlike, certainly not the sort of childlike people meant about someone forgetting their age, but perpetually youthful.

Of course, Great-Aunt Avis was Father's relative, not Mother's. It explained both the disapproval and the desire to please her. She had quite a bit of money, for all the house didn't really show it. Not beside the size and the location, and the amount of land attached to it, none of which were nearly as obvious as they might be in other people's hands. Thalia knew Father hoped to come out well in the will. And it wasn't as if Great-Aunt Avis had had children with

Father's uncle. Or as if there was much else in the family to give it to.

It made Thalia wonder if she could work up a story about this sort of house, the passing of the old ways. An old woman dying, and the house getting sold off, to become a girl's school, or a care home, or something of the kind. Not that it was really fit for either, from what she'd seen. This library might make a decent dining room for a crowd, but the rooms she'd seen upstairs would be awkward for dormitories, and everything would need renovation, especially the plumbing. The hot water had been glorious earlier, mind, but she was sure the boiler wasn't up to a horde.

Those thoughts, though, stubbornly took a turn she didn't care for at all. What drew her mind, what compelled her, was wondering what it would be like for a venerable house to be abandoned, with sparrows nesting in the rafters and a raven or crow perching on the crenellations. Animals might come and make their nest, with the eerie yipping of fox cubs or hissing of feral cats to go with the birds. That a place like this might die, and become a shell, no longer loved or noticed.

The library shelves absorbed her until mid-afternoon. Most of them were dated, as if any collection for the library, except perhaps about birds, had paused sometime in the mid-Victorian epoch. Great-Aunt Avis must be in her eighties at least, but her library had stopped when she was thirty or so, as far as Thalia could tell. Nothing at all recent.

It did avoid the terribly sentimental, though. Even the folklore tended toward the more wide-ranging, the collections of tales collected by amateurs around the country and those gathered by people with a titch more discipline. It still made for a curious collection, and Thalia wasn't sure what to make of the woman who owned it.

Also, she now desperately wanted some more recent novels. Nothing terribly improving, but rather the sorts of things she kept for reading late at night, when she couldn't sleep. She hadn't considered that part of her packing terribly well. Either she could get Hilaria to send some along, or that was the sort of thing a local lending library would have, or maybe a bookshop had a second-hand shelf. Mrs Harley must have an idea.

Thalia went back up to her room. There, she surprised - and was surprised by - a young woman in a maid's dark uniform dress. Her hair was up in a cap and a white apron over her front, and she was dusting with a feather duster.

"Oh, pardon'm." The accent was very much of the moor.

"I'm sorry. I didn't mean to startle you. You must be Bessy, yes?" Thalia was suddenly afraid she'd got the name wrong. The girl turned to face her, bobbing in what might generously be considered a curtsey, and Thalia waved a hand. "I'm Thalia Morgan."

"Mistress Morgan's, er."

"Great-niece. She married Father's uncle, a long time ago." Thalia could at least explain that part. "I don't want to be a bother. I told Mrs Harley that yesterday, so I hope you'll let me know if I make things harder for you?"

"Oh, I couldn't, ma'am. Miss." There was another little bob. "It wouldn't be proper." Someone had taught Bessy good elocution. Not fancy, but it was, as accents went, far more penetrable than the usual run in these parts could be.

"Well." Thalia shifted to perch on the arm of one of the chairs, testing before she leaned more weight, suddenly afraid it was going to pitch her to the ground. "I'm a visitor here, even if I might be here for a bit." She tilted her head.

"Do you have a minute to talk? Let me know a bit more about the place?"

Bessy glanced over at the door, as if expecting Mrs Harley to appear out of nowhere. "Yes'm. I have a few minutes, ma'am."

"All right." Thalia did her best to smile broadly. This was horribly awkward, but having asked a thing, now she really must carry through. "Did you grow up near here? Or - how long have you been here?"

"Grew up t'other side of the moor, ma'am. And I've been here near six months. Mrs Harley's kind, ma'am, and when I've been here a year or two, if I do well, she says she'll help me find a job somewhere else. Town or a big house, where there's ad, ad. Where I could do more, in time."

"I suppose a house like this doesn't need all the skills a big house does all at once. Or a busy household."

"No, ma'am." There was a twitch of the duster, as if Bessy wanted to be back at her work. "I was with the orphanage from when I was nine to then. They taught me how to do things, but each house, they have their own ways."

Thalia nodded. "And - you said Mrs Harley's been kind. You're happy here?"

"Yes'm." That, mind, came with a flash of a wary expression, as if Thalia should know better. Even if Bessy were unhappy, it's not as if she'd say so to Thalia. "I have my own room, and it was - well. Odd to be on my own, ma'am, but I like it now. And Mrs Harley helped me make curtains and a rag rug, just how I liked." There was a note of pride there. Thalia could definitely appreciate the joys of laying out her own room.

"I noticed there were a lot of books about birds in the

library. Does my great-aunt have a particular interest?" Thalia asked it almost idly. "I was reading the bit about owls, how they're thought to be liminal."

There was another sudden surge of emotion on Bessy's face. Thalia would have thought it was fear, but that didn't make any sense at all. Nobody could possibly be frightened of a shelf of books about birds. Whatever it was was potent, though. She wasn't good at hiding her thoughts. Unlike the previous expression, though, Thalia couldn't begin to make sense of it. "Mrs Harley deals with all that, ma'am. But Mistress Morgan spent a lot of time reading about birds, I know that. And there are photographs and what are they called. Prints? Upstairs, and in her rooms and things."

"Are there good birds around here, then?"

Thalia was watching more closely this time, and there was another of those flashes, before Bessy ducked her chin. "I should be getting on, ma'am. If you don't mind. Mrs Harley put out a map of the paths, on the hall table. If you want a walk before tea? And if you'd put out any clothes you'd like washed, we'll be seeing to the laundry tomorrow." As changes of subject went, it was wholly inelegant, but quite firm.

Thalia nodded. "The weather looks decent, doesn't it? I'll let you get on." She moved to gather up a sweater from the wardrobe, hesitated, and then left the room. Going down the stairs, she paused to look at the photographs. They all showed Great-Aunt Avis as rather younger than she must be now.

There were women who were like that, who clung onto their youth, and Great-Aunt Avis certainly had the sort of bones and figure that made it easier. It felt like the house was locked up in time. Not frozen, exactly. This wasn't something out of Russia or what was it, an ice palace in

Lapland or Finland. But still. Uncomfortably still. Thalia gathered up her coat, the map of the paths, and took off for a walk on the nearer ones, a circuit of the formal garden.

It was pleasant to be outside. The sunlight was surprisingly strong for coming into autumn, but the gardens had the same quiet stillness as the house. A breeze ruffled the leaves, but there was very little in the way of visible growth or the frothy liveliness Thalia had always thought the proper mark of a good garden.

CHAPTER 6
TUESDAY SEPTEMBER 20TH

T wo days later, Adam felt he could venture a walk to the village library, as well as to the orchard. He suspected he would regret it tomorrow, but he desperately wanted a bit more in the way of reading material. Especially the sort of thing he could read at three in the morning when his heart was still beating too fast and he couldn't possibly sleep.

Uncle Benjamin had waved a hand and given him brief directions to the library and some of the shops. Mrs Whitmore had, bless her, been a bit more helpful. The village wasn't magical. Adam knew that. It wasn't a bother to him. He knew how to keep his mouth shut, and not refer to his magic. He actually often preferred the non-magical communities. They didn't have nearly the same biases and expectations.

She'd suggested arriving around eleven, before the rush over lunch, and before the children got out of school. Adam had made his way down the street, using the walking stick. He probably should give up and find a cane, something a bit easier to manage in shops, but he definitely needed something to lean on.

The library turned out to be a small shop attached to the post office, though once Adam got into the room, it turned out that it went back further than it looked from the street. A bell jangled above him, making him start.

"G'day." The man at the desk looked up from where he'd been typing. Then he blinked. "New in these parts?"

Adam touched the brim of his hat. "Staying with my uncle, Benjamin Walton."

"Ah, heard he had someone staying. Bad break, I gather?"

Adam felt a rush of panic. He had entirely forgotten how to have conversations with someone new. Small talk had never really been his gift. He much preferred a good practical conversation. But he tried to remember how this went. "Quite, yes. Mrs Whitmore's a wonder, but better to have someone handy at night." Then, awkwardly, he added, "May I say you asked about him?"

"Oh, yes. Roger Dobbs. Please give him my best. Or if I can call round with some books, though I suppose if you're here, you could take some along. Your uncle's a good reader, keeps us busy." The man was chatty, apparently, which at least perhaps meant Adam could get by with a lot of nodding and making agreeable noises. Those were much easier.

"I'll ask what he'd like, then. May I - pardon, I don't know your rules. Can I borrow some myself?"

"Oh, oh, yes, of course. That would be why you came in, certainly. Uh. This form, please." Dobbs stood up, and made his way to the desk, rummaging for a form from a file. Adam caught the limp, and he could guess where it came from. The same place, roughly speaking, as Adam's unsteadiness and nightmares and everything else.

Dobbs must have caught something in his glance. "Trenches in Belgium."

"France." It came out too abruptly, neither of them specifying the name of their particular hell, and he swallowed. "Pardon."

"No, of course. Here you are. That table, there, has a pencil, if you want to fill it out at your leisure? Catalogue here, the shelves are labelled. Not a large collection, but varied." Thankfully, Dobbs settled down after that rush of comments. Adam took himself to the table, carefully willing his hands to produce legible letters this time.

He was only halfway through the form when someone burst through the door. "See here, Dobbs." His voice was loud, the door banged shut behind him, and then the man dropped a pile of books on the counter. Everything overwhelmed Adam, even though he knew this wasn't really a threat, not logically a threat.

Adam managed not to dive under the table. That was his first instinct. Somehow, he must have stood, he could hear the chair toppling to the floor behind him, something else crashing down, a book maybe. All he could do was bolt as fast as his legs would take him, down the row of shelves, toward the back. He just wanted to get further away, to be nowhere near that kind of noise. It was not quite blind panic, but it was near enough. By the time he was at the back of the room, now trapped there, the noise had faded a bit. But he didn't know if it was because of something Dobbs had done, or because the man had settled down. Adam couldn't really hear over the thumping of his heart.

He leaned his head against the flat end of the shelves, then his arms, bracing himself so the shelf took a fair bit of his weight. He could feel his breath shaking, like he couldn't get enough, and he had to remind himself of what they'd taught him. Counting. He could remember the count. More or less. Take as long breathing in as he did breathing out. He didn't remember why, not right now, not when it took everything he had to keep breathing.

Gradually, he got a grip on himself. He could feel how he'd been sweating, how his skin was clammy with it, especially in the small of his back. His fingers were tightly folded into fists, until he focused on uncurling them, finger by finger, breathing through the ache. When he finally managed to push himself fully upright, he heard unsteady footsteps coming down the aisle. "Pardon, sir?"

No more time to coddle himself, then. Adam cleared his throat. "Yes?" His voice cracked halfway through, even in such a short word, and Adam cursed silently, not even trying to vocalise those words.

"Pardon. Mr Oswald, he gets very... loud." Dobbs clearly had considered another word, but loud would do. They both knew what was meant. Then there was that deadly silence. Adam couldn't bear to look at Dobbs straight on, he knew what he'd see. Pity, probably, but also the look that Adam was dangerous, a caged animal that would lash out at anyone, without judgement or control.

"I'm sorry to have caused a bother." Adam worked on drawing himself back together. "I - look. I'll be in later this week, likely."

He'd apparently grabbed his walking stick out of pure instinct in his flight, as it was right there, unlike the abandoned paperwork. He gathered it up and made his way out of the library without looking back. He thought Dobbs might have tried to say something, but Adam just kept going. Once he was back on the street, he swallowed.

Going back to Uncle Benjamin's was no good. Mrs Whitmore would want to know what he'd thought about the library and the librarian. He was sure she'd get the gossip about it soon enough, but he didn't want to face that now. And Uncle Benjamin would give him one of those looks. The one that said it shouldn't be that hard to be around other people. The one that was ashamed he wouldn't buck up.

Adam grimaced, and then glanced at the lane that led along to the orchard. If he went there, at least he could grab an apple to snack on, he could sit down somewhere. He didn't have his cloak. If the ground was still muddy, maybe he could find a low enough branch to climb on. Or there might be a stone, somewhere. Whatever else, it would likely be quiet. No one around.

It took him longer than he wanted, his knee was giving him bloody hell. Half an hour later, he was perched on the remains of an old tree stump at the edge of the orchard, one apple eaten and biting into a second. He had seen no one else for at least twenty minutes, and that was an incredible relief.

Now, though, he could finally relax enough to look around. Not the quick scan for anything that might be a threat, anything that might demand something of him, but something more, well, useful. Even if he knew the panic had a purpose, somewhere in the seeds of it. He'd heard one of the officers, when they were on leave, going on about the Great God Pan. About a theory that primordial terror, as he'd put it, was a lot of what was at the core of shell shock.

Adam supposed it was a pretty theory. And it didn't put the blame on the men dealing with it, which was a novelty, honestly. Adam thought it must be akin to something with the Silence, the way fears pressed on you when you came too close to your oaths, the magically held ones. Either way, he'd come far too close to Pan's realm, over and over again, and now he couldn't stay away.

At the Gospatricks, one of the other residents had gone through a lot of fuss with appeasement rituals, little things done on the terrace by the pond. Adam hadn't seen the point. He certainly didn't want to draw more attention from any god—or for that matter anyone—with power to make men dance and beg for their lives like puppets on strings, to be discarded over and over when they didn't measure up.

And none of that helped what other people thought. Some were sure it was a moral failing. Some thought it was some lack in a man's training or parentage. He'd heard everything from having too strict a father to too doting a mother to too distant a parent proposed. Logic and reason suggested it probably wasn't all of those at the same time.

He sighed and chewed on the apple. The early varieties tasted like they should, at least. It occurred to him, only now, that perhaps eating them wasn't the more sensible thing he'd ever done. Every tale of fairy food, and a fair number of the Fatae legends besides, made it clear strange fruit held tremendous risks. Certainly, the sort of story and adventure Adam would fail at miserably. But if Uncle Benjamin had been selling the cider for years, presumably it wasn't actually poisonous or dangerous or anything. Not more than cider ordinarily was.

He took another bite, considering. A fine apple, in the prime of ripeness. No soft bits. A good bite, a crispness to it. It was quite a fine apple, really. Just out of its season.

It was as Adam sat there, contemplating the apple, that he caught a hint of movement. He thought it might have been a deer, or even a pony, wandering down from higher on the moor. He blinked at the shape several times until it coalesced into a woman. A skirt he thought might be unfashionably long for this year, not that he knew much at all about that. The woman seemed to be wearing a bulky cardigan, too, not the sleek lines Adam had seen on women at home.

Though, to be fair, it was a tad chilly out. It was the country, and if a woman couldn't wear something actually comfortable here, where could she? He couldn't see her well enough to catch her face. The light was behind her, but he didn't think she was much older than him. Solid enough not to be a wisp of a girl, not stout enough to have had several children.

He hoped she wouldn't come closer, and indeed she didn't, turning to go back up the hill after a few minutes, rather than venturing down to the orchard itself. And he was tucked back between trees. He was fairly sure she hadn't spotted him. He wasn't moving, anyway, and he supposed from a distance he might look like some unusually tidy branches.

When the light started changing, he finally picked himself up and made his slow way back home. Mrs Whitmore had gone for the day, leaving something warming in the oven, some sort of rabbit pie. His uncle was still napping, given the snores from the sitting room. Adam made himself a cup of tea at the kitchen table to avoid waking him.

About twenty minutes after Adam got home, there was a "You back?"

"Yes, Uncle. I went by the orchard. Did you hear any more about whoever's up at the house?"

Adam came and settle down where his uncle could see

him, after handing over the other mug of tea he'd made. His uncle took a long drink. "You see someone?"

"A woman, walking. I don't suppose Mrs Whitmore heard anything more?"

That got a grunt. "Did. Heard more than a bit."

Adam knew, suddenly, that she'd also heard about the library. He couldn't say why, it was just some note in his uncle's voice. He couldn't bring himself to own up to it. Anything he'd said would be an excuse, anyway. He had been rude, he had been obvious in all the ways his family found horrific. Calling more attention to it just made it worse.

After a long pause, his uncle went on. "Bessy, the maid they've got up there, was down getting a few things, Mrs Whitmore said. Gather it's a great-niece or something. Dunno her age. Name's ... Tallie. No, that's not it. Don't remember." He grunted again. "Don't you bother her. People live in a house like that, they're not our sort."

"Magical?"

"Dunno. Probably not. Don't ask." His uncle grumbled. "Just. We don't talk about anything except maybe a bit of flooding. Neighbourly needs. Never have."

"Even though the orchard runs along their land? And we must be one of the nearer houses to their road?" Adam asked. "It must, right?"

That got a grimace. "Even so. The border's that wall, to the north side of our orchard." Quite close, then, though Adam would have to look at a map again to get a proper sense. There must be an ordnance map in the house.

Just one more person to avoid, then. At least he knew where she'd likely be coming from.

CHAPTER 7
WEDNESDAY, SEPTEMBER 28TH

T halia grimaced. She had been working all afternoon. Her end result: three sentences she didn't like very much, a pile of discarded sheets crumped up in the wastebasket, and a cramp in her fingers. She'd tried to write the opening a dozen times, and all of the words fell flat with a thump. Nothing was coming out right, none of it.

She glanced over at her journal, frowning. Her friends had written, of course, but none in the last day except Hilaria. She'd not had much to say, and she certainly hadn't known how to respond to their worried little concerns. Yes, she was eating. No, she wasn't lonely. Yes, the landscape was lovely. No, she hadn't had uncomfortable interactions with the local village. All their own worries, writ large, none of the ones Thalia actually had. It hadn't helped the writing either.

She'd been trying to write another of the stories she'd tried before. Not moralistic and improving, the world didn't need more of those. But there was a fashion, right now, for bright and sharp stories with interesting twists. People liked a touch of satire, mixed with a dash of fashion and culture, and a tale that made them feel better about themselves. Like they were smarter than most, or more educated, or cultured. That sort of story had weight, it nudged the world in some new direction, or at least the right sort of reader.

Every time she'd tried, every sentence, had failed. Even the three that were not quite as awful as the others. It felt flat, like a badly painted set at an amateur theatrical performance, and the acting just as wooden and stereotypical and insulting. None of it felt real, certainly none of it would move the reader to anything beyond hysterical mockery.

It wasn't that the place disagreed with her, or at least not exactly. Curiously, she'd been sleeping well here. Much better than she'd expected. Some part of her had come to hope that would turn into words she liked. Nearly a fortnight here, and she'd barely written anything. A few scratches that might maybe turn into something better.

She was a writer because she wrote. And to be a proper literary writer, one wrote things that mattered, that somehow put a new light on the world. That was what she'd thought for ages, that was what she'd been told and shown. Every time she went to a party, people went on about it, about how they were bleeding on the page, laying all their pain out. It made her shiver, because how could she do that? She already knew no one was remotely interested in that from her. Not in writing, not in her life, not anywhere.

Which just brought her back to the queerness of being here. She still woke in the middle of the night - it would have been entirely unfathomable if she hadn't, at this point. But it was muted, like seeing her nightmares through a lace curtain, or slowed down. A bit less hectic and frantic, quite a bit more manageable. She would take every favour like that she could get, honestly. And it wasn't as if she could blame her writing troubles on sleeping better, she'd had trouble writing for near a year in London.

She stretched and heard something in her shoulder pop. That was also not a good sign. And it wasn't as if sitting here was doing any good. She wasn't one of those people who insisted that everything had to be perfect, the lighting, the desk, the inspiration, all of it, before she could sit down and write. She prided herself on her dedication to the work, to sitting down, every day, come rain or party.

But that didn't mean she produced things she liked. Truth be told, she hadn't for ages. If she were honest with herself, at least a year. That had been that last scathing round of critique, thirteen months ago. Not that she was counting, but of course she was counting.

She'd been trying to match herself to what they'd told her ever since. None of it had worked. She really should have a good sit down and decide what she was going to do differently. But she knew if she did that, she might never pick up a pen again. Or bring out her typewriter. Which, at the moment, was lurking at her from its case.

It wasn't even as if she knew what she wanted to write. Something that mattered. Wasn't that what everyone wanted, in some form? She envied Una, who bounced between travel notes and terrifyingly sharp-eyed satire with equal ease. Or Frederick, who had a real knack for sketching the interesting parts of someone's personality as part of an interview in a few precise phrases. They wrote things that made a reader see the world differently when they were done reading. Like a photograph or an engraving, giving some new perspective.

All Thalia ever seemed to do was bore people. She was

no longer new enough - or young enough - to coast on being novel. She had begun to fear, this past year, that she'd only ever been published because of that. Or because she happened to know what that particular editor had a soft spot for, and could write to that. Only, well. That only went so far. And it still didn't mean her writing was any good.

Thalia grimaced and went to find a cardigan. It had been her brother's, once upon a time. She'd snagged it out of his room before Mother had packed it all up, donating everything to veterans in need. She'd had to sneak the cardigan out of the house, but it made her feel, well. Something. Another thing she didn't have words for, another sign she was doing the wrong thing, trying to write. But it was also comforting, somehow. Or at least, when she wore it, she wasn't entirely alone in her misery. Maybe that was how to put it.

She went downstairs, slowly, to find Mrs Harley at the bottom of the stairs. "Oh, pardon." Thalia ducked her head. "I was going to go out for a walk on the grounds. Back before dark."

"Mind how you go, Mistress. There's a bit of mud from last night, I gather." Mrs Harley hesitated. "You let me know if you see anyone odd, would you?"

"Travellers, or something else?"

Mrs Harley shrugged. "Shouldn't be, but sometimes people get a notion in their heads. There are some bits of odd lore about the land about here. People sometimes get ideas." She considered for a moment. "Gather there's someone staying down with Benjamin Walton, he's the neighbour nearest. Had a fit of some kind in the library, Bessy heard all about it in the village. Quite queer in the head, from what Mrs Osborne was saying at the grocer.

Who knows what that sort of troubled lad might get it in his head to do."

The first part had a certain pragmatic sense. And if they stayed away from the house, it wasn't like people would bother Great-Aunt Avis. Thalia certainly wasn't going to tattle. And she didn't know how to ask more about whoever it was who was troubled. "There's quite a lot of land, isn't there? I should explore a bit further. Town first, I suppose. Maybe in the next day or two."

Mrs Harley said, a bit repressively. "It looks like rain tomorrow, Mistress. And the day after."

"Well. Eventually." Thalia frowned. "Is there any reason not to go for a walk today?"

Mrs Harley shook her head. "Of course not, mistress. Might get colder if you go down toward the village. You might want a cloak there."

"Oh, I should be fine. I don't expect to be out too long." Thalia suddenly realised she must be rather scruffier than Mrs Harley was used to. Every picture she'd seen of Great-Aunt Avis, and the memories she had from when she was little, her Great-Aunt had always been properly put together. Every ruffle pressed and every ribbon in place. Mrs Harley was certainly much the same, her dark dress tidy and orderly.

Thalia couldn't do it. Not anymore. She'd managed, during the War, as a VAD, to keep up with all the uniform expectations. At least until the point where no one was fussing about more than things being clean. There had been a point where, even in the requisitioned country home Thalia had been assigned to late in 1917, everything got faded and over-bleached. And well, not as sharp as it should have been. Certainly none of them were.

Ever since, certain scents or the starch in a dress

brought her back to earlier in the War, when she'd first volunteered. When all the VADs had been questioned and sniffed at, over and over, by the proper nurses, the ones with training and practice and skill. They'd had every right, of course, but that didn't mean those sniffs didn't still sting.

Thalia pulled the cardigan around her more tightly. "Back by tea."

It was a tad better once she was outside. Maybe it was the indoor air that was getting to her, and the way the fireplace was soothing but also stuffy, all at the same time. Vastly better than London, the air, but the moor had a dampness to it. The longer she was out of the house, the more at ease she felt, as if something that had got stuck was moving again, slowly. The light from the overcast sky was gentler than sharp flames in the fireplace, though it seemed almost a silly thought, given the light and warmth of the hearth was supposed to be the veritable literary representation of comforting rest.

She thought about what it would take to have a good ramble up on the moor itself. It might be inspirational. It had been for plenty of writers before her. It would, at the very least, be different. On the other hand, she knew there were risks up there, bogs and slippery places, and who knows what sorts of dogs or what have you.

And even if she were going to the moor, she had more sense than to start for it after three in the afternoon. Especially in autumn, when the twilight came earlier and earlier every day. She might be a woman of the city these days, but she had not forgotten all her good sense, nor left it behind with her dancing shoes. Such as they were.

Instead, she turned down the hill, towards the woodlands that ran along the road, further down. The property ran quite a way west from here, according to the maps, with a number of fields and foresty bits. Thalia wasn't sure, now, what the definition of a forest was, properly.

Certainly you needed more than a copse of trees to have a forest. But did it involve a certain amount of land, like a mountain involved a certain amount of rise from the surrounding landscape? Or was it perhaps a historical definition? Thalia half-remembered, the way she half-remembered a lot of things she had read, something about forests originally having belonged to the King.

If that were the case, maybe this wasn't a forest. The land had been in Great-Aunt Avis's family since near enough the Conquest, if Thalia had the history right. Whatever it was, she walked down the hill. It would at least have something different from the carefully tended grass near the house. Or the kitchen garden she'd spotted. That was clearly the realm of Mrs Harley and Bessy, and not for such folk as Thalia.

The walk down the hill was pleasant enough, and even involved an actual path, with a few stairs cut into the hillside at the steeper parts. There was a fence at the edge of the field, suggesting that something might occasionally be grazed on one side of it or both. Thalia could see nothing that looked like a grazing animal, nor any of the signs of their passage. At least she was less likely to be accosted by some unhappy ram or bull or cranky pony or opinionated goat. Well, goats only came in opinionated. That was an adjective she should cut from her internal manuscript, as it were. Redundant.

Thinking about her internal narration in that form at least kept her pleasantly occupied, not thinking about anything else for a while. Which meant that she got into the woods and through a path to the far side before she paid much attention again. Score several points for self-distraction, but lose several hundred for observation. Not the cleverest thing in a space she didn't know.

Thalia was at the stone wall surrounding what looked like an orchard when she saw something moving at the edge of the next field. She couldn't for the life of her make out what it was yet. The light was coming from her left, as the sun was setting, and there was a huge tree near in the middle that cast a sizeable shadow. At the edge of that shadow, she could see some movement on the ground. Thalia couldn't make out how tall it was or how many legs it had, for a good minute. It might have been a deer, or a dog, or a person, or even some combination.

Only after she'd been blinking at it rather owlishly, and for long enough to also be wondering if she should figure out where the nearest optometrist was, did it resolve into a man. He had a walking stick, that was part of the problem. It made him look, from the angle she had, like he wasn't quite human. It was only when he'd turned and she could see the stick at arm's length, about up to the height of his head, that she could make sense of the shape. He didn't look up toward her. He didn't actually seem to be doing anything.

Lurking, maybe. That was a good word, it had weight to it. Lurking. He certainly wasn't doing anything with the apples, nor did he seem to be doing much of anything else. Just standing there, the stick planted down close to his feet, angling a bit away from his body. Very curious.

More to the point, she'd thought this was still the family land, and yet, here was an orchard, and a person in the orchard. Thalia suspected that might be the sort of thing she would need to deal with, as part of whatever Great-Aunt Avis thought needed a representative from the family. If Mrs Harley were sufficient, why have Thalia to stay?

She grimaced, but waited, wondering what the man would do, while the shadows shifted. If he were a Traveller, he was on his own; she didn't see any signs of children or wagons or whatever. If he were someone from the village, he seemed very idle.

She hadn't thought there were other great houses near here, at least not on this side of the village. And she'd thought most people there would need to be earning their living, not standing near motionless in an orchard for - goodness. It had been three when she left the house, it couldn't have been more than a ten or fifteen minute walk down the hill. Twenty, at the outside. But when she glanced at her watch, it was nearly half-four.

Not that she was any better, come to that, at not standing about looking like an apparition. All she needed was a proper fog and she was prepared to be a bit part in a tragedy. She shook her head, and turned to climb back up the hill and see what Mrs Harley might say. The house looked odd in the light, now, not just the orchard. It was as if there was a shimmer, like a heat haze from a radiator or an unusually warm summer day. A trick of the light that made Thalia have to blink and clear her eyes again.

CHAPTER 8
THURSDAY

Adam was feeling somewhat improved. Not better, better implied things that he was certain he didn't feel. It had been raining, and something in the quiet sound of the rain on the roof over his head, that had been soothing in the night. Just a little.

And now, the day was clear and bright, and his uncle was busy working on sketches for next year's projects. Adam packed a lunch and took himself off to the orchard. It was what he was supposed to when it wasn't raining, the orchard.

He didn't dare brave the library again. Not for a bit, anyway. With any luck, Mrs Whitmore and enough time for the village to produce different gossip would cushion things. Adam thought she didn't mind him too much. Certainly, he was trying not to make things difficult for her. He was glad to pull the sheets off his bed and his uncle's for washing day, though he wasn't quite competent to make them up again. And he'd twice helped her with a jar that she couldn't get open.

He wasn't much use, not anywhere, but he could at least stay out of the way and avoid being a bother. An odd duck, as people put it, but perhaps seen with a touch of fond bemusement rather than disgust. It gave him something to work towards, anyway.

Adam had made it to the orchard without incident. Or, for that matter, without coming across anyone other than a duck, which had left him thoroughly alone. Perhaps the duck was as lost as he was, since as far as Adam knew, there wasn't a lake or even a meaningful stream anywhere nearby. There wasn't even a pond, just the Reddaford Water. He felt a certain sympathy for the duck, but he had no idea how to help. Not that he was in a fit state to be much help to anyone, as an odd and out of place duck himself.

The orchard was more or less as it had been last time. A few more apples ripening in their own sweet time, some small branches blown down in last night's wind, but nothing very big. This time, he had brought his sketchbook. His hands were doing a bit better today. Perhaps his parents had been right, and the country air was a help, even with the changes and the stress of settling in to somewhere new. Maybe it was a false improvement, a passing moment, and tomorrow would be awful.

Whatever the reason, he'd take advantage of it while he could. It had been a long time, a very long time, since he'd done a proper naturalist's notebook, but he had loved doing them at school. They'd been part of his training. There was a lot that went into proper farming, and even more that went into it if you were magical. Knowing everything that lived on your land was just the first step.

He had wondered, after his last visit, whether the slowness of the orchard might be due to some magical creature. There were tales about the Dartmoor ponies, whether they might be magical. There was certainly more evidence about the Exmoor ponies. They could, for lack of a better word, flick themselves from place to place across the moors when suitably motivated. And suitably fed, he remembered one of his teachers at Snap talking about some research into particular properties of one of the purple moor grasses.

But Exmoor was milder in climate, wetter, and had generally better soil. Besides, whatever was going on with the orchard, it didn't seem to have much to do with ponies. He hadn't seen any down near here, anyway, at least not so far.

He knew that the moor itself was an entirely different place, too. Maybe he'd figure out a way to get up there. It rose up from the surrounding fields and farms. He knew that, on a clear day, he could see it looming at him from the southwest.

That meant looking for other options. Bees, he'd heard the bees the first day here. He wouldn't disturb them, but observing a hive, if he could find it, might do it. Signs of the various mammals. It was far too early in the day for bats. And he would need the birding guide he'd brought with him to do much with the birds, but he hoped for something else, perhaps a fall flower, or even a tree's leaves beginning to turn.

He could certainly sketch plants. He might see a newt or something of the kind, and perhaps insects. There might be adders around, though he thought not as likely in the orchard itself. And besides, he made more than enough noise coming and going to give them fair warning, as long as he didn't stick his hand into any dark holes.

Adam didn't know why, exactly, he was so insistent on this orchard. His uncle wasn't fussed about the unripe apples. Mrs Whitmore hadn't been either when he'd asked her yesterday. It was just how things were; it was how things always had been. Those apples ripened late. Made it easier on the harvesting. And if he found a few eating apples ready to pick, well, she'd make him some Eve's pudding. He'd loved that, back when he was a boy, out visiting his grandfather and grandmother who'd had the cottage before his uncle. Apples in batter, drenched in custard. There was nothing quite like it.

Circling the orchard got him a few sketches. There were a few flowers he'd need some more research to identify. He'd found a bird's feather, and some scratches on a tree that suggested some sort of mammal. Possibly a dog, possibly something else. He didn't think there was much in the way of a weasel population locally, but he might have missed something in the notes. Once he thought he'd heard the cry of a fox, but he hadn't seen anything, no matter how hard he'd looked.

There was also a pleasant range of mushrooms that had come up thanks to the rains. He'd have to check with his uncle and Mrs Whitmore. And brush up on his mycology. He knew mushrooms as well as any Snap-trained forager, or at least he had before the War. But mushrooms weren't a thing to take on trust.

Perhaps Mrs Whitmore knew someone in the village who could look them over as well, for peace of mind. Besides, he didn't have gloves with him, or a basket that would suit, just his satchel. He did sketches as best he could, noting the colour and the angle of the gills as precisely as possible.

As he was taking a break, he thought he saw a movement back toward the hillside. He froze. Something about it startled him. Not that anyone was close. A good two hundred feet, maybe more. Though, of course, he remembered when two hundred feet was the distance between life and certain death. Numbers didn't sort out in his head the same way they used to. Before.

Whoever it was didn't come closer. They didn't even come as far as the orchard wall. She, probably. There was a skirt, which certainly implied a woman. And she was slim-shouldered, that too. But he couldn't see her face, or anything much else about her. The light was more behind her than otherwise.

After a few minutes, whoever it was went away. That was good. He didn't want to be bothered. He rather vehemently didn't want to be bothered, actually, now he thought about it that way. It was more than enough to walk to the orchard, observe the creepingly slow passage of time, wonder about it a bit, and go back to his uncle's for tea. Any capacity for something more complex had burned out of him, and had no more fuel.

He made his way slowly back along the lane, frowning as it curved away from the hill rising up to the big house. That tree there was turning a beautiful gold, and that one was tipped with red. All south of the road, away from the moor. He turned, at a curve in the lane, to look up toward the moor, and the line of trees stretching up was green. A fair few evergreens, he was sure, but surely not all.

As he turned back to the lane, he saw a flash of white, a shift of the light that made him lean hard on the walking stick. He didn't topple, barely wobbled, but it was a near thing. Something about the light and the speed made him feel like there had been a shot, a burst of flame from a gun or a charm, flying at him again. Or worse, at someone near him.

Instead, his mind scrabbled to make sense of it, before realising the spot of white had slowed, then stopped, a good twenty feet away. He blinked at it, without moving, and it resolved into a white rabbit, or perhaps a hare, sitting up on its hindquarters and peering at him. It was eerie. Not just the colour, Adam knew perfectly well that happened, including in wild animals. But it was something about how it looked at him. Deliberate. Knowing. Like it saw him and weighed him and found him wanting.

He barely breathed. He didn't move, for a good minute or two, until one of the church bells rang, and the hare leaped away, disappearing into the underbrush. He waited until the bells had stopped echoing before he considered moving forward. Adam was feeling like a skittish horse as he moved to the far side of the lane, well away from where the hare had disappeared.

Right. Now he was terrified of hares. Coming to the country had not, perhaps, been a good idea in terms of recovery at all. Worse, the hare had been judging him. Which was a ridiculous sort of thought, unbecoming of a proper sort of man, even if he couldn't get it out of his head.

Adam made his way slowly back. To his surprise, Mrs Whitmore was still there. Or apparently returned. "Sent me back, he did. My Billy's got plans with his mates. Darts match at the pub. Himself said I could do my knitting here, just as snug. There'll be a meat pie for supper in an hour."

Adam nodded. The lighting was likely better. Uncle Benjamin didn't live lavishly, but he was generous with the reflecting lanterns that made the most of charmlights. A necessity for his work, but a pleasure in the evenings as it got dark. "Are you busy now?"

"Just with the knitting." Which she didn't look up from. "I can talk and look at the same time." That came out tart, but amused. "You've a question, then?"

"I was wondering about stories, about the area. There must be some." No one had mentioned stories about an orchard stuck in time, but perhaps there would be something else.

"Here, now? Or up on the moor?"

"Here, please." The moor was a different country. Adam was sure of that. It might be one he should get to know if he stayed here too much longer, but that wasn't a question for right now.

"Well, there are fair few tales of haunts and ghosts. To be fair, most of the old houses have one. And there was a monastery, not too far, people see the ghosts there. Or what was it now? Some tale about a family taking the staircase from the abbey, and all the ghostly monks trooping up and down at night, all in a row."

She sounded more amused than anything else. Adam nodded. "That sort of thing. Or along around the orchards, or the house up on the hill?"

"Ah, well. There are a few legends. One about a maiden, around the time of the Crusades, it was. She was left all alone, and thought herself betrayed, the story goes, and died of it. Or killed herself, or something. To be honest, I'm none too clear on the details. But the tale goes, she goes about as a white hare, still. I can't say I've heard more specifics about ghosts up there, beyond the hare, but they must have one. A grey lady or somewhat."

That was rather too on the nose for Adam's comfort. "Anything else about hares? Or any of the wildlife, really. I got to thinking about what I was seeing in the orchard."

"Ah, there's a long tale, more up on the moor proper, about a witch who'd go into a hare to make a bit of coin."

"To make a bit of coin?" Adam blinked. "That makes no sense."

Mrs Whitmore looked up and laughed, amused at his confusion. "Ah, she'd set her grandson up, turn into a hare. The boy would go tell the local lord or whoever there was a grand hare to be hunted. The boy would get a bit of coin for it, you know? Pointing out a good hunt. And the lord would loose the hounds, she'd give them a grand chase until they were exhausted, and she got away safe. Clever woman, until she got found out." Mrs Whitmore tsked. "That's the sadder part of the story. Some say she was whipped, some burned, some that she repented."

Adam nodded, silently. She'd made the best of a bad bargain, he thought. And if he could turn into a hare, he might still have problems, but they'd be rather different ones. The thought was tempting, certainly. "Any others?"

"Oh, aye, quite a few. There's the one about the Mistress of Birds, now, there are a few versions of that, the sort that don't all make sense put together. But a woman who calls the birds, or maybe a bird, the stories don't agree, and makes it give her favours, or grants the favours. You know the sort of thing, aye?"

Adam nodded. Not a class of tales he knew well, but there were plenty he'd heard here and there that had that touch of the wild magic to them. That made him think of something he hadn't asked before. "And the house? The Morgan house? Are they magical? Seems the sort of spot that might have some lore, especially if they were."

Mrs Whitmore blinked at him, and rearranged her glasses on her nose, peering over them. "You know, I don't rightly know. We do our shopping in the village, both Mrs

Harley and I, but we don't talk. And we'd not talk about that. How would I be knowing a thing like that?"

In some places, the gossip might carry that far, but Adam supposed it was just a sign of how isolated the house was. Or perhaps how indifferent his uncle was to magical society in the area. Quite possibly both.

CHAPTER 9
FRIDAY

T he next day, when Thalia came down for lunch, Mrs Harley cleared her throat. "Pardon, Mistress, would it be a bother if I were gone for the afternoon? There are errands I'm needing to do in Newton Abbot. I'll be back by tea. Bessy has the regular shopping to do and we've knives for sharpening. That will be a bit of time."

Thalia shook her head. "Goodness, no, not a bother at all. There's a kettle in my room if I need anything. A late tea would be fine, too, or whatever's easy for you. Sandwiches." She waved a hand.

"We've soup on the stove for the tea, mistress. I should be back by half-five or so."

Mrs Harley seemed a little ill at ease, shifting from foot to foot. Most curious, and even more curious, as the phrase went. It was as if there was a thread of a story there, something Thalia couldn't understand, never mind articulate.

"I do hope everything goes well. I expect I'll be writing away all afternoon." Thalia left it at that. When she was done with lunch, she retreated upstairs. Her sitting room gave her a decent view of the front drive. Half an hour later, she saw the two of them setting out, both in good frocks and hats, down the long drive.

Thalia gave them another thirty minutes, watching to make sure neither of them came back for some forgotten item. Then, her curiosity wouldn't wait any longer. It was the first chance she'd had to explore the house without worrying about one of them seeing. In the last hour, she'd put together a plan.

She had regular access to all the ground floor except the kitchen and kitchen garden. She was curious about the garden, but that was last on her list. If need be, she could claim the cream had gone off, or something of the kind. Though it seemed to do that far less than she expected, even with a cold box in her room for her. Never mind the cream, she thought, pulling her focus back. She wanted to look at the other rooms on the first and second floors, and whatever attic there was.

The first floor had her two rooms, a sitting room and bedroom. She'd explored most of it as she'd put her things away. If there was a secret passage or a hidden doorway, she hadn't found it. There was another bedroom next to hers, set up as a smaller guest room. Perhaps where one of the other women slept when her great-aunt needed someone right on hand.

That left Great-Aunt Avis's rooms. Thalia paused outside one of the two doors, painted a muted grey-blue like the others in the hallway. She heard no signs anyone had returned to the house. The doors were locked, of course.

She wished for lock picks. Or Hilaria, who had a knack with hairpins. To be fair, Hilaria often forgot her latchkey, and she was always misplacing the keys to her trunk. And long hair meant never being without a few hairpins to spare. It would improve one's skills rather a lot. There might be a set of keys down in the housekeeper's realm. But Thalia didn't think she dared risk finding them, getting them, investigating, and getting them back into place in time.

Thalia pressed her ear to the door, straining to hear if there was anything in there. She didn't know why there should be, of course. It was ridiculous to think it. If Great-Aunt Avis had a dog or a cat or something, it would have the run of the house, or someone would have mentioned it.

Though that was curious. Elderly great-aunts, statistically speaking, tended to dote on small pets. Thalia had done a whole series of profiles at one point, for one of the women's magazines. Not much money in any given one, but you could go on for years. She, though, had not had the fortitude for endless cups of tea and the most minuscule details of a dog's life. Each of which, of course, had to be presented exactly as described.

And Mother had vociferously disapproved of Thalia drawing on family connections for crude pecuniary purposes, otherwise known as having supper seven nights a week. It had been at that point that Thalia had taken the secretarial job, which was tedious and fraught, but did come with a regular and predictable pay packet. A rather small one, but regular.

No use staring at a locked door. Thalia took one more turn around the floor, peering into a closet, then went up the stairs. She'd not dared before. There was no reason for her to be up there, after all.

This time, the doors were a pale green, much like some of the ground-floor rooms. Surprisingly, though, even the hallway had the sense of being used, far more regularly than Thalia would have expected. The floors were all recently swept, no signs of dust at all, even less than in Thalia's own room, which was quite spick and span. The carpet runner down the hall wasn't muted by dust or sun damage.

Thalia went around, testing each of the doors. The ones over her own rooms, below, opened. They were unexceptional guest rooms. One was still set up as the nursery that Thalia remembered from her childhood visits, with a rather memorable Edwardian rocking horse, all dappled grey and red leather fittings. She'd mourned that horse after they'd returned home.

Now, though, it seemed an odd thing. Great-Aunt Avis had no children. Why did they have a fully fitted nursery? Had there been children on her great-aunt's side of the family, perhaps who visited more regularly than Thalia and her parents and her brother and sister?

She remembered Pierus riding the horse, talking about bold cavalry charges and heroic battles. That made her shiver and turn away, rubbing at her face with her hands. War was nothing like that, as he'd learned. As they'd all learned. It never had been, mind, but the Napoleonic wars had been blunted by distance and travel time, and a lack of immediacy in the news arriving home. Not like the sudden telegram out of the blue, a scant day after Pierus had been killed.

Dwelling on it wouldn't do her any good. Or him. Thalia sucked in a breath and turned away, making sure to leave the door closed, exactly as she'd found it. She circled back, glancing nervously down the stairs before she tried the other doors, the one above her great-aunt's rooms.

They were also locked. But this time, she heard something on the far side. It was a burbling sound that made it sound almost as if water was running, splashing into a near-empty bathtub or something of the kind. Only it wasn't constant. It started and stopped.

That made Thalia a tad less worried about an imminent flood. It wasn't coming from outside; the weather was clear enough, there had been no storm in the last day. But what was making it? She tried the door again, rattling the handle this time, and the sound got louder.

It wasn't a sound she could make out, not clearly, as if it were coming behind a waterfall or through a storm. Not water itself, but something behind or surrounded by water, that might be the way to put it. There was something fierce to it, and uncanny. As if something were pulling her closer, wanting her to give in to whatever it was. Uncanny was not a word Thalia had much truck with, usually. This didn't feel like any magic she knew, though, and after a moment, she pulled her hand back, cautiously, wondering what would change.

The sound ebbed away, and so did that almost slimy sense of magic pressing against her, like a bog ready to trap her. There was something there, she was almost sure of it, but she couldn't imagine opening that door now. Not the way it made her feel. Instead, she turned away, to look at the room next door. This one was in that state of temporal preservation that Thalia had begun to assume from the house. As if everything had been near-frozen back, oh, forty years ago. Perhaps fifty. There were photographs on the walls here, but they were the same ones of Great-Aunt Avis and the family. Every one with Great-Aunt Avis looking like she was perpetually thirty or so, even as the ages of the family around her changed.

This time, Thalia could linger a bit. She'd only been investigating for an hour or so. It was a good four-mile walk to the village. That would take an hour and some, then the market day, then getting everything brought back. She still had at least an hour, likely two or three, before anyone would be back on the grounds. Thalia glanced at her watch. At least two, she'd only been half an hour so far, though it felt much longer. She'd have to keep an eye on it, and the light.

Not that it entirely helped. There was nothing obvious in the room. No way through into the next room, either. No hidden doors, no balcony or even a railing to permit her to entertain the ridiculous idea of acrobatics to peer into the locked room. She could, she supposed, consider a rope out of the window to peer in the room below, but there was nothing she trusted as a sturdy anchor. And, honestly, she wasn't at all sure she could get the window open. It looked like it had been painted over long ago.

Her Great-Aunt had not been one for entertaining, Thalia thought. Which made those childhood visits even more curious. Two of them, when she was six and eight. Before Phoebe had gone off to Schola, and before Pierus had gone to the tutoring house, but after they had much patience for her at all.

Had there been visits before she could properly remember? And why had they stopped? That was around when her great-uncle had died. Though that wasn't entirely an explanation. And besides, as far as she could tell, he'd been nearly entirely stripped out of this house in the twenty-odd years since. Few of the photos included him, and the ones that did were large family scenes.

Thalia diagnosed an unhappy marriage, though of course, unhappy marriages were unhappy in hundreds of ways, and she had no idea which it was. It was curious, though. The house had been Great-Aunt Avis's.

None of this was any good. Short of finding a way down from the attic, she'd seen all she was likely to see. That meant she went back downstairs. She paused in the little study dining room, looking at the clock. She'd noticed the weights, three days ago, a third of the way down. If it were a seven-day clock, they should be near the bottom now, but it looked as if they'd barely moved. If Mrs Harley had wound it, surely they'd be nearer the top. That was curious, but the clock just kept ticking away.

It wasn't wrong, exactly. There was no need to wind a clock that didn't need it. But it felt - oh, like lines of stilted archaic prose, in the middle of something that ought to be more pastoral and flowing. Unexpected, a break in the genre, that was the word. The house wanted to be a quiet hermitage, and then she'd turn around and notice something like this clock, and the shadows seemed to get bigger.

She turned away from it, back into the hall, before passing through the green baize door that separated Mrs Harley's fortress from the rest of the house. It was a tidy space, everything labelled and put away. Thalia didn't dare touch anything, but she circled through, making note of where the sugar and cream lived, in case she needed an excuse in the future. No spare sets of keys hung on hooks, unfortunately.

That just left the kitchen garden. She ducked through the back door, out into the garden, and then frowned. There was a greenhouse that seemed like more of a structure than she'd expected. Perhaps that was why tomatoes were still doing well, glowing ruby red through the glass. The garden was still abundantly full of food, at a time when she'd have thought everything was getting muffled up for the coming winter and the long, dark nights.

The whole thing was terribly odd and also rather confusing. It felt, honestly, like she'd walked into some sort of fairy-land, where nothing worked quite as she expected. It made her want to go reread some Edith Nesbit again. The whole place, the rattling empty house, made her think she was going to stumble over a psammead or a phoenix egg or something of the kind. Something Fatae touched, perhaps, one of the stories from before the Pact, when fae creatures of all kinds abounded, at least if one thought all the tales true. She'd heard all the teaching stories, about why the Pact mattered so much, and none of them helped right now. She hadn't done some forbidden ritual, or tried out a dangerous new magic.

Though that was ridiculous. It was a perfectly ordinary house, perhaps in an odd bit of landscape that made for milder weather.

By supper time, everyone was home, and Mrs Harley seemed to be in better humour. Certainly, she seemed to be less on edge. Thalia couldn't make sense of why, though. It was as if the housekeeper had transferred all her nerves to Thalia, like handing over an old burden. And Thalia couldn't shake the feeling she'd had upstairs of something deeply and fundamentally wrong. She wondered if Mrs Harley knew what was there, or if she only had guesses.

At the very least, it seemed like Mrs Harley hadn't discovered her explorations. Or if she had, she was ignoring it for reasons of her own. Thalia couldn't even think about it, because what if the women could in fact read minds? Thalia had retreated to her room well before either of them returned, and so could stretch and smile and say she'd got a bit of writing in. All fine, so long as no one asked about what she'd written. What she'd written was awful. That was how it went.

The whole adventure had reminded her of something

from yesterday, however. When Mrs Harley had brought in soup and a fair bit of a cottage loaf and fresh butter, Thalia cleared her throat. "Pardon, Mrs Harley?"

"Yes, mistress?"

"I know you asked about anyone down in the fields. I did see someone in the orchard, I think, but it might have been a trick of the light."

"Not close up Mistress? You'd know a traveller, I suppose, even being a city lady as you are?"

Thalia felt that 'lady' was clearly something of an insult here, or rather as much of one as the housekeeper would permit. On one hand, it was entirely accurate. And even by implication it was, she was not from here, and they all knew it. "I would."

"Might be the nephew." That was Bessy, coming in with a fresh pot of tea.

"Might." Mrs Harley nodded. "Tall man?"

"Probably. He had a walking stick, as tall as his head?" Thalia looked from one to the other. They were being obscure and mysterious. Probably not on purpose, though honestly, this house was making her suspect near everything.

"Might be." Mrs Harley considered. "Young man, staying with his uncle, down in the village. Bessy heard Mrs Whitmore, who does for Benjamin Walton, talking a bit today. Had a bad War, from what she said. Made him more than a bit unpredictable, from what she didn't say. And there was that event in the library, earlier, you recall of course. You be careful, mistress, if you go out walking."

Again, infuriatingly, Thalia couldn't tell how to take that. Was it disapproving, commiserating, something else? Mrs Harley repressed so much emotion in her voice that it was impossible to tell. Thalia nodded. "Has his family been here long?"

"Oh, aye. His grandda was well known in the village. He had the orchard. His wife, now, she made a fine batch of jam, won first prize for it, in the village, a dozen years running. They died, oh, years ago now. The summer we had the flooding." That jam was impressive, somewhere like here, where the competition was likely fierce.

"And the nephew?" Thalia brought the conversation back to the original point. She'd wondered, hadn't she, earlier, about what happened to him. It sounded like he'd made it through, but not quite all in one piece.

"Gather his uncle broke his leg, badly, a few weeks ago. It'll be some time mending." Which was rather a lot. Thalia knew from her own time as a VAD that bone injuries were one of the easier things to sort out, comparatively, but a bad break hurt the muscles as well as the bone, and that took far longer.

"I'm glad there's some help then." Thalia said. She then suppressed a shiver of memory, of men coming in to the Temple of Healing with horrific breaks that pierced the skin and twisted the whole leg into a wreckage. Clearly the man was not so bad off as that. "I'll see about another walk tomorrow if the weather holds. And this soup is grand, Mrs Harley, thank you."

That got her left alone for a solitary end to her meal. Thalia spent rather more of the night than she'd intended rummaging in the library for something suitable and reading it. No Nesbit. If there were any here, it must be up in the nursery. But there were plenty of folk tales of Dartmoor, which just got her worrying over large black hounds and dangerous lights that lured you into bogs.

CHAPTER 10
SATURDAY, OCTOBER 1ST

Adam continued what had now become a routine. He spent the morning reading and tending to whatever small things the household needed. After luncheon, he'd make sure his uncle was settled in for the afternoon, and go off to the orchard. He didn't need to worry about running into anyone else, most likely. Maybe a passing farmer on the lane, but that had only been the once.

Today, the weather loomed ominously until he crossed over into the orchard proper, where the trees seemed kissed by sunlight, more like summer than starting into October. A few apples showed some signs of ripening, and Adam slowly made a circuit of the place. The mushrooms had not disappeared overnight, nor had many new ones appeared. There were again some signs of something scratching at the ground here or there, but he couldn't tell what that might be.

This time, Adam had brought a book. Reading outside, in decent weather, certainly had some pleasure to it. He'd planned to alternate reading with some more sketching, but his fingers were being a challenge today. Turning pages he could manage, a pencil, not perhaps so much. That kept him occupied until well past two.

When he looked up from the cloak he'd set down on a dryish patch of ground, he found someone watching him. He could see her better now, but she was staring not at him, but at the apples. Then he must have moved. Perhaps he'd twitched without noticing it, because she turned her head, looking at him.

She waved tentatively, as if she wasn't sure what was done here. Adam reached up and touched the brim of the flat cap he was wearing. It was much simpler for him, in a number of ways, that social nicety.

There was silence, even the birds were quiet for a moment. Then, deliberately, she came closer, toward the low stone wall, before she glanced along it and found the gate. Not asking permission, but he supposed that she wasn't the sort, and it was a public way, technically, the path around the orchard.

As she got closer, Adam got a better look at her. Wool skirt in a dark green, some sort of blouse in a finer fabric, not made for hard work. And a deep blue cardigan over it that was far too big for her shoulders, and darned in a couple of places. The hat on her head had a ribbon that matched the skirt. It made the whole effect rather smart for the countryside, but her boots were rugged enough for a good ramble. She had the sort of brown hair that made him think of undistinguished tree bark, but it was a colour he found restful on the whole.

He looked rather different, he suspected. Sturdy tweed trousers and a hat to match with a heathery-green jumper that had been patched three times in the elbows. A tie with the Snap colours, deep green and tan. And, well, his unpre-possessing self.

"Hello. Goodness. I hadn't expected to see anyone else down here. Though, were you here two afternoons ago? I thought I saw someone, but I wasn't sure until rather later."

My, the woman chattered. Adam thought, at first, she was just a fluttery sort. But then he caught a note in her tone, the kind of anxious that wasn't sure about being alone in the quiet.

"Adam Walton." That was the sticking point. He extended his right hand, hoping it would behave itself. His left was usually worse, but he wasn't sure about either today. She glanced at it, and then put her own out and shook his hand with a surprisingly strong grip.

"Thalia Morgan. I'm staying up the hill, my great-aunt's place." She gestured with her chin as she released his hand. Then she tilted her head. "You're not from around here."

"Nor are you." The accents said it all, really. His own marked him as being from Surrey, near enough. And hers, hers was somewhere in the Southeast, but he was fairly sure she'd spent most of the past decade in London. It had the speed of London, for one thing.

There was a flash of something, not a smile, but then she nodded briskly. "London, all my adult life. Except for..." She shrugged, and Adam could fill that in. Something in the War. He wondered what she'd done. Something tame and clean, most likely. She seemed the sort of woman who'd rolled bandages and perhaps staffed a canteen near a training camp or something of the kind. On alternate Thursday after-noons. Nothing terribly demanding, certainly.

The woman tilted her head, then glanced at his tie,

before deciding something. It was a brisk nod, filing him away into some category in which he was forever lacking.

It made him wonder if she placed the tie, or not. On the one hand, perhaps the people up the hill weren't magical. There were plenty of obscure and remote country houses that weren't. And plenty of ties, for that matter, that had green and tan.

He knew the Devonshire Regiment was close enough to the Snap tie, for one thing, though the patterns were a tad different. On the other hand, it wasn't as if she were going to be measuring the width of the stripes, either. Adam brought his chin up, refusing to fold beneath her gaze.

"Army?" Her voice was clear, sharper than he'd given her any cause for.

"Yes'm." He let the last sound draw out, not quite a boy tipping his hat to his betters, lined up along the road, but near enough.

She went entirely still. It was rather like a bird who had been spotted by some predator, a hawk or eagle or something much larger, with great talons. Then she gave a tiny shrug, the sort he'd seen on society ladies, as if even movement was far too much effort to spend on someone like him.

That hadn't worked. He cleared his throat and tried to sound like an ordinary person would. "I hope your great-aunt recovers quickly?" It sounded feeble as soon as it was out of his mouth.

She nodded. "She's away, an illness. My parents have her somewhere in the south of France. I think." That last seemed like it slipped out without her quite meaning to.

The woman was baffling, and that was very annoying. Adam swallowed, then said, "It's my uncle's orchard." Perhaps he could get her to just go away. Surely that would be easier for both of them. And his knee was beginning to complain again.

She looked around, then blinked several times, as she was considering some new and startling fact. Then she brushed her hands off and held her hand out again. "Hello. I'm Thalia. Have you noticed anything odd around here?"

What on earth was the daft woman doing? Starting over like that. Like she'd lost a bit of time, and she was picking up where it seemed sensible to her. She didn't look like she was addled, but you never knew. Certainly Adam didn't look as badly off as he was some of the time. And telling her she was one of the odder things he'd seen today probably wouldn't do.

Adam looked down at her hand, back at her face, then over her head at the apples. The unripe apples that should have been harvested weeks ago. The mushrooms that hadn't changed. The grass that still looked like late summer. A dozen other things. The too fast hum of the bees. Then, slowly, he reached for her hand a second time. "Adam."

"Right." Her voice was brisk now. "You're really staying with your uncle? And this is his orchard?" If she noticed he hadn't answered her question, she didn't seem bothered. "It's just that I noticed there's lots of apples here, still growing, and it's not as if I've been all through the village, not yet. But I thought that mostly apples were harvested by now, isn't that right? Is there something odd with the apples here, then?"

And how was he supposed to answer that? He didn't dare reach to feel the Pact, the oath he'd made as a youth that protected magic, kept any of them from talking about it. He couldn't bear the touch of that, not for a decade, like it rubbed on skin that was far too raw and never healed.

"He says it's normal. Others ripen earlier, this one ripens later. That is how it's been for decades. Longer, maybe. The family's only been here since 1860 or so." He could play the game of sounding non-committal.

"And you?" She glanced at the apples, looking away from him, and he took a breath. "Do you know about orchards?"

It would be a great deal easier if he knew that she'd identified him as being one of Snap's yeomen farmers. The brightest of the men and women who lived and died by the land.

"Not so much, but a bit." He shrugged. "I've been reading up." What he wanted, and what he feared, was an omen.

Thalia leaned forward, looking at him directly, now. In the eyes. No one had done that in ages, and he wasn't at all sure he liked it. Certainly, he didn't have any idea what to do with it. Then she drew back a bit. "What do you think?"

Adam coughed and looked away. Apples. Apples were odd, but they didn't stare. When he didn't say anything, she said it again, as if she actually wanted to know. "What do you think, then? About the orchard."

Adam blinked at her, startled. She seemed in earnest, the way women got when they got the bit in their teeth. Which was a ridiculous saying. The bit went where horses didn't have teeth, definitionally. Then he swallowed. "I could understand a week or two's difference. We're in the lee of the hill. It stays warmer a bit longer, perhaps. Gets sun longer, though we're on the north side of the moor. But this is - this is near a whole season shifted."

"And that seems odd to you. It does to me, but I admit, I don't know a lot about, well, growing things. Orchards. Farms. Domestic animals. I mean, I like a cat, or I would like a cat, if I thought I could keep a cat properly. But that's entirely different, isn't it? Especially in a city. It's not like they keep mice out of barns there."

"Kitchens." It popped out of him without warning. "Also good for kitchens."

She beamed at him, as if, for some benighted reason, anything he said delighted her. Which was, in the list of things that were odd, also odd. He was gathering a rather long list. The apples, certainly. But those scratch marks in the dirt, and the way he'd seen fewer birds than he should, and the hurry of the bees. The hare, though he supposed there was enough folklore wandering around the place that people must bump into it from time to time.

She cleared her throat. "Anything else odd?" It so exactly mirrored his thoughts that he knew he looked startled, then he coughed again for an excuse to cover his face. "How long have you been here?"

"Three weeks or so. You?"

"About the same. Before this, not for ages and ages. I was eight, the last time we came. I rarely came down this far, though. Nanny preferred the garden up near the house, all tidy." Thalia wrinkled up her nose. Adam could just see the sort of girl she must have been, in a pretty dress and perhaps a pinafore to keep clean, and shoes meant for indoors, not woodlands. Perhaps a straw hat and hair in long plaits, which was decidedly not what she looked like now.

"Huh." Someone had to say something. That was what he had. "What are things like up at the house?" He hesitated, before implying oddness anywhere else. People took offence at that sort of thing.

"Also odd. But not so obviously odd as the apples." She

flicked her fingers at them. "Are they, I don't know. Lurkingly wrong? Dangerously wrong? Or are they just odd?"

"Does it make a difference?" He felt his fingers twitch and jammed his hands in his pockets. Better to be a slight bit rude than draw that sort of attention to his failures. He wasn't at all sure what he thought about her worrying about fairy apples the same way he had. It meant there was likely something to worry about.

"Well. It does make me wonder what sort of narrative we've wandered into. I was thinking, yesterday, that I half-expected to come across a psammead."

Adam blinked. "A what now?" Not an animal he'd ever met, he knew that.

"Edith Nesbit. *Five Children and It*? And there's two sequels. You know the sort of thing, even if you don't know that one, children coming across a magical creature, each of them with their own tidy personality traits, neatly labelled. The clever one, the kind and good-hearted one, the joker, the one who's a little sensitive or frightened, the unformed baby."

Adam couldn't stop himself blinking more. "Do you, I say, do you dislike it?" It was also not helping him at all decide whether or not she might also be magical. She was quite right about the whole range of literature, and it confused things utterly.

"Oh, they're quite good books for what they are. A tad simplified, but that's a risk of children's books, isn't it? I blame the publishers, even more than the authors. There's a whole set of assumptions about what children must want to read. Which honestly are at least as much about what people are willing to buy for children." Thalia shrugged. "You don't want to hear about that, surely?"

Adam thought it at least had novelty to recommend it

as a topic. It was not about apples, cider, garden design, or him hiding or failing to hide his frailty, which had made up most of his conversational range for some time now.

"And a, what, sammyad?" Adam asked instead.

"The collection of children finds a creature that grants wishes. The Psammead." She spelled it out, letter by letter. "I'd have to find a copy to look up a proper description. But I remember it being that sort of overly detailed that makes you sure someone is having you on. Haven't you noticed that, when someone becomes exceedingly detailed without any particular reason for it?"

Adam swallowed again. "Um. Yes?"

Thalia beamed at him, as if very pleased to be agreed with. She might chatter along, but she had some sense to her, or at least the parts Adam could sort out seemed to. He honestly wasn't sure what to make of her. The way she seemed a whole different person after she forgot the first half of the conversation did not help him figure her out at all.

CHAPTER 11
SATURDAY IN THE ORCHARD

T halia wasn't at all sure what to do here. She thought the tie meant he might have gone to Snap, but it wasn't as if she knew anyone from Snap. Where she'd grown up, they moved in entirely different circles.

Her people might socialise with a few from Dunwich or Alethorpe, those at the top of their professions. A number of the best healers and apothecaries had gone to Alethorpe, and a number of trading families, including the Pelagius clan and the banking families, usually went to Dunwich. Being in trade might be a tad, well, lower class, but it was also so terribly handy to know someone who could help you get something special back to Albion. Or find it in the first place, for that matter.

And second, she could feel Mother glaring at her from across the Channel and down in the south of France. If that was where they were, the place had fallen out of her head with all the scramble about getting to the house and packing things up.

Which, now she thought about it, was also odd, at least

six ways round. That distracted her, rather a lot, so that the next thing she knew, Adam was clearing his throat, and he'd just mentioned something she had missed.

"Oh, pardon. You must think I'm daft." She saw his reaction, before anything else, the way he withdrew, just a hair, like that was a personal insult. Even though it was about her. Thalia was not at all sure what to do with that.

She was fairly sure he was real. For one thing, she had seen him two days ago. For another, there was gossip about him. Which, well, there was gossip about ghostly hounds, and ghosts of other kinds. And she'd heard a story she couldn't believe about hairy hands. They would appear from nowhere and grab the handles of whatever you were driving and steer you off the road, up by Postbridge. She made a note not to bike anywhere near Postbridge, wherever it was. Again.

Then she realised Adam was still staring at her.

"Um." Thalia straightened her shoulders. "I suppose you don't know what to make of me. That's fair."

Adam gaped at her for a moment, then cleared his throat, uncertainly. "I couldn't say."

In a Schola man, it would have come out plummy and puffed up. In him, though, it was more like he had the good sense the Gods gave the gifted not to stick his foot in his mouth and get in trouble. If his uncle owned the orchard, it wasn't leased land. He wasn't dependent on Great-Aunt Avis's goodwill. But that wasn't helping either.

"Well. Most people look at me and think I'm not good for anything. And I'm sorry, I do go on, I do that sometimes." Often, to be honest, but she was a writer, she could choose her words with purpose.

Adam considered, then spread his hands. "I am, pardon, ma'am, not sure what you want here?" The ma'am rolled off his tongue like he used it all the time. That might suggest the tie wasn't Snap. Why weren't people like in stories, where you could give them easily identifiable features? You had all the different stock personalities, the daft scholar, the ingenue bent on a romance, the elderly man who lectured everyone and got things ridiculously wrong. Or, in this case, the honest farmer might do, though what that made Thalia, she had no idea.

That was fair. She had no idea what she wanted, honestly. Or, to be more precise, she wanted a lot of things. Fame, a steady and sufficient income from her writing, a place to live that didn't require buckets under leaks when it rained hard. Perhaps a cat. But none of them seemed terribly likely. Except perhaps the cat.

Certainly, none of them were on offer in an apple orchard. She glanced around, and then said. "Could I eat an apple?"

The question made him blink, but he nodded, "Moment." He shifted his weight, as if testing his balance, and then took several steps toward one of the trees with more visibly ripened fruit. There, he peered at several apples within reach before twisting one off. He had that odd sense of movement she'd seen a couple of times when she had been at the Temple of Healing.

Men whose minds had got shaken up. Where whatever magics the body used to tell your feet where to go and your hands what to do had got so jangled, none of it quite worked right. She'd been told by one of the nurses that it was all in their heads, the problem. But another nurse, what was her name, Sister Pomegranate? Sister Parthenope. Sister Philomela. No, none of that was right.

"Pomona!" She said the name out loud, then clapped her hand to her mouth. She'd startled Adam as much as she'd startled herself. He dropped the apple he was holding, with a jerk of his wrist that sent it flying to split against a tree. He looked after it with a moment of some deep hurt or resignation, then plucked another without saying anything.

"Goddess of apples?" It came out of the silence, as if he were just now catching up with what she'd said. Then he frowned at the apple in his hand, and said, "Moment." That he placed it that quickly made her think he must have gone to Snap again. But it wasn't as if you could interrogate someone about the breadth and depth of their mythological reading. Some people got very obsessive about that sort of thing, whatever their background.

He went off to another tree, across the path from where they were standing, peering up at it. Now she could see him walk a good twenty steps or so. She could see that one of his feet didn't quite want to follow along evenly. It was a little like watching a sheepdog with a flock of sheep. There was always one who wanted to stray and had to be nudged back with the others. It was quite an image.

She didn't say anything else until he came back, holding out two apples. Then he frowned at his hands. "Um. Can I offer you a rock? A tree stump? Thought." He glanced up at her. "Two different sorts. Thought you might want to taste both. And I wanted to see how they tasted."

"Do you know what varieties they are?"

"Well. Yes and no. It's an orchard, the trees are grafted, Uncle Benjamin has records. But there's a few wildlings in here, and sometimes apples just get minds of their own, you know?"

She didn't, so she blinked at him. He turned away, stumping over to fold himself down onto the cloak he'd apparently been sitting on earlier. Joining him was not the done thing at all, so she perched on an old stump, nearby.

Adam pulled out a small knife from somewhere. A belt pouch or pocket, maybe. He seemed the sort to use one every five minutes. If she were writing about someone like him, she'd put that detail in. The way he either held his hands out of the way, or seemed to have something in them. Apples, at the moment, and he pulled out a bit of wax paper, and a book for a flat surface. Then he used the wax paper to cut the apples up on.

The slices he held out were slightly uneven, but better than what Thalia managed most of the time. The pen was mightier than the sword, and also the kitchen knife, in her case. It was a terrible problem that no one had ever actually taught her how to cook things. Everything she knew was guesswork, and sometimes one of her friends taking pity on her and showing her something in passing.

She missed when she'd been working during the War, and she could just rely on the refectory or whatever other meal they got together. Even if the food wasn't terribly good. To be fair, it had been the War, and nothing was terribly good. Not the food, not the laundry, not the clothes, not the shoes. Certainly not anything going on in the world that needed tending to.

Then he was holding out slices of the other apple to her and taking a bite of one of them. The expression on his face was going to bother her for weeks, Thalia was sure. Not that it was a bad expression, anything but. The problem was, she had no idea how to describe it, and now she wanted to.

You saw people writing about lust and passion and anger and all sorts of other emotions. Thalia had often considered those attempts a bit overwrought, while admitting she did exactly the same thing, and probably more often. Whatever Adam was feeling, it wasn't any of that. It was a certainty, being confident of what he was going to get, leaning on that known pleasure like he did on the walking stick.

He took a bite, then another and another, until he finished the slice. "Sops in wine." he said.

"Pardon?" This conversation was apparently going to be partly about random words that made no sense. On the other hand, she'd started it. She couldn't blame him for that.

"The apple. The variety's called Sops in Wine. It's an ancient apple, as apples go, sometime in the 17th century. End of it, if I remember right, but. Quite venerable."

"And you knew how to figure that out? That is clever. I'm awful, looking at plants. I mean, I can do the obvious ones. Churchyard yew. Apple tree when there are apples on it. Or blossoms. Lavender. Rosemary. Though it helps if they're in a kitchen garden."

Adam considered her, tilting his head, as if he weren't sure what to make of someone that ignorant. "Not a part of your growing up?"

She shook her head. "Or since. Part of it's London, of course. There are allotment gardens, but not very near me, and no one sensible would trust me to grow anything. I've killed every indoor plant anyone's ever given me. I tried to learn a bit at school, but..." She shrugged. "It didn't take."

Adam opened his mouth, then popped a bit of apple into it. She couldn't decide if he'd meant to say something or not.

"Actually, what I took wasn't very practical? Really, I wish I'd done a course in, well, taking care of people. That would have been useful." She hadn't done the Healing course, it hadn't seemed remotely relevant at the time.

Of course, she'd written, during the War, begging them

to make sure everyone got at least the basics. Enough to help in an emergency. More importantly, to know what sort of things they had the stomach to help with.

There had been so many VADs who'd just fainted at things that were, in the grand scheme of the Temple of Healing, rather mild. And then someone had to make sure they wouldn't trip anyone up, and they hadn't bumped their heads, and it just made everything all the more awful.

Adam popped another bit of apple into his mouth, chewed and swallowed. "What do you do with yourself in London, then?"

She shrugged. "I write. Work as a secretary to pay my bills. Moth - my parents, they wanted me to do the proper finishing school sorts of things." Wanted to make that her apprenticeship, near enough, before she was shunted off into an equally appropriate and entirely tedious marriage.

"Anything I might have read?"

She blinked at him, startled. "That depends what you read, doesn't it? I mean..." And now she really couldn't answer because near enough everything was in one of the magical community magazines, such as they were. She fumbled the apples in her hand, and then ate a slice to help her balance them, cradling the others in her other hand. "Oh, I say, that's quite good."

"Known for the colour, like it was soaked in wine." He displayed two of the slices on a large hand. The way the pink was deeper on the skin, and faded as it got toward the centre, gave that impression, definitely. "The other one is Beauty of Bath. Both early apples."

"Only here. They're only barely ripe, a few of them." She glanced up at the trees. The second one was sweeter in taste, to the bittersweet of the Sops in Wine, and she alternated bites for a moment, trying to figure out how to describe it.

"Mmm." He gestured with a thumb. "You said Pomona?"

"Oh, I was thinking of someone. A Sister Pomona, one of the nurses I worked with." She cut it off there. For one thing, she daren't say 'At the Temple of Healing'. That was a dead giveaway. And for another, she didn't know how to explain the rest of it.

"I thought you said you didn't have much practical?" He was looking at her now, like he knew things she didn't want anyone to know.

She shook her head, a slight motion. She could feel herself now, the way she was drawing back, like she was narrating her own life inside her head.

"Oh, no. I helped during the War. Everyone doing their bit, all that." Helping wasn't the word for what she'd done. Well, yes, some of it had actually been helpful, she was sure of that. Other parts had been a long, awful slog, and the people she'd done it with had divided into three tidy groups. The ones who actually had talents at healing, but who had been kept from going into it by family assumptions. That wasn't her. The ones who made a show of doing it, and were bloody useless. Also not her, or at least she tried very hard to avoid it.

And then there had been the ones like her, who desperately wanted to do something useful. And if that meant all the awful work, cleaning and bandaging and writing letters for men who were dying slowly and awfully, well. She could do that, and she did. She'd learned far more than she'd ever wanted about burns and lungs that would never heal, and what the Healers said should help, but never did.

CHAPTER 12
THE ORCHARD

Adam was not at all sure what to do with this woman. Or the situation. Frankly, he wasn't too used to dealing with strangers at all, and hadn't been for nearly a decade. He was, however, fairly sure this wasn't how things went. Whether or not she was also magical, she was baffling.

But there she was, perched on the tree stump, and here he was. He couldn't just walk away. That was rude, undeniably. He might not be the sort of gentleman who went to Schola and spoke like she did. All the crispness of her words, even when there was a flood of them. But he could avoid being rude.

He coughed. "Look. Um."

"Yes?" Her voice was chirpy and bright. The note caught him off-guard, the way it was such a change from just a few moments ago. The way he'd claim everything was all right, when it absolutely wasn't.

Oddly, though, it didn't bother him the way Mother did, or some of his aunts. It wasn't the false chipperness of someone who was refusing to notice all the things that were wrong about him. He wasn't sure if she was simply so oblivious to half the world she hadn't noticed, if she was ignoring it, or what. Certainly not something he could ask about.

He flailed around inside his head for something to say. "You're a secretary? Besides the writing?"

Thalia nodded, a bit grimly. "Well, I was, and I'm sure I will be again. Except someone had to come here and keep an eye on the place. Which is actually rather ridiculous. There's a housekeeper and a maid, and they're both perfectly competent."

"Perhaps your great-aunt didn't trust them alone? Or needed someone to sign off on things?" Adam was not at all sure how he had got himself into this conversation.

"Mrs Harley's been here for ages and ages. Decades. And I'm sure she knows just where everything is. If there'd been something legal to tend to. Great-Aunt Avis must have a solicitor or a man of business or something. Having me down here is... odd."

"To go with the other oddness." Adam had to admit it sounded queer. "And how long are you going to be here? Doesn't your work, I mean." There he was assuming things again. Maybe her work was just a way to keep busy.

"Father's paying me a stipend while I'm here. I'm saving it up for when I get back. A bit of a buffer. I was getting fed up with my last place, one of the men, well. I'll go through an agency to find somewhere new whenever Great-Aunt Avis is, well, whatever happens. When I go back to London."

Adam frowned. That wasn't what he expected from someone like her. Like she seemed to be. "An agency?"

She kicked one foot out, rolling her ankle and looking away from him. "Great-Aunt Avis lives in a huge house, with staff. I live in an attic room in a Georgian town house made over into flats full of writers and artists and whatever, and someone's subletting my flat while I'm here." Then she looked up, something stubborn and fierce there, as if she expected him to be difficult about it.

Adam wasn't sure he knew how to be difficult about that kind of thing. Oh, he knew about social snobbery, but he hadn't been inclined to it much before the War. And since then, he'd been on the receiving end of it, over and over again, as a 'temporary gentleman'. One of the officers who'd earned it through his own actions, but not really One Of Us. Capitals strongly implied.

And then, of course, he'd gone and lost his mind, and none of them would talk to him. Cowardice was contagious, or the next thing to.

He missed the next sentence entirely. Perhaps several sentences, because when he managed to focus on her again, she had that look on her face. The one his mother got, routinely, that he hadn't been paying any attention. "I beg pardon?"

"You said something about, what was it earlier? Gramping?"

"Grafting." Gramping, good grief. "You don't know about apples, then?" Adam peered at her.

"That," Thalia said, more acerbically, "Is why I'm asking you. You're the one that knew what kinds there were. And that it's odd they're not ripe yet."

Adam leaned back on one hand. "Grafting." He swallowed, then rummaged for his flask of tea, and swallowed some of that. He should, properly, offer her some, but he only had his flask, and she could go find her own tea. Somewhere, in the back of his mind, a little voice noticed the rising edge of irritation lurking around the edges. He ignored it. "You know you can't just take an apple and plant the seeds and get the same kind of apple, right?"

"I do not, in fact, know that." She was leaning forward, blinking at him, as if he were pulling her leg.

"'It's true. You have to graft to get more of a particular kind. Cut a branch off, properly, cut a slit on a different tree, and graft it on, binding it up - or there are other options - so it grows strong." At the last moment, he avoided mentioning charms. "Give it a few years, and you have predictable fruit. Near all of these were grafted. There are a few wildlings here and there, mostly around the edges."

"You realise that makes no sense?" She brushed her hands off on her skirt, suddenly, too quickly.

He shrugged one shoulder. "It's how things are done. Have been done with fruit trees for ages. Roses, too. Olives. Grapes for wine. Not that I've grown those. It goes back to China. They taught us." He cut off where he might have learned that, his self-control was slipping.

She shook her head again. "Why?" Her voice had an edge to it, the wrong sort of edge.

"A lot of plants can't self-pollinate. Apples among them. Male plant, female plant, need both. You can get it by grafting a male scion onto a female rootstock, or the other way round. And then, sometimes, you want to use the blessings of a rootstock, hardiness or sturdiness or established growth, but you want to get something specific from the fruit. Or you can use grafting to get several varieties on the same tree. That one has Sops of Wine on this side, and I think that's Devonshire Quarrendale on the other."

Thalia looked at him, still entirely dubious. He shrugged. "You don't have to believe me, but I'm right."

"It doesn't make sense." It didn't fit into her tidy view of the world. That did what she wanted. If she lived in an attic, he was quite sure it was at least substantially because she chose to, at some level. She was on good enough terms with her family that her father was willing to give her a stipend to be here. And for her to be here in the first place. It made him even more cranky. She had choices, and she didn't see them.

He didn't say anything, just looked at a point in one of the trees. He didn't know what to say, and she certainly wasn't making it easy to carry on a conversation.

"How old are the trees?" The question popped out of her mouth and into his ears rather suddenly. As if she'd set aside the earlier bafflement and was trying some new attack. On him, on reality, both.

"These? All older. Nothing grafted recently. I mean, you can see if there's been a graft in the past few years, usually. Even if the rag holding things together is gone, you can see the joins. But you also wouldn't get fruit off a graft for a few years, most like." He waved a hand. "But all of those? Decades, probably. My uncle's records make it clear there hasn't been much grafting in - oh. My lifetime."

"Was it his for ages? Has it been his?"

"My grandfather's, his da's." Adam shrugged. "He'd come up from a farming family, became a grocer, built a small empire. Kept the family cottage, retired there." It was an awkward place to retire, actually, if you wanted to keep up with much, being on a less than frequent train line and far from any useful portal. Unless there was a private one tucked up at the great-aunt's house, or some other nearby estate Grandda had had the use of. Or perhaps his grandmum, who had been both charming and from a more established family.

"So nothing's changed much for a good while." Thalia waved a hand at the house, and again, some flicker of the movement caught his eye, or caught the light. It made him close his eyes.

"The house?" Even to him, it sounded weak. Feeble. She'd say something awful, soon. As always, he couldn't decide if waiting for it was worse than hearing it.

"The house looks like it hasn't changed since, oh, Queen Victoria's coronation. Other than a few things like photographs." Adam wondered for a moment if she'd meant to use some other date, and if so, which one. The rise and fall of monarchs in the non-magical community affected them all, but it wasn't the same as before the Tudors. Nothing was.

Sometimes, in the dark, late at night, when he couldn't sleep, he read about that history. It had been such a complete and dramatic change, like the one he'd lived through. He kept thinking something there might give him a rope to hang on to. Even if it were the kind of rope that was dragging him behind a large and fast-moving object. Might show him a way through, even if it were battered and faded and twisted out of all recognition.

Once more, he lost a sentence or two of what she said, and this time, he didn't look at her when he said, "Beg pardon?" again.

She went quiet, then suddenly she was pushing herself upright in a flurry of movement and speed that he couldn't match, even if he'd wanted to. Her body was all elbows and knees and scowling, now. The little flashes he caught, because the light behind her made shadows that made his head ache. He caught a word, here or there, mostly the last one, "alone" before she stormed off back across the stone wall.

Adam flinched, and then he froze. He could feel it come over him, the way his body wouldn't answer to him, how his hand trembled against his leg. Everything locked up, like some automaton that had run out of fuel. It was the disapproval that did it, more than anything else, these days. The angle of her head, the tilt of her chin. The sound in her voice, more than anything else.

He stayed there, his eyes closed tight against the world, for what felt like a long time. And probably was, this time. His hands and legs got colder, he grew stiff, and it wasn't just the muscles clenching against an anticipated explosion. Slowly, painfully, he worked through the exercises the Gospatricks had worked out, bit of body by bit of body. Toes, first. Ball of the foot. Working his way up from the bits of him that froze least to the ones hardest to move, his jaw and neck and shoulders.

By the time he got his eyes to open properly and focus, the day had shifted, tipping over well into late afternoon. He heard the bark of a fox nearby, but no birds, nothing else that hinted at the season or time of day. Even the bees had gone quieter. That was a bad sign, for him, for the orchard. For everyone, probably.

Incipient dread, that's what one of the poor chaps at one of the homes had called it. The lurking sense that everyone was doomed. Lurking certainty. There was no use fighting it when it set in like this. He could only hope he could pry himself upright, shuffle home, and at least be in utter misery inside, on a soft bed, rather than out in the wilds with who knew what.

CHAPTER 13
SATURDAY NIGHT

T halia had come back up the hill, worn out and drenched under her cardigan, to find tea had been served.

The tea itself had been welcome, but she'd found herself unable to stomach any of the food. Her insides seemed to be doing flips, like she'd run endless races or got through the worst of the intake at the train station. When Mrs Harley was out of the room, she held out her hand, and it was trembling.

The housekeeper came back, all brisk and proper. Thalia wanted to ask a dozen things, but what she managed, between sips of tea, was "The nephew. Do you know where he lives? The one who was visiting?"

"Why, mistress?"

"I think I met him, down by the orchard. Adam Walton?"

Mrs Harley sniffed, softly. "Believe that's him. About your age, mistress? I've not seen him, heard a bit in the village. I told you that. He's none too steady on his feet, I gather. Might be the War, might be drink, who knows. And he near broke a chair in the library, from what I heard. Not that I've heard anything about him hurting someone direct. But I suppose Mrs Whitmore wouldn't say, she's known to be fierce about Benjamin Walton. She works for his uncle, there's a house to the west of town, on the main road. Nothing fancy, a cottage. Upstairs and down, gardens, some chickens."

That, at least, was some help. She hadn't wanted to leave him, but there had been something there, lurking, that made her entirely unsettled. Not uncanny, not the way the house was, but something with expectations. Something grasping.

He hadn't reacted any of the way she'd expected, not through the conversation. Having another sip of tea, she tried to think about it more clearly, and kept failing. She hadn't felt any threat from him. He'd been kind, really, certainly patient with her ignorance. And then things had changed. He'd gone still, and she'd had no idea why.

Coming back up the hill hadn't made it any better, which meant the whole thing was either a trick of her mind, or was the house itself. And if it were the house, well, that was a problem. Seeing as she didn't have anywhere else to eat or sleep. And the house had her typewriter.

She swallowed. "I'm sorry, the weather must be catching up to me. Would the boiler be up to a hot bath, do you think?"

"I'll send Bessy up to run it, mistress. Do you need someone to be around after?"

Of course, they wanted their own little cosy cottage and privacy, and whatever it was they did in the evenings. Thalia very much wanted company in the house, but she'd be painted blue before she admitted it. It wasn't as if her relations with either of them had led to confidences, much as she was sure they were perfectly pleasant women in their own way.

"Oh, no. Running the bath is grand, but please, go off to your evening as you would normally. Though." She glanced at her food. "I'm afraid I'm not very hungry at the moment. Could I bring up a tray for later?"

"Yes, mistress. I'll take this, pop the soup in stasis, we've some rolls and cheese and apples." Mrs Harley was at least efficient about the whole thing, and Thalia was able to escape back to her own room.

The bath had, in the end, been something of a help. It was a proper copper tub, broad and ancient and comfortably curved. And better yet, fully charmed to let her soak as long as she wanted without going cold. She'd read a good half a soothing book, one of those she remembered fondly from her girlhood, and which hadn't been horribly warped by later experience. By the time she'd got out, the house was quiet, with just a few lanterns in the hall.

She thought back on the afternoon, and after a moment, her thoughts settled out more evenly. Calmly, as if the afternoon had been a long time ago, instead of just a couple of hours. It felt as distant as the War. No. Before the War.

Thalia opened the door from her room, then closed it again. She turned back to the desk, where the tray waited. Soup, with a little domed cover to keep it piping hot. Bread and butter. Cheese. And an apple.

Of course, there was an apple. It sat there, taunting her on its plate. It looked innocent, but she was beginning to be certain she didn't understand apples at all. And if she didn't understand apples, what on earth was she doing with her life, and why was she even attempting to write anything that mattered?

She shook her hair out, feeling the damp strands loose down her back. Then she coiled them on top of her head and stabbed a hair comb through it to hold it up. Thalia rapidly pulled on her nightdress, dressing gown, and slippers. There was a library downstairs. Even if it didn't have much recent in it, it had to have things about apples.

If nothing else, birds ate apples. Adam hadn't answered her question earlier. Before he'd come on all odd. She'd wanted to see him home, wanted to tell his people where he was. To ask could someone make sure he was all right. But in the end, there'd been something forbidding about him, a wall between him and the world. Maybe she'd insulted him, far more deeply than she'd thought or expected, about the apples. She couldn't think what else she'd said.

Asking about a bird shouldn't be a problem, should it? The sound of the chirping, like it was an adult and baby, the back-and-forth call and response of it. She pulled her attention back to what she'd actually said, and it came sharp again, in her memory.

She'd asked about the sound of the birds, and everything had come crashing down. Or crashing in. In was the better preposition, yes. It was like a wave, rolling downhill from the house, bringing a sucking tide as it pulled back. Like the riptides off some of the coastline. A wall of water, then everything, toppled and dragged away by the force of it.

Still. She rather hated herself now for being dragged. For leaving Adam in the orchard, even if she'd been very clear he didn't want her there. He hadn't needed to use words to make that known. It was the way he'd looked at her. Like he'd been caught up in something much larger than he was, some unknown magic or tale. It wasn't that he needed rescuing, it was that he thought no one could.

Her thoughts were all a tangle, like brambles that had grown up for years. Something like Sleeping Beauty's castle, surrounded by thorns, a space asleep for so long it was untouched by time. That felt entirely too close, all of a sudden, as if the thorns were pricking into her skin.

She curled her arms tight around herself again and forced herself to go downstairs to look for books in the library. If nothing else, she could likely find something soporific, the sort of thing that would not entice her to read on and on. When she got back to the ground floor, it was dark and quiet, except for the charm lights in the hallway, just enough to see by.

She brought the lantern with her, with a charm light that illuminated a good fifteen feet around. Looking through the books was actually rather soothing. She'd always appreciated a library. Not enough to want to work in one, and besides, these days, they wanted certificates and training she didn't have and wouldn't find easy to get. But the order of the thing mattered. Knowing there was an order, even if, as here, it didn't entirely make sense to an outsider.

Great-Aunt Avis had been arranging her life to her own desires for a long time, really. It only made sense the library was more of the same. At any rate, there were some local histories that had looked promising and not entirely full of ghosts and legends. And there was a biography she'd had recommended to her, enthusiastically, by three different people. A classic of its time, about one of the 18th century actresses in Trellech, who'd apparently had a gift for adding a touch of illusion to her performances.

Thalia was thoroughly entranced in the shelves when

she heard the sound. At first, it sounded like something small. A cat knocking something off a table. Only.

Only there was no cat in the house. No cat, no dog, no monkey, no small child.

The thump came again, and this time, something that sounded, for all the world, like slow heavy footsteps. They came from upstairs. Not behind the locked door to Great-Aunt Avis's room, but somewhere nearby.

Thalia couldn't run outside. She was in slippers and a dressing gown. It was cold, she couldn't. And it was probably nothing. It had to be nothing.

The noise came again. It wasn't exactly like footsteps, but it was moving. Something was moving. She hesitated, shifting from foot to foot, trying to decide what would be worse. She had three choices, and only three. Flee to the others, in the farmhouse, outside. Flee to her room, and cast whatever protective charms she could remember. Stay where she was.

A thump came again. At least it sounded like it was closer to the library. She ran, the lantern swinging in her hand, banging into the doorframe as she flew through the door and barrelled up the stairs. She didn't so much as look at her great-aunt's room. She just flung herself into her own, slamming the door shut behind her and then turning the key in the lock with a trembling hand.

When she opened her eyes, the charm lantern had toppled to the floor at her feet, but the room was as she left it. Apple. Soup. Bread and cheese. Bath making the last faint gurgles as it fully drained. It was warm enough. The fire Bessy had made earlier was still going well.

Everything seemed normal. But she could hear her heart pounding, loud in her ears, as if her chest would burst. She could feel the weight of something powerful and ancient, like that wave, earlier, pressing. It didn't seem to be seeking her out, to be personal. It was just there, insistent, demanding, unyielding.

Thalia put her back to the door, and sank to the ground, her full weight against it. She stayed there for ages, long enough that the fire began to burn down, that she would need to add another log. Her hands ached, where she had her fists clenched in the skirts of her dressing gown, and her foot twinged, as it did in bad weather.

Finally, though, she had to move. Had to do something other than clutch her robe and her knees and listen. It had been quiet for ages by then. She hadn't heard anything new since she'd slammed the door to the room. And that relentless pressure, whatever it was, seemed to have receded. Slowly, moving just one foot or hand at a time, she got up, testing the door to make sure it was locked. Finally, she went to put another log on the fire, before sitting down on her bed and pulling her feet up, knees to her chest. She watched the door for a long time, feeling like a child who'd had a prescient dream.

Something was wrong. Or if not wrong, certainly not ordinary. In her childhood, she had wanted to be brave, to go on adventures. She hadn't wanted to be the scared one, the little one, the one who never got to do anything interesting. Even if, in her family, that's who she was. Who she always had been.

Thalia didn't want to think about it, but the one time in her life she had been at least a little brave had been the worst of the War. There had been a comfort, then, being with the other VADs. Women like her, who'd volunteered to do what they could. She'd expected discomfort, and short sleep, and no time to herself. But she hadn't known about the other bravery that would be demanded.

All the times she'd been on the edge between a comforting lie and the truth, for men who were dying of things no men should die of. No women, either. All the times she'd asked, hoped, for someone to hang on a little longer, while knowing they were in excruciating pain. When once, Healers might have helped. But all of them, all the proper nurses, were drained down to the last dregs of their magic, over and over again, with each new horror. The way it felt when she did her part there. Letting them use her magic to keep people alive a little longer, heal them enough it was a grinding raw slog to some recovery, rather than a gruelling death.

This had the same feel. Of something she was caught up in, vastly larger than she was. Just as impersonal, just as demanding. It was a kind of bravery she was sure she didn't have left. She didn't know how to call it to her, not anymore. Not even the shaky form of it she'd used early in the War, made of false confidence and a true desire to help. All of that had burned out of her long since.

And it made her terrified of what she'd find, what she'd learn, if she stayed here.

CHAPTER 14
SATURDAY, AT UNCLE BENJAMIN'S

Adam made it back to his uncle's somehow, making a muffled excuse that he wanted to wash up when he got in to avoid talking to anyone. He took a long time in the loo, running water over his hands. Hot, first, because he was trembling as much with the chill as with anything else, then cold once he'd warmed up. Cold worked better to bring him back to himself, overall.

He stood there with the cold water running over the insides of his wrists until he was cold again, but at least he felt his body now. For all the good it did him, since half of him ached, and the other half trembled. It was the little things he'd learned, each one painfully gained. Like every inch of ground in France. It certainly felt like each piece of self-knowledge was a scar and a blotch in his memory. An explosion of things he didn't want to think about.

Only. He didn't know another forward. Magic knew he'd tried everything he could think of, as much as he could. Without a lot of progress. Oh, he might not be an obvious quivering wreck anymore. He hid it better. But he knew how fragile it was inside his head. How any little thing could make him feel rage and despair and terror and a desire to end it all, tangled up together.

By the time he came out, he could smell something warm for tea. Soup, at the least. There was a beefy vegetable warmth coming from the kitchen. When he came in, his uncle was propped in his chair, and his arms were full of something. A moment later, the something yipped and twisted, and it resolved into a puppy.

It had been a terribly long time since his rounds with the veterinarian, back at Snap, the training he'd got in how to judge how serious something was. One of the nights he'd followed the man around, one of the bitches had had her puppies. They were tucked into straw in the barn, sheep dogs to be trained up and sold on. This puppy was just old enough to leave its mother, he judged. Ten or twelve weeks or so. It was hard to tell, given the wriggling.

"Ah, there you are. Are you fit to drive a cart up on the moor t'morrow?" Mrs Whitmore had a bowl in her hands, beating some sort of batter with a whisk.

Adam blinked. "I. Um. Been a while." He'd been out in a cart a few times since the War, nothing complicated. He didn't trust himself to hitch one up, more than anything. Driving, well, a pony had a sense of self-preservation. They could probably manage.

"That there's a pup. His mum needs to go back up on t'moor, with Miss Brock. She lives up near Widecombe."

Adam must have looked blank, because Mrs Whitmore tsked at him. "Widecombe in the Moor. Fine church there, she's got a cottage, two miles outside. Nine miles or so from here. Himself has a pony cart arranged, a steady pony, be all day going and coming back."

"And the pup?"

"Pup stays here. We'll keep Master Benjamin busy

training him, won't we now." It wasn't a question at all. Apparently, Mrs Whitmore had a plan, and her plan would be followed.

"And the mother?" Adam was trying to keep everything straight, but his head was spinning.

"In a bad way, something she ate. Doing better now she's been seen to, but she's too big for a bicycle basket, and much too big for Miss Brock to carry. So the cart it is. Can you do it?"

Adam swallowed. "I'll give it my best. When?"

"You be up and about by nine, then. We'll be packing a proper lunch, and I'm sure Miss Brock will give you some tea or somewhat before you come back. Wear a cloak, it'll be a chill wind up there."

Adam gave in. "Does the pup have a name?"

Uncle Benjamin looked up. "Still sorting that out, aren't we?" It seemed to be doing him good. Granted, even Adam had to admit a puppy was compelling. And it would certainly encourage his uncle to get up and about in manageable doses. He suspected he might be pressed into service as well, to walk or clean up after, or whatever was needed. He ought to resent it, but he couldn't quite.

The evening was spent keeping the puppy from chewing things, taking him out, and in the end Adam fell into bed exhausted. The following morning, Miss Brock turned out to be a tiny woman in perhaps her fifties. She had her silver hair up and covered by a scarf or bonnet and a series of layers of cloaks and jumpers and long skirts that entirely enveloped her. She stood by a pony cart, a governess cart, meant to be driven from the back corner.

She took one look at him, and said, "This is Mate." The pony, he assumed, who was an undignified sort of red roan, splotchy in places. "And this is Doris." That was the dog, who was nestled in a box on the front seat of the pony cart. Miss Brock waved him in. "I'll drive."

"Pardon?" Adam cleared his throat.

"I know where we're going, don't I? Your first time on the moor?" The sentences came out briskly but not unkindly.

Adam nodded, uncertainly. "First in a long time. We came up when I was little. Twenty years, now, more. Twenty-five." He was stammering like a schoolboy. It wasn't that she was aggressive or unpleasant. She wasn't even particularly setting him on edge. But she had a way of taking control of the situation, undeniably, like an iron trap.

"Well, in you get, that side, mind Doris. There's a lunch packed for us. We'll see how far we get before we need a pause. She might need a bit. Or we might need to rest Mate. He had a hard summer, working, didn't he? Well, get in. You've a cloak, I suppose that will do. There's a good wool blanket, a bit mended, tucked in there if you need it."

"Yes. Um." Adam glanced from one side to the other.

"You in there, on the left. I drive from over here. You will on the way back, but that's simpler, isn't it? Mate knows his way home and you won't have Doris to fuss over. Really quite simple, a child could do it."

Adam was fairly sure a child shouldn't be coming back across the moor in a cart by themselves.

"Well, go on, get in, there you go. Mind your feet. And that stick, yes, tuck it there, it should just fit. No? Well, how about those hooks there." She charmed it into place with a touch, so it didn't jostle. He'd have to remember to fetch that, too, though on the way back he could probably wedge it diagonally across the seat.

A moment later, she was checking the harness one more time, with quick deft touches, murmuring something to the pony. Then she swung up into her seat, glancing at him. "All ready? Walk on, Mate, walk on."

The pony obediently picked up a steady walk. It was ungrudging, actually, given the pony was pulling two grown adults, a dog, and a basket. Miss Brock drove along in silence until they were well out of the village, passing up the road. Adam could see the house, the ever-looming house, for just a moment, through trees, then they passed some workings that looked like some sort of ruined building.

"Copper mine. Not mined in more than fifty years now. Not for long, either." She sounded disapproving.

"Not fond of mines?" Adam kept his voice even as much as he could.

"There're a terror on the land when they're like that. Now, a well-tended mine, that's a bit different. Still a terror, but some things ought to scare a man, and going down into the deeps with the Belin is one of them. My father's people were miners before they came out here." She caught Adam's look, and said, amused. "I've magic in my fingers, same as you."

Adam looked down at his hands in his knit gloves. He'd prefer leather. The wool felt entirely too much like the War, even if these were currently dry and not full of mud or worse. Something about the texture got to him. But leather cost money he didn't have. What money he did have was on grace, and no one cared that knit gloves made him itch in ways that weren't at all physical. "Ma'am."

"Aren't you a polite one?" She drove on a bit further, beginning to climb up to the moor. "I'd ask you to be getting out to walk this bit, but I gather that's a bit much for you." Unlike nearly everyone else who'd commented about it, her voice was neutral.

"Ma'am." He made it obliging. "My balance, usually. A few aches, I can work with those. The balance is harder."

"And more so on an incline, and this isn't the best road now, is it?" It wasn't, there were some ruts and some holes, though she mostly steered deftly to avoid that. "Mate will manage. We'll take it slow and steady."

By the time they got to the top of the rise, Mate was indeed breathing hard. Miss Brock tsked. "We'll walk along a bit to let him cool down. Don't want him taking a chill, and then we'll give him a little pause. There's a bit of a stream where he can get a breather."

She put action to words, and drove on in silence, rather focused on the pony. Adam had no idea what to say to any of that. He didn't object to her being in charge. She was making sensible decisions. He supposed many men would have been annoyed, but that had all burned out of him a decade ago. Right now, it was a relief to have someone competent making the decisions, so he didn't have to.

They stopped, letting Mate drink. Miss Brock leaned against the carriage, considering him. "Not so many of us with magic round these parts. A few. Mrs Whitmore said you'd asked about the great house. Them too, not as they show it much."

Adam blinked, wondering how she knew he'd been curious. Besides Mrs Whitmore, who was a channel of information. "Anything I should know about them?"

"They're a queer lot. The old lady, there's a stillness to her. Like everything's pulled in tightly. Unchanging. Mrs Harley's steady, but she keeps private, and teaches the orphanage girls to be too. Don't know about this great-niece or whoever it is." Miss Brock considered. "Gather she's got more than a touch of the sight, or something of the kind. Kenning beyond the physical, but I don't know if

Mrs Harley went to one of the Five Schools or what. Not a woman who talks about herself. "

"I met her. The great-niece, I mean. Down in our orchard. She seemed pleasant enough." That wasn't the right word for it, but he didn't know what was. "Didn't say I was magical, and she didn't either."

"Ah, well, a person might be cautious. And who knows what sorts of things she knows or doesn't. There's some odd tales around that house."

"I heard the one about the hare, wasn't it? The Crusader one."

"Ah, that's an ordinary sort of tale. There are others, about someone who calls the birds to her and takes their magic, stealing it. Or borrowing, at least. Not the sort of story has a woman cloaked in feathers. That wouldn't be practical, now, would it?"

Adam offered. "Possibly beautiful, but not the sort of thing you could sit down in?" It came out a little tentative, but Miss Brock smiled at him, as if he'd actually made a joke. Mate snorted at that point, breaking the mood, and they rearranged themselves back into the cart, at Miss Brock's pointed "No need to waste the good light."

Off they went again, picking up a trot part of the time, walking part of the time. Miss Brock didn't offer particular conversation, not until they pulled up into the lane of her small cottage. It was well kept, the garden turned over for the winter and some burlap around more delicate bushes, to protect them from the wind. Two, near the end, looked a bit more faded and battered than the rest.

As he got out to help her get Doris down, he offered, surprising himself, "Your bushes. I could have a look. See if they could use a touch of something."

"You went to Snap, your uncle said. Should I trust you?" The question came sharp and clear.

Adam swallowed. "I don't know. Honestly. It's been an age since I tried anything like that. But I can have a look. Tell you if you ought to get someone up here who's competent."

She looked him up and down. "Let us get Doris into the house, and then we'll look." That took a bit of time, getting a fire going, putting a kettle on for tea, but after a good half hour, she led him outside again. She stood back, not crowding him. Adam took a deep breath, and pulled off his gloves, then stuck them in his pocket, reaching out to touch the leaves.

He'd touched dozens, hundreds, of plants in the ground since he came back from the death and the mud, but this was the first time he'd deliberately reached out magically. He hadn't dared, in the orchard, too afraid something was wrong. It was one of the first lessons they taught at Snap. It was the one they began with before anyone was assigned a dormitory, before they'd even managed to give their names.

And it came flooding back to him now. Rather literally, the roar of knowledge flooding into his head was far too much, and he staggered with it, dropping his hand. That quieted everything, but he went down to one knee, heedless of the dirt.

Miss Brock didn't fuss over him, though she did take a step closer, where she could probably see his face. It took him a minute, two minutes, to get his breath and his words back. "Rootbound. Maybe crammed up against the foundation and a rock, I don't know? Might be a trick to fix."

"Ah." She nodded once, precisely. "I can get Young Jimmy up before the ground freezes, see if we can dig out a bit, give the old girls more space. He's good with a rock,

Young Jimmy is." She then looked Adam up and down. "That's a good deed."

Adam shrugged. He'd been told to come up here. Looking at the plants, in context, was. Well. Odd to be doing again, but not so outlandish as all that. Miss Brock considered. "Due a favour. You wait here with Mate." She went trotting off back into the cottage, and she was gone long enough Adam was beginning to wonder what happened.

When she came out, she was holding a pair of deep brown leather gloves. "Try these. I think your hands are about -" She cut off, and held them out.

Adam pulled them on, carefully. They were just a hair on the loose side, but he preferred that, and lined with something that made the leather feel smooth against his skin. Comfortable. He pulled on the other one carefully, then stretched out his fingers.

"There. You take those." Adam looked up. There was an odd note in her voice. "They were my brother's. They should do some good." Adam didn't know what had happened to the man. Nothing happy, clearly. But he knew enough what to do with that.

"Thank you. And for the drive. I'll take good care of Mate."

She nodded, then turned away, to go back inside the house without another word.

CHAPTER 15
MONDAY AT THE LIBRARY

The next day passed without any incident. Thalia didn't think it showed too badly, how terrified she'd been. In the end, she'd curled up at the head of the bed, her back to the wall, watching the door. Nothing came, but she didn't fall asleep until it was properly daylight.

She'd got no writing done, and only a short walk outside, and she had sworn to herself she wouldn't do that again. That night, she went up to her room while Mrs Harley and Bessy were finishing cleaning up. She could hear their small noises downstairs, the door opening and closing several times as they cleared the table and did the last round of endless tidying.

When she came downstairs the next morning, she found Mrs Harley dusting the library. "Pardon, Mrs Harley. Do you know if there's a library in the village? And is it the sort of place I could walk to?" No, that was foolish, there was a library, she'd said Adam nearly broke a chair in it.

"Goodness." The housekeeper dusted her hands off.

"There is, and it should be open this afternoon. It's a fair walk, though, near four miles, and the hill coming back."

"I'll manage, I suspect. And leave myself plenty of time. There's no bicycle? No, wait, I suppose that would be worse on the hill, wouldn't it?" Thalia waved a hand. "It will be good for my legs, I'm sure, and I've gone up and down in the fields a few times and not died yet."

As a humorous comment, it felt flat, but Mrs Harley smiled. "Well, that's true enough. Would you be willing to take a letter or two for the post? It's two doors down from the library. And I can draw you a map. How's that?"

Curiously, going off to the library seemed to have unlocked something in Mrs Harley. She added a note here or there about what else was in town. Which tea shop was better if Thalia wanted a snack before coming back, and a warning not to buy fruit from that Mrs Douglas. She hid bruised spots deliberately. For fruit, you apparently wanted Mr Thorn across the street. Thalia let it wash over her. If she'd been in London, it would have been the same. London was a city of villages, each handful of streets having their own customs and traditions and gossip.

Right after lunch, she set off back down the lane, and an hour later she was in the centre of the village. It was a good size, actually, and there was quite a lot of pottery on sale. The first three conversations she had were quite proud of it, made locally and used all over the world, apparently on Navy ships, as well as elsewhere. Thalia wondered if a story with a conceit about where a bit of pottery went might work, but it would be sentimental and cloying almost immediately. Not the sort of thing she wrote.

By two, she'd found the library, a pleasant space attached to a shop, and she heard a bell ring as the door opened. A man looked up from the desk, then blinked, as if she weren't at all who he expected. Which was only sensible, since she'd never been to the library before, and she'd only really decided to come down this morning.

"This is the library?" Good grief, she sounded dim. It was visibly a library. Every space, flat or otherwise, had books or magazines or newspapers or something of the kind. Some sort of pamphlets there.

The man stood. "Yes, miss?" He cleared his throat. "Roger Dobbs, librarian, such as we have. Are you new in the village?"

"Staying up at the house while my great-aunt is away. Avis Morgan? I'm Thalia Morgan."

"Goodness. My." Dobbs wrinkled up his nose, a bit like a dubious rabbit. "I didn't know she had family. I'm local, but my family has a place about three miles outside of the town, away from the moor."

"Oh, yes. More or less. She married my father's uncle, so it's a rather distant sort of family? But she'd been poorly and was told she ought to spend some time somewhere warm. So my parents are in the south of France with her, and I'm here. Well. Keeping an eye on the place, though Mrs Harley has everything superbly in hand."

"We see her in the village every few weeks, and the maid, of course, for the market." Dobbs nodded. "Well. Are you staying for a while, then? We can set you up with a library card if you are, but also—" He hesitated. "There's a dance coming up Saturday week. Nothing fancy, of course, but you could meet some others here. We could likely arrange a cart back up to the house, or there's an inn could put you up for a night there? It's quiet this time of year."

That was rather a lot to take in, and Thalia honestly wasn't sure what she thought. On one hand, talking to different people would entirely be welcome. She was doing rather badly with that. She was quickly coming to the conclusion that while some writers might embrace solitude and do their best work as ascetic hermits, she might need a conversation here or there.

On the other hand, it was a country village, she'd utterly made a mess of things with Adam, and who knew who many other catastrophes she could stumble into. And on the third hand, the number of possible catastrophes that might happen at a village dance was surely exaggerated in the popular literature.

She nodded. "I'd love to, so long as it won't put anyone out. Let me check with Mrs Harley, that's the housekeeper, about what's convenient. I don't want to make things harder for her. That's unkind, isn't it?"

"Ah, you come from the sort of family that thinks about that." Dobbs was clearly approving. "Are you here for a while, then?"

"Oh, it depends on how Great-Aunt Avis gets on. But likely a few weeks more, at the very least."

"It's very kind of you to uproot yourself and come down here. We're rather the back of beyond. You must - well, I know you're not local, but I'm being nosy."

Thalia smiled. It was not very deft flirting, but she had to give the man credit, and it was pleasant to have someone want to talk to her. "London, usually. I scrape by as a secretary, but I write. Not much published, I'm afraid."

"Ah, that explains why you were drawn to the library. We don't loan out our magazines, unfortunately, but you're welcome to read them here. Bit of competition for *Country Life* and *Women's Weekly*, of course. Some for *Punch*, and less for the literary magazines. Those are there, those shelves. And the books, of course. Any topic you're particularly interested in today?"

Thalia nodded. "Actually, I came in to see if you had anything about the local folklore. Especially anything written in the last few decades? The library up at the house is sprawling, in some ways, but not recently updated."

"Well, first, have you read anything by the late Reverend Sabine Baring-Gold? He was the parson up at Lew Trenchard. Unfortunately died three years ago, nearly. Amazing man, mind like a trap, and a great fascination with the moor and her people."

"I saw some books in the library, but I - there were rather a lot of them, and I had no idea where to start."

"A few? Dozens? I suppose she must have the ones about Devon. Here, let me pull some out for you. Let you see what looks interesting." Dobbs stood up from his desk, and it was obvious as soon as he took a step or two that he limped. Which made it more curious that he'd invited her to a dance, actually, but perhaps he danced anyway, or perhaps he wanted some new company when she wasn't dancing.

She almost protested that he didn't need to find her things, but the man looked resolute. Fierce. And she certainly wasn't going to call him incapable. Thalia nodded. "Shall I sit down over here, then? Or put my things down, and browse?"

"That second table might be best. Miss Fulton often comes in around three, and she's very particular about her preferred seat. Yes, that one is fine."

Thalia supposed that in a small town, such things might matter quite a lot. And it wasn't as if Mother and Father weren't horribly picky about which table they got at their preferred restaurants, or the box at the theatre. Rather ridiculously so, actually. She'd usually preferred varying where she sat. You saw different things, different people, that way. More stories.

Five minutes later, she had a small tower of books, about ten, next to her, and she'd gathered a few of her own from the shelves. She spent the next hour or so working through them. She wasn't a swot, not by any stretch of the imagination, but she'd learned how to do that efficiently. Not entirely at school, which had encouraged her more free-ranging sorts of ideas. Or at least not squashed them.

In the end, she checked six books out, making a note of the other titles. Really, she'd have to think about getting another notebook. At the rate she was going through failed ideas, she'd need one. Two books about local folklore, one of Sabine Baring-Gould's novels, and two books about fairy tales which had drawn her interest and refused to let it go.

And one of local poetry. She wasn't much for poetry, and so much of it was rather awful or sentimental or convinced everything had deep meaning. Sometimes all at once. But seeing how people described the place, that might be a help or something.

Dobbs was agreeable about signing them out to her. "I'll send a note by post about the dance, and you can let us know the same way. Or you're welcome here any time, oh, let me put in a slip with the hours." He tucked that into one of the books, then patted the cover a bit protectively.

Thalia was the sort of person who loved books, but rather more actively. She didn't turn the pages down in any book she didn't own. She wasn't a heathen. Nor did she break the spines open and lay them flat. But she did tend to read while snacking. A fair few pages of her own copies had a hint of a tea stain, and she was forever putting whatever bits of paper or cardstock she had handy as a bookmark. It made a number of her friends and social circle despair utterly.

Once she'd managed to take her leave, she had the long slow climb back up the hill, getting back just before tea-time. She brought her new trove of treasure to her rooms, settling down in the comfortable chair to read a bit. At supper, she came down, changed into a cardigan and slippers.

"Did you enjoy the village, mistress?"

"I'm glad I went." Enjoy wasn't the right word, and besides, it didn't have the proper emotion behind it. "Mr Dobbs in the library was very helpful. He mentioned there's a dance, the next Saturday, if I wanted to come down for it. And that he'd be glad to see about a cart to get me back, or there's an inn?"

"Oh, you don't want the inn, mistress. Terrible gossips, they are, and they've never been kind about Mistress Morgan. There's a lady I know in town. She might put you up for the night, or you could come back here. If you don't mind paying a bit, of course. Not too much."

Thalia inclined her head. "I think my funds can stretch to that. Would - how do I see what the options are?"

"I'll send a note down with Bessy tomorrow, and we should know in a day or two. I suppose someone like you might want to be meeting other people nearer your own age."

Thalia nodded, then tilted her head. "Could I have a friend out to stay for a few days? Maybe a week? I don't want to put you out, of course." Asking this was so terribly awkward, in her nebulous place that mixed being a guest in the house with the person nominally in charge. With one hat on, she should be asking permission, hat in hand. So not on, then. With another, she should just be telling the staff what to do, and they would presumably cope.

That meant at least one hat too many, a lot of guilt and confusion, and honestly, now she was entirely in a tangle. "What sort of friend, mistress?"

"Hilaria Thomas. She has the flat next to mine, in London. We've become good friends."

"Oh, a woman friend. Of course, mistress. We could make up the room next to yours, and with simple foods, that wouldn't be a problem."

"I am quite sure Hilaria would be as delighted by the food here as I have been. Which is to say, very." At that, at least, Mrs Harley let her be, to inhale a sturdy sort of soup and thick well-buttered bread.

CHAPTER 16
WEDNESDAY MORNING

"You should get out a bit." Mrs Whitmore was sitting at the end of the kitchen table. She was doing something with a pot of grains or beans or some such and a smaller bowl she kept dropping things into. Sorting out stones from the grain, most likely, but Adam hadn't actually got close enough to see.

"And where should I go?" Adam wasn't going to fuss at her about it. He was used to people telling him, subtly and not so subtly, that he should buck up and get moving and be back to his old self. His old self was dead and gone, and he was a shell who looked the same. Well, mostly the same.

"You've not been to the orchard for three days. Himself mentioned it when I took him a cuppa."

"I was up on the moor with a dog and Miss Brock for one of those." Adam felt he should point this out. "And a pony." And he'd been in bed near the entire next day because of it, not that he'd say that.

"And a kind thing that was too, but that doesn't get the apples tended, does it." Mrs Whitmore went on with her sorting, without pausing.

Adam was not at all sure what to say here. The truth was that the whole place unsettled him. Both its subtle and not-so-subtle wrongness, or at least oddness, were bad enough. But how did he tell someone he'd run into the girl from the big house, and it had also been wrong and odd and awful? And that he couldn't stop thinking about her.

He considered, after his examination of the woodgrain on the table refused to yield any answers for a good minute. "Do you know much about the people at the house? In general?"

"Well, I did hear a bit yesterday. I gather the young woman, she's a Morgan, like the old woman, up there. The lady, I mean, not our sort of lady. It's not a proper demesne, now, is it?"

"Do you know if they're magical?" Adam tried to make the question easy, as if he didn't have a reason to ask. Miss Brock had said so, of course, but it would be good to confirm it.

"I suspect they are. But they don't associate with the likes of us, never have, other than the shopping. And I think that Bessy's got just enough magic to make her Pact with the Silence, but not much more than that. The place she came from, it's not the sort of place someone with strong magic would end up. All the work done by hand, that sort of thing." Mrs Whitmore, as far as he could tell, approved of the work ethic, but not of the situation that led to it.

Adam nodded slowly. "And the younger woman?"

"Ah, yes, well. She came into the library yesterday. I heard all about it from Miss Fulton last night at choir practice. She goes in to the library every afternoon, three on the dot, and of course she tells me all the news. It was the meeting about the holiday planning, making sure the little ones in the area all have some sort of gift. She's a pillar of the local parish, of course, and her family have been, oh, quite far back." She dropped several stones in the smaller bowl, then let the grains pour through her fingers, rattling a little.

"And Miss Fulton?"

"Well, she had a nice chat with Roger Dobbs, the librarian. He's a good sort, though his people are terribly snobbish, don't associate with the village much. Differently from the Morgans, now I think of it. Have their own pew in church and never talk to anyone properly." She was clearly in a chatting mood.

"Both in large houses, but not associating with each other?" That also struck him as odd. "There hasn't been a family or anything up there? Children?"

"Oh, goodness, no. Just Avis Morgan, and Franklin Morgan, her late husband. He died, oh, fifteen years ago? Twenty, like. Well before the War. They'd been there for years. Not going out, occasionally having people visit. Family, mostly. The Morgans were his side, of course." She chattered on, amiably.

"Did you ever see any of them?"

"Oh, goodness, no. You might have, actually. Your uncle was telling me you played with the children. That must have been the nephew's girls. And a boy, too, I think. I seem to remember hearing he was killed. I know I saw that housekeeper with a black armband, and someone asked. Not Miss Fulton, she wouldn't be demanding like that, but that's why women like Hespasia Dutton were put on this earth now, weren't they? To ask all the awkward questions."

"Is Miss Dutton - Mrs Dutton? - around I could talk to? I'm a bit curious about where the land meets theirs."

"Will you go along to the orchard as well? She's most of

the way there, to be honest. Mrs Dutton, widowed, in the War. Not fighting, him, but a factory."

Adam sighed and spread his hands. "You are a far better strategist. Yes. And then you can tell Uncle Benjamin I've gone to look at the apples."

Mrs Whitmore smiled the smile of someone who had come up trumps. "She's in the last lane on the right, as you come to the end of the village. If you go in twenty minutes, you'll catch her when she's having her elevenses. Let me pack you a lunch. You can eat in the orchard. It's a perfectly good day out there."

Adam did not argue. He did not, to be fair, have the energy to argue. And he was going to need all the energy he didn't have to make it out there and back in one piece before midnight. Instead, he spent twenty minutes finding his most comfortable socks, the newly gifted gloves, making sure he had the cloak tied onto his bag, and a warm sweater. And then he tucked the packed lunch into his bag. "Back eventually, I suppose."

"I'll tell himself." She settled down, going back to sorting stones from grain, and Adam went out. He passed a few people going through the edge of town, but no one who showed any signs of wanting to speak with him. The directions Mrs Whitmore had given him brought him to a small cottage on a side lane with a pleasant garden, tucked behind a plaster wall. He could see the curtains twitch as he made his way carefully up to the door.

He knocked twice. A querulous voice from inside said, "We don't want to buy anything."

Adam cleared his throat. "I'm not selling anything, ma'am. Mrs Whitmore suggested you might be able to help with a question."

He waited. There was a long silence, a good minute,

then the voice again. "Who are you?"

"Adam Walton. Benjamin Walton's nephew?"

The door opened, revealing an older woman, the sort who got shorter and thoroughly themselves with age, with her hair pinned up properly and a flowered frock. "Well, that explains how you know Millicent. Come in. I was just about to have a cuppa, and there's some scones, my, you're a tall one, aren't you? Leave your stick there. And your bag. Don't want you knocking anything over."

Adam wanted to leave neither, but he knew how absolute that order was. He would get no answers if he didn't play by her rules. It was rather like the old fairy tales. Enter a cottage of a woman like this - or to be fair, a man - and mind your manners, or you would regret it later. He left stick and satchel on a hook by the entrance, making sure the door was closed, before following her into a sitting room.

Part of him couldn't help adding up what he saw. It was a cottage, technically, but rather more like Uncle Benjamin's cottage, with additions made over the years, so that there was a sitting room besides the kitchen. Possibly two, with a parlour kept for more formal occasions. Stairs led up to the private spaces, and he could smell some sort of soup wafting through from the kitchen.

A minute later, she brought out a fussy tray with a floral design, and a ceramic tea set. He frowned, trying to place it. "That looks familiar."

She beamed, then tsked at him, shaking her finger. "It ought. This is from the Bovey Tracey Pottery. My Wallace worked there, bless him, until he went to the War work. You served?"

Adam managed not to flinch. Well, not too much, though he was suddenly sure it had been a test, and he'd not quite failed it. "I did. In the trenches, in France, then made an officer."

Mrs Dutton nodded once. "You take care of your men?"

That question haunted him. He'd done the best he could with what he had. But his tools were mud and death and rot, and it was impossible to make anything worthwhile out of any of them. Even the mud wasn't clay. When the silence had gone on far too long. "Not as well as I wished I could."

She looked him up and down, then poured the tea without comment. This wasn't the chattery perhaps flighty woman he'd expected from Mrs Whitmore's description. Though she was, to be fair, doing well with asking the awkward questions. Once the tea was poured, she pushed a plate with a scone across to him. Currant, perhaps, or something like that. Small red berries.

"The pottery was good to Wallace. And to us. But that's not what you're here about. If you were a fiend for pottery, you'd have spotted it first off. Distinctive." Her pride in it was blindingly obvious.

"No, ma'am. I was curious about the house up on the hill. Above our orchard. And Mrs Whitmore said you were exactly the person to ask."

"Well, now." Mrs Dutton was pleased. "I suppose I know a few things. There's a history of the place. I think I can lend that to you. It comes from one of the local societies. There's one in the library, and I know it by heart. Let me find that." She went tottering off to a bookshelf across the room, coming back with a slender volume. "You can bring it back, or give it to Mrs Whitmore of a Thursday. Our knitting circle, you know. Knitting for the orphan children overseas, now. I'm just finishing up a muffler."

Adam suspected many of the orphan children overseas

would do better with lighter clothing than a muffler. But he supposed that was a problem for whoever was sending the final objects along. "Mrs Whitmore said you might remember more about the family, though a history of the property is a great help. There was - the nephew, and then his family?"

"Ah, yes. They came, oh, twenty years ago? Twenty-five? Let me see, it was the summer Wallace and I put the roses in out back. I remember that. That must be twenty-five years, yes. They're still doing very well. I feed them properly, you know."

"Blood and bone meal?" Adam couldn't help it slipping out.

"Yes!" Mrs Dutton seemed delighted. "Do you - oh, of course, your uncle."

"I don't have his touch with design, and I've not had a garden to enjoy for, well." Ever, really. His mother had a firm grip on the house. Or rather, she refused to consider Adam's suggestions, and deferred to the elderly and opinionated head gardener.

Which, on one hand, was fair. The man got to earn his living. And it wasn't as if he was bad at the job, not exactly. But he was very regimented about it. Adam had felt all his life that a garden wasn't an army to be marshalled. Even a farm, relying on growing things, wasn't. It was more like a village, different pieces playing different parts.

He felt even more strongly about that now, but people were even less likely to listen to him.

"Well, now, they're not at all in their prime. I really do need to finish preserving the rose hips. We just had the first good frost. Late this year, isn't that the way of it?"

Adam nodded, considering how to ask what he really wanted to get at.

CHAPTER 17

WEDNESDAY MORNING

" I was wondering about that. Uncle mentioned that his orchard ripens late, and always has."

"Oh, yes. That stretch of woods, it takes forever to turn colours. Well into November. And the orchard, that's more of the same. I remember your grandmother commenting on it. Handy, actually, it spreads the harvest out. One of those things." She narrowed her eyes. "Your grandmother, she said you were at Snap."

Adam nodded, uncertain where this particular conversation might be going.

"And you don't have a garden."

"No, ma'am. Mistress." He could give her the proper title.

She beamed at him. "Not so many of us here, with magic. Or more than a touch of it. Us. The Whitmores. It's a kindness for your uncle to have her in. The family's had a hard time of it." She tsked amiably over it, but of course she didn't explain. Adam expected it was something a while ago. Besides which, he knew Mrs Whitmore had been tending to his uncle's housekeeping and cooking since before the War. And she'd been a help with his grandparents before that. "A half-dozen other families. Not the Dobbs. They're the other side of things. The Morgans, though."

"You're sure they're magical?"

Mistress Dutton nodded. "Quite sure. We magical folk, we don't see each other socially, always. But we know who's who. Always been in magical hands, that place, quite a long way back. There's a legend about a woman turned herself into a hare."

"I've heard some of that. Though the version I heard had a ghost. And then there was a tale about a witch, up on the moor, giving hounds a tremendous chase?"

Mistress Dutton nodded. "Just so. Now, I don't know what the Morgans do with their magic. My Wallace, he was a foreman at the pottery, and he helped keep things safer. Your uncle, it comes out in gardens that grow well. Mrs Whitmore makes a tremendous healing soup. You're looking better since you got here, for one."

Adam had not particularly considered the food as a factor in anything. It was tasty; it was filling. She didn't pour scant bowls of decorous clear broths, as his mother preferred. But now that Mistress Dutton put it that way, he did feel like the food was a help. "I'll pass that along. I'm sure she'll be pleased. She is a grand cook. I try to appreciate that properly."

That got a nod. "So, you were asking about the Morgans."

Adam nodded. "I met the great-niece, briefly. Makes a man curious."

That was apparently the proper tone to take, because Mistress Dutton beamed at him. "Well, there, let me fill up your cup. Now, they've always kept to themselves, all the way back as far as I can remember. Avis, that's her name, and her husband. He died decades ago, rather young, I think?" Though as she said the words, she didn't sound entirely sure. "You saw her, sometimes. Always in the late spring and always at a distance. They'd lend out one of the fields for a spring fete, but neither of them would actually come to the thing, not even to present a prize."

Adam considered. "That's a little odd, isn't it? It's different where my family is now. We moved there recently enough. Not the established family, and all that. And people don't go to the Dobbs?"

"That's the autumn fete, dear. The midsummer one is here in the village, on the green. Though I suppose I do hear it's done otherwise in other places." She clearly had no patience for such variations and changes.

"Of course." Adam frowned. "And the rest of the family?"

"Well, dear, some families would come visit regularly, wouldn't they? But I can't remember the rest of the Morgans coming out since - well." She tsked again. "When we put the roses in. The nephew, I think, came out a few times, but not at all after his uncle died. Or if he did, he got there on his own."

"They didn't travel or anything like that?" Adam was considering. His parents were well-off these days, had been most of his life. His mother flitted back and forth from home to a fashionable seaside town to London. Then back home, before going off to Trellech or perhaps somewhere on the Continent. His father travelled less. There was the business to see to, but in the right place, with a portal close by, he could get to wherever he wanted in Albion on short notice. Which made Adam think.

"And there's no portal up there?"

"Goodness, no. There ought to be one somewhere near, properly, but there are tales about it disappearing. A bit of bog on the moor. There's a legend about it spreading and taking down the portal, though I don't recall where, exactly." She shrugged. "Near one of the tin mines, I believe."

Adam nodded slowly. "And the Fatae? Or I suppose anything like that? I know sometimes mines are uncanny."

"There's a whole slew of elder trees, up there. And a few tales, spots best avoided. There are the sort of stories children pass along, how if you go through a pair of them, you'll find yourself not able to get back for hundreds of years, or come out some far distant place, as far as China." She shrugged. "A few tales of the tors. Some of them certainly look like the rocks were shaped by magic, with some purpose. Sensible folk don't linger, not after dark."

Adam suspected that did not narrow it down much. At any rate, there was no portal. The vagueness wasn't much help either, not about the concerns nearer to home, like the apples. That was not helpful. "And no one's seen Avis Morgan in ages?"

Mistress Dutton shook her head. "Not more than perhaps through a window, on the day of the fete. You'd think it was some sort of fairy tale or legend, a princess in a tower. They have money, certainly, the grounds are well tended. More servants, when I was young, even though they didn't entertain much." She seemed about to say something else, but didn't.

"And now just the housekeeper and maid."

"Oh, and a groundskeeper and some day help in the gardens. They don't tend themselves, you know that."

"No, they don't. But not in the house." That was curious. Two servants for one elderly woman wasn't that unusual, but honestly, Adam would have expected, oh, devoted old retainers or some such. Someone like that should have had a lady's maid or a companion or something of the kind. "And the great-niece? Or her family?"

"You met her, you say?" Mistress Dutton poured herself a little more tea and raised an eyebrow at Adam. Adam shook his head. He still had half a cup.

"I did. Near enough my age, give or take a few years, I suppose." He described her, though he stumbled over how to talk about her clothing. Any woman's clothing.

"That seems like, well, she'd be the youngest. Older sister, I don't know. Eight years older? A proper miss. A brother, in the middle, a few years older. He's the one died in the War. I don't remember the details now, but we all talked about it after the housekeeper came down with a black armband and mentioned there'd been a death in the family."

"Because she'd have worn mourning for her own family." Adam pieced that together carefully.

"I don't know about her people at all." Clearly not local, then. Not that Adam could throw stones on that particular count, of course. He was thinking about the brother and wondering what sort of death he'd had. The options on offer ranged from awful to horrific. And coming down, that might have been necessity. Or it might have been making a point of showing the armband, if there had been any hint the brother hadn't died honourably.

"Anything else you might remember?" Adam spread his hands. "It - well. They touch on the orchard. I suppose I've got curious now."

Mistress Dutton shook her head. "If I think of a thing, I'll let Millicent know, and you can stop by again. Though." She looked him up and down. "You could be a dear and get something from a top shelf for me? Save me the stool."

Adam didn't trust himself on a stool, but it turned out the top shelf was comfortably in his reach, and he handed down a baking pan she wanted. "There you go, go along now, and bring the book back when you can."

The weather was rather dingy grey when he got to the orchard, not promising at all. However, it wasn't raining, and he rather thought it wouldn't be until this evening. He was beginning to get a better sense of how that worked here.

The orchard was much as it had been four days ago. The apples were a bit more ripe, but now he looked it, it was more like the progress he'd expect in a day, maybe two, rather than four. Which fit with the overall speed of the thing. If they were a month behind now, that meant what.

It was like measuring how much a grandfather clock lost time over the course of the week, the optimal time to wind it again. Also, it was going to require scratch paper. Maths had never been his best subject.

Take the Beauty of Bath. His reading suggested it ripened around early August, give or take a fortnight. That put it two months behind. The Court of Wick took longer to ripen, but it seemed to have progressed a little faster. A month or so. Given the beginning of the growing season, that meant things were progressing at the rate of...

This was where the maths got hard. Four months for the Beauty of Bath, five months for the Court of Wick, give or take, in what he would call the expected schedule. He couldn't quite solve for the key factor, which was when they'd stopped blooming and started working on fruit. But they should be progressing at a rate of five days to four or four to three.

Adam shook his head. He was going to have to work that out later, at a desk, possibly with an abacus or something he could move around. His uncle had one in his office, he could borrow it. Feeling it under his fingers often helped with this sort of puzzle. Though it had been a long while since he'd done it for plants.

That made him think of what Mistress Dutton had said, asking about how he didn't have a garden of his own. He wanted one, but he wanted a great many things he didn't have and wouldn't get. If the garden was a tad more complicated, well. That was also the way his life was. He stood suddenly, nearly overbalancing himself, and went off to walk along the edge of the wall, to see if he could see anything else.

The stone wall felt like a temptation, somehow. A demarcation, and not just for the property line, that was too simple. True, but also too simple. He walked along, peering across it, before he heard chirping from up above in a tree just on the other side. He hesitated. Crossing into their property, well, that was the kind of thing that kept warding and protection specialists in business, wasn't it? And someone so devoted to their privacy almost certainly had some sort of something.

He heard the sound again, like a falcon in distress. He couldn't bear that, especially if there was a chance he could do something to help. If it had got snared on something, perhaps. People left wire in the woods, or there might be a poacher who'd laid a trap, or something of the kind.

Adam got over the wall in one piece, largely thanks to the walking stick. What he found was a bird who was barely balancing on a branch. A falcon, yes, but clearly juvenile. The way the feathers stuck out, the line of the head. He knew instantly this bird was far too young for the season.

Younger than the apples were. A fledgling certainly, but it should have left the nest two months ago, near enough, and it looked like it might be another few weeks yet. This was a bird who couldn't live on his own. Couldn't properly hunt yet.

A moment later, an adult bird swooped down, crying out at him. Considering him a threat, keeping him away. She kept herself between Adam and the fledgeling until the younger bird managed to take flight again, beating his wings strongly somewhere up the hill.

It was, horrifyingly, like the feelings Adam had about watching men go over the top. Wanting desperately to tell them not to, it was hopeless, while knowing there was no other option.

CHAPTER 18
WEDNESDAY AFTERNOON

"So, why am I here all of a sudden?"

"Restorative country air?" Thalia had come down to Newton Abbot to meet her, and take the train branch back to Bovey Tracey together. However, that didn't leave for two hours. Plenty of time to find a park, have a packed lunch, and talk without anyone overhearing them.

"You sounded rather urgent in the journal." Hilaria took a bite of her sandwich, then swallowed. "This is the usual run of food?"

They were particularly good sandwiches, actually, with a chutney relish and sharp cheese, and a glorious loaf of bread. "Mmhmm." Her mouth was still full.

"Well. All right. I'm in. I won't flee into the night for at least a day or two."

Thalia snorted. "Good. I mean, I think they're pleased to have someone else in the place? All things considered. Mrs Harley seemed pleased."

"She's the housekeeper. Bessy is the maid. Assorted

people on the grounds, which are expansive." Hilaria laid out what Thalia had written.

"Exceedingly expansive. Out to the road, you'll see that side. Down the hill nearly to a north-south road, a good mile and a bit of a downhill steepness. And then across, rather a long distance, though the farmed bits are mostly on the far edge. A lot of woodland and meadow and things."

"All right. So. Large house. A lot of land. Sounds almost like home." Hilaria leaned back.

"Does your family home come with terrifying thumps in the night? A lurking presence?"

Hilaria shook her head. "The ordinary sort of ghost stories. A white lady. And a grey lady. Not the same lady, of course." She was about to say something else, then she leaned forward. "You're terrified, darling."

Thalia hadn't wanted to name it. But yes, she was. She nodded, once.

"So why me? Of all the people you could invite, why me?"

Thalia swallowed, then paused. A bit of tea from the flask would be a good idea, she could feel a frog in her throat. She swallowed, then set it down. "You understand this sort of house. And most of the others don't."

"I've never been sure about Una, to be honest. But mostly not, no. At least our usual circles." Hilaria considered. "And you couldn't invite Oswald down here."

"Goodness, no. For one thing, I'm fairly sure he'd be ahead of me running from any ghost. And for another, it would give him ideas about whether I might be encouraging him. He's a nice enough man, but I do not wish to encourage." Oswald was the sort of man who wanted a woman to keep his papers in order, type his stories, and make sure supper was on the table every night.

He was well enough off, she thought, that whoever he married wouldn't have to do the cooking herself, or the cleaning. But she'd have to spend all her time making sure everything got handled. And that was not what Thalia wanted from her life. Also, if Oswald wanted that, he should have the decency not to look for it among women who had artistic projects of their own.

Though not worrying about if it was going to be another eggs and toast week would be nice. She let out a sigh.

"So. Not Oswald. But why me? Besides the fact you run faster." Hilaria didn't take offence at that.

Thalia gestured, feeling incoherent. "I want your eye for the thing. I don't know if I'm imagining it, or fantasising it, or if I'm going batty. Or all of the above, I suppose. There's no reason it couldn't be more than one." She hesitated. "You know I - well. I get fancies." Moments where the world swarmed over her, and it wasn't real, for all it made her feel real fear and panic and scrambled her thoughts for ages.

"Or if there's something actually there." Hilaria pointed this out, dryly.

"Yes. And I don't know which. And also." She shrugged. "It's worse at night. Knowing you'll be there is reassuring."

"Even if we both end up crammed in your bed. All right. You can show me around the house, and we'll see what I think of things. Do you want to tell me anything about what you've seen or heard or whatever? I suppose it would be better if I weren't predisposed. Is that the right word?"

"It works as a word. I think I'd rather not tell you details yet. If you notice the same things, then that's telling. Look, I wrote up a list on the train down, and here, I'll seal it up. Let me add one or two things. You write up your observations after a day or two, and then we'll compare them."

"That," said Hilaria, "is a sensible way of going about the thing. I approve. You knew I would."

Thalia nods. "It has a very, I don't know. Fairy tale feel. Locked doors and hidden rooms. I got a copy of a collection when I was at the library, tiny little place, but a surprisingly good selection, considering? And then I couldn't stop thinking about all those stories about Bluebeard and opening the thing you're not supposed to open."

Hilaria blinked. "Huh. Not a story you hear people talk about often. It's one of the..." She flicked her finger. "A lot of fairy tales, the versions we have are so overblown they don't seem real? That one always got me, though. Or the one about the sisters and the harp made from bone."

"You have a very visual imagination, you always have." Thalia spread her hands. "So. That's the main reason you're here. And the air - I don't know. I feel better. The food is grand, and they don't skimp, even though I'm sure Great-Aunt Avis must have eaten like a bird. She's tiny in all the photos. And very young looking."

"Older photos?" Hilaria finished half her sandwich, and set to work on the other half.

"It's hard to tell. A number of them are with Father, and suits didn't change as much. At least not Father's suits. And you know him, he has looked perpetually dignified since he was about twenty. And he dyes his hair, that's no help. Resolutely refusing to age, that's him."

Hilaria looked up and blinked. "He doesn't!"

"Oh, he does." Thalia leaned back. "Every fortnight. He hates when his roots show. It's a shampoo paste with a charm to set it. Really quite ridiculous. His moustache, too, of course."

Hilaria shook her head. "I would not have figured your father for that sort of vanity." She grinned. "If you ever need to bait him, that's a grand one for a blind in the gossip columns."

"You'd know." Thalia grinned. Hilaria occasionally wrote pieces for them, though she was mostly an artist.

Her friend just laughed, all good cheer. "All right. How else are you? Besides feeling better. Honestly, being out of the fogs is a good start. We had a bad one on Sunday again. I was glad I didn't have to go out."

Thalia shrugged slightly. "I haven't written much."

"Do you want to talk about that now, later, or not ever?" Hilaria laid out the options even-handedly. Or perhaps that was odd-handedly, seeing as how there were three of them.

"All of those?" Thalia admitted it, then peered at her watch. "Better now than later? I don't know. I keep typing things and tearing them up. Or trying with a pen and tearing it up. There's a small mountain of crumpled paper, and it's not as if good paper grows on trees. Well. It does, technically, I suppose, or it is trees, goodness."

"I prefer a good linen paper. Or cotton. But we're still at plants." Hilaria leaned forward. "You're ducking the question."

Thalia was. And she didn't want to talk about it. But if she didn't talk about it with Hilaria, who was she going to tell about it? They both knew dozens of writers and artists and sculptors and musicians and dancers. She could talk about the craft of writing, or analyse a piece well enough with most of the writers. But finding someone you could talk to when the writing wasn't going well, that was a rare thing. They both knew it, even if they didn't talk about it much.

"I think." She swallowed. "What I've been doing doesn't work. Not anymore. And I'm not sure if it ever did." It was horrible to admit that it felt like she was giving up any hope of ever actually being a writer. Forever and ever.

Hilaria, though, leaned back. "It's certainly not making you happy. And it hasn't for a while. That piece you sent to *The Second Pan*, that was the gates of the factory, right?"

Thalia nodded. A set piece, the lives that walked past, the neighbourhood, a thread of drama and recrimination that swirled around. It had some good turns of phrase; she had thought, at the time. And the people in it felt like people to her. Independently minded.

"There are good bits in that." Hilaria considered choosing her words deliberately now. "You know that. I'm telling you that. But it didn't..." She turned her hand over, palm up. "It was all line art, not shaded in. No heart to it."

She closed her eyes, curling her arms around her waist, feeling herself withdraw the way she'd always withdrawn. The way she'd always felt with her family, especially since the beginning of the War. As if she were on an iceberg bobbing in the ocean, a long way from anything else, forever.

A moment later, there was a hand resting on her arm. Warm, Hilaria always had shockingly warm hands. No good for pastry. The passing thought flitted through her head, and she made a wordless noise of frustration. Then she swallowed even that. It wasn't ladylike. It wasn't proper, it wasn't what was done.

"When you're at your best, you're making things real for people. Showing them what's there. A new way to see it, or think about it. I've seen you do it over and over again. I know you hate them, but you've a knack for obituaries. Seeing what makes someone interesting, what they did that was their own."

Thalia did indeed hate writing obituaries. She'd had to do five, for fellow VADs, at one point or another. When the ones from their families left out all the important parts of their recent lives. And then two others, for writers in their larger circle, when no one else would touch it. She'd felt a sense of pride at doing a good job, and a sense of terror that she might have got it wrong.

Whatever an obituary said about someone, it should be solid. About them, not some fantasy of who they were.

She didn't catch what Hilaria said then, not until there was a tap on her wrist. "What are you reading right now? Besides Perrault." Bluebeard, of course, Hilaria would place that.

"Local folklore, various authors. A novel by Sabine Baring-Gould, who was one of them. A few random things from Great-Aunt Avis's library." She shrugged. "Rather a lot about bird folklore. Did you know there's quite a lot of odd folklore about birds? One of the books said that if you pluck wild peonies during the daytime, a green woodpecker will come and pluck out your eyes. It doesn't even make sense!"

Hilaria snorted. "A lot of folklore is tosh, you know that. In that case, I have a proposition. Don't try to write anything for a few days. Don't even pick up a pen, unless you simply must leave a note. 'Going out, mind the ghost on the stair' or what have you. See what you enjoy reading, what you keep coming back to. And then try something more like that. Nothing long, just a beginning or a scene from the middle or something..."

Thalia opened her eyes and peered at her friend. "Something you've done?"

"The only good thing I got from my art tutor at school." Hilaria said. "You remember how awful she was about everything else. Right, sometimes, but also awful. But she said, when you have a block like that, you need to back up, and see what you're interested in now. Then come at that from a new angle. It's worked for illustration. And painting. You could, I don't know. Write a fairy tale. A satire. A limerick? You're very good at limericks."

"There is only so much that fits in a limerick." Thalia tried to be stern about it, but she was smiling as she said it.

"See? What have you been thinking about, for books?"

Thalia made herself answer, before she second-guessed the whole thing. "Edith Nesbit. *The Five Children and It.*"

"Have you read it recently?"

Thalia shook her head.

"Well, then. First thing is finding you a copy. Right. We should wander back to the train, and we will see what happens."

CHAPTER 19
SATURDAY

"All right. Here I am, here you are. There is a moor." They had walked uphill and along the road. They had meant to get to Widecombe in the Moor, and have a proper lunch at the inn. But Mrs Harley had wisely insisted on giving them a sturdy packed lunch as well.

She had been concerned that the two would find the walking too much. It was, in fact, a lot. Thalia's calves were aching, but not nearly as much as her thighs were. The satchel with lunch was not terribly heavy, but was, in fact, annoyingly full. And there had been a fair bit of climbing uphill, though at least that would be different going back.

It wasn't just the lunch. Hilaria had brought her sketchbook and watercolours and far more pens and pencils than any one person should need to make sketches. That many for detailed work, Thalia could understand, but it wasn't as if Hilaria had even used more than three.

They had not made it to Widecomb, in fact, because Hilaria had seen some rocks. They were, to be fair, exceedingly dramatic and impressive rocks, rising up from the top of the hill abruptly and demandingly. While Hilaria sketched, Thalia had been thumbing through the copy of *A Book of Dartmoor*, the accurately named work by Sabine Baring-Gould.

She had already read, some days ago, his section on the tors in general, great masses of granite that apparently littered the moor like the discarded toys of giants. The names intrigued her, too. There was Fur Tor, and Leather Tor, and Hen Tor, all apparently with a scatter of stones at the bottom. The illustration of Vixen Tor was rather striking, but that was on the other edge of the moor.

She had also got through several passages about the joys of living on the moor, which involved rather rustic living. However, it was recommended for poor lungs, and she certainly had to agree it seemed to help. She wasn't coughing nearly as much, and Hilaria had agreed it seemed most agreeable. And being out with the birds was pleasant. She'd missed hearing them close by, somehow. It made a place feel real, and the silence down near the house kept echoing.

"Does your book say anything about them, then?" Hilaria was erasing something with a rubber. The distraction was decidedly welcome, before Thalia got caught up in less pleasant trains of thought.

Thalia thumbed back to the place she'd stuck a scrap of paper and read out the quote. "Hey Tor Rocks form two fine masses, and are unlike most of the moorland tors, in that the granite is very consistent, and is not broken into the usual layers of soft beds alternating with hard layers."

"That's quite reasonable of him." Hilaria noted.

"He adds that the view is fine, which understates things a bit. That's Grea Tor, I think, and over there is Bone Hill. I wish I knew more about where the names came from. I mean, what's Grea when it's at home? On the other hand, this is a man who also said, and I quote, 'But what are gloves for, but to cover dirty hands when we go to town to make display?'"

"And he doesn't talk about the names?"

"Oh, some. He has a whole section on various names for large stone objects. And he has attitudes about people in other places that I don't think are entirely proper. You know, tweedy British." It was one of their private phrases. Not that this one wasn't easy to guess. The kind of man who ran the Empire from the comfort of his club, never venturing out of his routine or comfortable environs. With a man to bring him a fresh drink, and a housekeeper to see to everything else.

Thalia flicked through the pages. "He spends quite a long time on tombs, actually. Of which there are quite a few prehistoric ones. Also, a number of sketches of pottery, flint arrowheads, and so on. And he has no patience for a lot of local superstition about the tors or what they might have been used for."

"Well. Do we go on?"

Thalia shook her head. "I don't much want to be up here when it starts getting dark, and that means we shouldn't go off and look for more things that draw your eye. Eat here and go back?"

"Eat and talk." Hilaria waved a hand. "You have the envelopes? And here, hand me that. There are perfectly good places to perch and we can use that one for something like a table."

Ten minutes later, they had dealt with the most immediate hunger and thirst, and Hilaria solemnly held out her hand. Thalia put one envelope into it and opened the other, reading Hilaria's hand. It was artful, a mass of curling lines that took far too long to put to the page for Thalia's preference.

When she'd read it, she looked up to see Hilaria still reading. It made sense. Her letter went to three pages, describing everything in precise vertical letters and tight sharp strokes. When Hilaria looked up, she gestured. "Much the same, only you've seen more of it. The first night, in particular."

"Were you - were you scared?" Thalia hadn't known how to ask. She'd heard something herself, or at least she thought she had. But if Hilaria had heard it, surely she'd have said something in the morning. Only, no. Mrs Harley had been bustling around all day, making sure Hilaria was finding everything comfortable. And one of the Dartmoor ponies had wandered down into the drive, and there was a great deal of fuss about shooing it back out. Then a pig.

Which, now Thalia thought about it, was an additional oddity. A house like that wouldn't normally have livestock up against the house, but she'd expected to see a bit more in the way of farming. Other than the kitchen garden, there didn't seem to be any of that. No chickens, no stables. If they needed a pony cart, one got brought up from near the village.

Hilaria was taking her time answering. "Scared isn't exactly the word. Aware of something uncanny? Yes. I don't know. It's like a painting's varnish going yellow or brown or even black. Changing everything you see of it, even though the paint underneath might still be fine. Some colours do that, you know."

"You had a fine rant about it last time we went to, oh. Who was it? The man with the absurdly bushy eyebrows, you had to go to make nice about something."

"Don't remind me." Hilaria grimaced. "Roberto. Who

thinks entirely too well of himself, and also he uses abominable materials and his work will be worthless in time."

A cattier woman than Thalia actually was might have said something about how they were worthless now. But she and Hilaria had made a pact, quite a solemn one, blood oath and all, that they weren't going to do that sort of thing. Art and writing rose or fell enough on its own merit. There was no need to tear something down without being asked. One could always say that it wasn't to one's taste, or perhaps one didn't entirely understand it. No need to go on and add that was because it was an incomprehensible mess.

It meant they got more invitations to gallery parties and other amusements than many of their circle. Often with quite lovely food and drink and entertainment. And, as a lure, the possibility of making useful connections.

"So. What do you think is going on?"

Hilaria considered. "You mentioned some of it. The isolation. The oddness of the house. You're right about those pictures of your great-aunt, she barely seems to age, except her hair changes colour a bit? Though even that's hard to tell. And the way the place is decorated. Do you remember what it was like when she was married?"

"Not terribly well. I was rather young. But - very much his areas of the place and hers. I wrote about the upstairs. I wonder if that might have been her space, principally, when he was alive?"

"And they never had children." Hilaria was chewing on something. "Was there any family gossip about it?"

"Only that it was a pity Father was on his side, not hers, because it made it less likely we'd inherit the place, whenever that happens? All this, them taking her off to the south of France, might be in aid of that."

"Even though it's just you and your sister now." Hilaria frowned. "Anything else?"

"I - there was a nursery here, when I was little. I mean, it's still there. Which is odd. I don't know if they had other parts of the family to say her side of things? If there's some other cousins by marriage. If so, I've never met them that I remember."

"And how much of the grounds have you walked? I know we went over the fields yesterday. You said there's an orchard?"

"That's the other side of the wall from our bit. Great-Aunt's bit, I mean. It belongs to someone in the village. I met his nephew." She winced.

"Oh, Thal." Hilaria reached out and patted her hand. "What sort of bad?"

Hilaria, at least, was familiar with Thalia's bouts of uncertainty and awkwardness. Thalia knew perfectly well what to do in the social circles she had been born to. She wasn't always deft at it, rather the opposite, but she knew what the rules were, and when she was breaking them, and when she was bending them. This had been something different.

"We'd been talking about apple grafting, which I still don't understand, though I've read more about it now? And then I mentioned hearing a bird and a chick, and he went all over odd. The way -" Thalia swallowed.

"You know it's better if you talk about it a bit." Hilaria sounded careful now. Which was a good thing. Half the time Thalia talked about it, she ended up a sobbing mess, which was fine when she was home. Well, for values of fine. It was, however, distinctly a problem when they were miles from the house and walking was the way back.

Hilaria, though, had a theory that not talking about the

War only made it worse. That things built up, until they flooded out without any controls. She was ruthless about it in herself. She'd turn her own personal nightmares into drawings and jagged lines in a sketchbook she never let anyone see. When Thalia had tried the same thing in words, she'd hated herself. It came out either sentimental or hateful, and she couldn't bear either.

"It was like being back there." Thalia looked away, down across the moor, the rolling landscape. It was a huge space. It could absorb a bit of horror and not feel it. "Seeing him. He had a bad War, I'm certain. That kind of look. You know the one."

"Where they're lost, and there's no coming home." Hilaria nodded. "Like you said, early on."

Thalia had thought about that a lot. It was like being adrift in the ocean, no compass, no stars, no way to know which direction you should go. Something like that, anyway. A flat landscape, water stretching unbroken from horizon to horizon. It was being unmoored but in the largest, grandest sense. The rolling grasses and bracken of the land, like the featureless ocean, making it near hopeless to find your way anywhere else. Though, mind, they were on a moor at the moment, so scarcely unmoored in reality, no matter what it felt like.

Only now, she found herself turning that around in her head. This was a different sense of a moor. It had its anchors. She didn't know what they were. She had only the faintest glimpse from the reading she'd done, and being up here. But there were ancient places, where you could feel like others had gone through horrible times and come out on the other side.

Not better, not wiser, not stronger. Not any of the things in the perky and overly sunny magazines that thought you could cure shell shock with cheer and company. But something more like making a space for yourself, whatever it was, in a place that would hold it. Could hold it. World without end, amen.

"What do we do now?" Thalia looked up, finally, to see Hilaria had begun sketching her.

Her friend tucked the sketchbook away. "We go back, and we keep observing, and we talk about it. We'll have to keep taking energetic walks, but I suppose it's safe to talk through the details together, going back."

"We will certainly see anyone coming a good way off." Thalia agreed. "You ready?"

"My fingers are getting cold, so yes." Hilaria stood and brushed off her skirt, as they packed up the remains of lunch and the sketchbox.

CHAPTER 20

FRIDAY

A dam had returned the book to Mistress Dutton, and been gifted with several scones still warm from the oven. It was a kindly gesture, and he was not at all sure what to do with that kindness. It had been a long time since anyone had been that apparently uncomplicated around him.

It made no sense. He knew Mrs Whitmore must have said something about him. Something accurate and kind enough, but the sort of comment that would provoke pity and distance. And surely Mistress Dutton had heard the gossip in town now, from the librarian, from everyone else who had a hint of an opinion. It wasn't that Adam was the centre of anyone's world; he knew he wasn't. But he also knew how gossip worked in a small community. As far as he could tell, he was the only new thing this month, besides the woman up the hill.

Two women now, they seemed to be multiplying. He'd seen them yesterday. Walking north across the fields, hundreds of feet away. Thalia had her hands in her pockets, the other woman had an arm through hers, and they were deep in conversation.

He supposed people had friends like that. Still. He hadn't, not for a decade. Oh, certainly people he could nod to, who didn't know about him, the few times he made it to the Veterans in Trellech. But he didn't fit there, nor at The Arthur. He technically qualified for membership at The Arthur. But that didn't mean they needed to make him feel comfortable, among all the officers who had been born and bred to it.

It made him wistful, at any rate, that Thalia had a friend. Taller, dark-haired, striking, what he could see at a distance. But not nearly as comfortable on a hillside. Thalia hadn't seemed rugged or outdoorsy, but she had a comfortable ground-covering walk, a certainty about where she put her feet. While he was at it, Adam envied that too.

They had disappeared, and today he'd kept an eye out for them, but he hadn't seen any sign of them. No sign of birds, either, at least nothing close enough for him to get a good look. That worried him. It was autumn, certainly, and well past time for a number of birds to migrate.

He wondered, suddenly, how far that went. If there was something odd, could you use the birds to locate where the problem was? Quite possibly, they avoided whatever it was. The difficulty was that birds moved rather faster than he could, and it was impossible to tell without a great deal of work. Tracking charms, and all that, he knew the theory of it, but he'd only ever used it on sheep. Sheep, on the whole, were less prone to vast, swooping journeys.

Today, he was trying to focus on an actual task, figuring out how close the bulk of the apples were to ripening. He thought the earlier varieties might be just about ready in a few days. A week, perhaps. It was hard to tell. Once those actually ripened, he thought it would be easier to sort out the details for the others. He'd drawn up a proper layout of the orchard, as he'd been taught, got his uncle to help identify a few of the apples he brought back. And Mrs Whitmore, who had been surprisingly helpful.

He had been doing another pass, trying to get a good look at the higher up apples. He turned to find Thalia standing on the other side of the wall. She was a good twenty feet away, but he should have spotted her. Normally he noticed, whenever anyone came close, no matter how well he knew them.

Thalia lifted a hand, then let it drop, awkwardly. She looked, for a moment at least as awkward as he felt. But she didn't go away. She didn't come closer, either. It reminded him a bit of the lore about vampires, about them needing to be invited in. He picked up his stick and came over, stopping about five feet on the other side of the wall.

"Yes?" It came out sounding peevish, which he didn't entirely mean to do.

"Afternoon." She stopped, then said, the words coming out in a flurry. "Look, I'm dreadfully sorry about last time, but I couldn't think of anything I could do that I was sure would be a help. And you looked like what you needed was no one fussing at you. And besides, even if you wanted someone fussing over you, I'm a stranger. How would you know if you could stand it? I hope you got home all right?"

That was not what he'd expected from her at all, and he gaped, openmouthed for a good ten seconds, before swallowing. "I." He coughed and tried again. "I got home all right." Then, hesitantly, he added, "Thank you for worrying."

It wasn't the sort of thing one said to other people, particularly strange posh women wandering in fields like ghosts. But at the same time, the fact she'd worried was novel enough to derail his usual reactions. He considered. "May I offer you a tree stump again?"

"Oh, very kind." She glanced at the stone wall, at where he was. Before he could think about whether offering her a hand over the wall was a good idea on several counts, she had stepped over it. She wobbled slightly on a bit of uneven ground, and found her footing. When she was steady on her feet again, she smiled at him, and went off to the tree stump, letting him follow at his own pace.

She seemed, to Adam, to be very independently minded. And as if she didn't care for the usual social graces and polite touches. The way a man was supposed to help a woman, and a woman was supposed to imply that she needed it, whether or not she did. It seemed particularly perplexing from a woman of her class, who surely was used to expecting her lessers to attend to her.

Once she was settled on the tree stump, he found his rock and coughed before he sat down. "I have a scone or two? Or there are apples."

"Oh, apple, please." She looked delighted at the offer. "And I do like a scone. So long as it's not your tea or lunch or what have you?"

"Mrs Whitmore sent me with plenty." Adam considered, then brought back two apples, two of the Beauty of Bath. It gave him something to focus on, for a good minute, rather than slice his fingers. Then he handed the pieces over, and she drew out a handkerchief, clean, to drape across her lap and hold them. "I didn't expect to see you again."

She considered that question for a moment. "Did I do something that hurt you? I'd like not to do that again."

It was stunningly blunt, even brutal. The kind of no-

nonsense forward movement that he'd seen in the nurses he'd liked best. "Again." He echoed the last words.

"Last time," she paused, looking at him as if evaluating something. "I asked about a sound, and it seemed to upset you. You didn't speak, you - went away."

"Oh." He looked down, wanting to flee now, and knowing that he couldn't. Physically couldn't, but also, as much as he wanted to be elsewhere, he didn't have the wits together to make himself stand up and move.

She coughed, gently. "People judge, don't they?" It was almost conspiratorial.

Adam looked up. He could move that much. The deadly weight that settled over him sometimes hadn't lifted, but it was as if someone had shifted the corner of a heavy blanket off him. A taste of freedom. "What do you know about that?" He tried to make the question neutral, but he was sure it came out bitter and harsh.

He saw a flash of something in her eyes, certainly, as if he had handed her another piece of information. She considered, then tugged something from a chain under her blouse and jumper. "I went to school in Wales." It seemed for all the world like a complete change of subject.

But then Adam made his eyes focus. Silver pendant, a greenish blue stone in the midst. Aquamarine, he thought. Stamped around the edge, in letters he was sure were Latin. She'd gone to Schola, the place the best and brightest and best off of the magical community went, a far distance from Snap in every possible way.

When he met her eyes again, she smiled briefly. "Less awkward if we both don't have to talk around that problem, right?"

He nodded once. "Snap."

"Oh, that explains why you know so much about the

apples. I think they like you, too. Did you make a proper offering to the Old Man of the orchard when you came? We talked about that in one of my classes. Two of them, actually, now I think about it. Of course you did, you're not going to turn your nose up at perfectly sensible long-standing customs. I know that about you already."

"You can't possibly." The words came out of him in a rush.

Thalia shrugged. He didn't know what to make of her. She was something like one of the corvids, the more he watched her. Quick, sharp, and he suspected rather more clever than was obvious at first or second or tenth glance. She didn't miss much, even as she chattered along. "The apples seem happier. At any rate."

She took a breath and let it out. "I was a VAD at the Temple of Healing through most of the War. Not just the tidy bits, that was my sister. All of it. Burn cases and dreadful wounds, and the people who were hurt most inside their heads. And their hearts. That's what Sister Pomona told me once, and I've done my best to hold on to it."

Adam felt overwhelmed, like water had flooded over him, buffeting him and near drowning him. She must have noticed something, because her hand came up to her mouth, as if she were forcibly keeping herself quiet. Unexpectedly, it worked. There was a good minute of silence before Adam could venture a question. "Why?"

She gave that the seriousness it deserved, but the first thing she said wasn't what he'd expected. "Almost no one's asked that. Most people assume. Or tried to talk me out of it."

Her family, he guessed. Other people of her social set, the people who had money and all the time in the world for civilised pursuits. He wondered what hers were when she had a chance. Flower arranging, perhaps, or porcelain painting. She had delicate, precise hands. She might do well with either. She'd said she wrote things, but he didn't know how much of her time that took. "Why?" The question had worked the first time. He'd try it again.

"Not the done thing." Now, her voice sounded completely posh, the sort of person who would pass Adam on the street and assume he was nothing. "And seeing men at their worst, that's not suitable, either."

Adam had not considered that part of things. Most of the people he'd been around, until much later in his recovery, had been proper nurses with training. Who knew what to expect. Or so one assumed. He wondered, all of a sudden, what kind of training she'd had, if it had been uneven, like his. Some parts structured to the minute, if not the second, every piece laid out with pages of rules to follow. And other parts, utterly bodged together, or left entirely to chance.

One more time, he ventured a question. "Why do it?" Three words this time. At least he got them out without freezing up.

She looked up, meeting his eyes again, but looking at him softly, deliberately, not staring. "Because it mattered. Because my brother went off to fight. I wanted to think there'd be someone kind if he needed it. I didn't know much, but I thought I could do that. Be kind."

Then she swallowed hard, suppressing a sob or something else of the kind. He wouldn't ask about that, he couldn't. He glanced to the side, up toward the house. "Your friend?"

"Hilaria. She's the other one who asked."

That wasn't entirely what he meant, and he gestured. "She's on the hill."

"Oh. Oh!" Thalia fumbled the apples. "Thank you. For the apples. Look. The house is still very odd. Can - you didn't seem to mind that part. Before."

He felt now like a toy boat, bobbing along in a stream, going with the current because that was all it could do. "If you'd like to talk more about it. The next clear day?"

"Please. Yes." She made quick work of tying up the handkerchief again, folding the apples into it. "Pleased to meet you properly. Next clear day. Later."

Before he could think of anything to say to that, beyond nodding, she was gone back over the wall. She took quick ground-covering strides up the hill to where her friend was standing, waving at her.

CHAPTER 21
SATURDAY EVENING

That night, it rained. And all through the next day. Thalia and Hilaria were in the library, as they had been since they got up, with pauses for meals. Mrs Harley had tended the fire before she went off for the evening, and it was still going strong, making the room cosy and not too damp. Thalia had filled several lanterns with charm lights, enough to browse the shelves comfortably. She had been going through the shelves again one by one while Hilaria sketched.

"Merrylees, Milson, Molson, Montgomery, Morris, Mystor, Nanson, Nelson, Nesbit. Wait." She pulled the volume out, an omnibus collection of several novels in one binding. It looked as if someone had had it privately bound.

Hilaria looked up lazily from the rug by the fire. "Yes?"

"A book."

"Those happen in libraries." Hilaria stretched, but Thalia turned back to the shelves, peering at them and then moving the lantern stand closer. It was a clever device, letting her have the light right with her, rather than fighting with the shadows.

There was something else back there. Part of her wasn't at all sure about sticking her hand into a dark space, especially in this house. Instead she said, "Can you come here and hold some books?"

Hilaria stretched again, and stood up, coming over and holding out her hands. "Sure."

Thalia stacked four books, then added two more, enough for her to shift the light and see the back of the shelf. No mice, no leavings from mice, no spiders. She did, however, see a soft-bound journal, curved from being pressed between the books and the back of the shelves. She pulled out her handkerchief, glad she'd got in the habit of always having three clean ones on her person, and dusted it off.

Hilaria coughed, and Thalia smiled, putting the books back on the shelf. "What's this?" She peered at the volume. It was bound in an unusual spring-green leather, not a shade that you saw very often.

"Bring it back to the sofa. Here, I'll get the light. Or do we want to go upstairs?"

They both glanced at the fire as one, and then at the stairs up to Great-Aunt Avis's rooms. Hilaria nodded. "Let me bank the fire." She set about doing that promptly, and Thalia let her. Hilaria had spent six months, mostly over the winter, living in a farm cottage for her art, and she was much better at the task. Safer, too.

Once they were upstairs, they curled up on Thalia's bed. It was the bigger of the two. The light was better, and there was more space to spread out. Thalia hesitated, though, before opening the volume. "What do you think it is?"

"Isn't that my question? Something important, or something trivial. Something lost, or something hidden. Something old or something more recent. How do you tell?"

Thalia snorted, but she could feel a tension building up in her. Fidgets, as Nanny would have said. "It was tucked back there deliberately, I think. Out of the way."

"What was the section?"

"Fiction. Novels and such. The volumes of Nesbit I grew up on were smaller. Cloth bound, I remember how they felt. My copies fell apart. I mean, they'd been hand-me-downs, twice over. And I think cousins, before us."

Hilaria tsked. "Proper children's books ought to be kept around. We'd be better people if we reread stories of being kind and curious and good-hearted more often."

"But then people might expect us to reread all the sentimental, moralistic tripe and be improved by it. And very little of that holds up against reality, does it." Thalia ran her finger along the edge of the leather, trying to decide what she thought.

Hilaria grunted. She'd had her own experiences with that. "Old?"

"Older. I don't think I've seen something bound like this. Not since the War, though I suppose it could be a particular maker. The colour, though."

"It's an odd green. Like the arsenic greens. I don't know that that is, I'm fairly sure it works differently on leather? But wash your hands after we're done?"

"I was going to do that anyway. It's all over dust in bits. The leather's in quite good shape, though." She felt like a detective out of a serial novel, drawing out the investigation. On the other hand, she didn't have a wealth of knowledge about the precise dye shades of leather made whenever it was made, so she might as well press on.

"Go on. Open it."

Thalia did, slowly, cradling the book in her lap with a wash towel under it. If it were an old book, opening it could damage it. She at least wanted to keep all the pages together. But no, the leather opened easily, and the paper felt supple under her fingers, not brittle at all. It had barely yellowed, either. She'd have to look at it in better light, outside, but it seemed rather brilliantly cream. It was thick, too, like the best writing paper.

The front had "AV" in an ornate calligraphed monogram, precisely centred on the page, with an M added below in a slightly different ink. Thalia could see how the later ink had a little less depth to its black.

"A, Vee?" asked Hilaria.

"Great-Aunt Avis was a Vesta before she was a Morgan." Thalia said. "So that would fit. And suggest it was hers from before she married."

"Do you know much about her people?" Hilaria peered at the book, then leaned back, as if she were thinking and too busy doing so to focus her eyes.

"A long line, trailing down to her, in the end, I think. She had a brother, but I think something happened to him in India? A snake or a tiger or a boar or something. I'd have to look it up. So it was just her, and she didn't have children. The family goes back forever, though."

Hilaria nodded. "You told me that." She nudged Thalia with her elbow. "Go on, then. Open it up. Turn the page."

Thalia felt that her world would change when she did. It was when, not if. She knew she was going to. But she wanted to hang here, in this moment before everything shifted, to feel what it was like. That moment of potential, the weight and the depth of it. She wanted to be able to describe it later, properly, so other people would know what it was like.

Hilaria didn't rush her. That was the thing about Hilaria as a friend. When it mattered, she got it right. Often at other times, too, but her great gift was knowing when something had shifted from fun to earnest.

Then, slowly, Thalia opened it up. The beginning items, at least, were more or less diary entries. They were brief, a few lines for each day, but the dates weren't easy to read. They were in small cramped writing, much more so than the notes themselves, and blurred, as if someone had wanted to obscure that.

"There's a reference here to the Irish famine. And the Crimean War." Thalia let her thumb trace along, as she skimmed down pages. "So 1850s, maybe? I'd have to look up the details."

"That's..." Hilaria did the maths, quickly. "That's seventy years. Is that something she wrote as a child?"

Thalia leaned in, peering at the handwriting. "It sounds adult. No, she mentions her husband, here. So an adult. How queer." Now she definitely felt like they had wandered into some sort of story.

"She doesn't look very old in the photographs, you said. Any of them." Hilaria chewed on her lip. "So if she were twenty, then..." She gestured at the book. "She'd be ninety something now. She definitely doesn't look that in anything I've seen. Forties, maybe, though that can't be quite right either, can it?"

"I think Father would handle it very differently if she were. Take her somewhere in England, not to France, for one thing. Or he'd have been - well. A lot more diligent about visiting? But surely he must have some idea how old she is?"

Only, well. Maybe he didn't. Her father was, in fact, fallible, much as he hated to admit it about anything. And if he'd only known Great-Aunt Avis when she was an adult, and he was a younger adult. Well. Women of her approximate age never talked about their age. There were no children to measure time against.

"How do we figure this out?" Hilaria said, glancing down at the book.

"I think the first thing is to, well. Go through it, and look for references. Anything that might have a date, or indicate how old she was, or how recently married. I suppose there are records somewhere for marriages, but it would look very odd if I went and asked. Even if I could go and ask, without that being obvious." Thalia grimaced.

She thumbed through again, turning the pages, peering at the text early on. "It talks about Mrs Harley here, I think. I can't quite make out the first name. Fortunata? Florentia? But that's definitely Harley, and she's talking about the Irish famine, how Mrs Harley has opinions about it. What opinions, I don't know. But that's not possible. I mean, she's talking about her having known people from over there, and the years don't make sense. Like Mrs Harley was an older woman then."

"Maybe it's a different Mrs Harley? An aunt or a mother or grandmother or something? You are getting overly complicated. Find out what you can from there. We'll look at photographs as we can, see if there's anything that helps date them. I'm better with clothing than you are, as a rule, but there must be clues. And when I go back to London, I can go round to Somerset House."

"Getting time to look here might be the trick. I mean, not being obvious about it."

Hilaria shrugged. "We could look once they've gone off in the evening. Or get up very early. How early do you think they start?"

Thalia groaned. "Six in the morning, can you believe? It's an evil hour. No, not evil." She strove to be more precise in her language than that. "Not a time with which I am willingly familiar." Certainly not anymore, though she'd manage to convince people she preferred evening and overnight shifts for much of the War. Coming at dawn from that angle was entirely different.

"We'll try the alternatives, then, before that." Hilaria snorted. "Besides. You want me for the photos. So maybe I'll get up very early sometime. And come back to bed after. I will say the beds are quite comfortable. They feel almost new sprung, had you noticed?"

Thalia considered. "I did. The style of things is rather old-fashioned, though I suppose that's to be expected. But they don't feel it much. The towels, the bedding. The sofa. Even the chairs don't creak much. Which might just be the fact there weren't people using them, and competent staff to see to the place."

"It does make me wonder a bit about Mrs Harley." Hilaria said.

"She's been here a long time. Not as long as that, I think?" Thalia gestured at the diary. "Though I suppose she might be mentioned somewhere."

"We could ask her?" Hilaria was dubious.

Thalia considered. "If there is something odd going on, asking her tips our hand, doesn't it? Better to see what we can find out first, and then ask later. Speaking of, this should go in my trunk, tucked away. And I will wash my hands, I haven't forgotten."

Thalia clambered out of bed, slipping her feet into her slippers. She used the charm on her trunk to open it, then the hidden compartment that would open only to her touch. It wasn't large. That sort of thing took more money than her parents would have spent on a trunk for her, even if she'd been a more obedient daughter. And they hadn't wanted to bribe her, either. But it was enough for a small book or two, or enough bank notes to travel with, or carefully spread out coins.

When she came back, Hilaria blinked up at her. "I should go off to bed."

"They won't come in. If you'd rather company." They'd slept like that, plenty of times, after a late night when neither of them wanted to move. And, honestly, because two slept warmer than one, and there were days when that made a difference.

Hilaria let herself fall back on the bed with a soft thump. "Right. Turn out the light?"

Thalia lay there in the dark for quite a few minutes, listening closely to the noises of the house. Hilaria's sleepy breathing. Again, that faint noise, from somewhere upstairs, that she couldn't quite identify.

CHAPTER 22
TUESDAY

The next clear day was several days later than Adam expected, even given the fact it was coming into late autumn. The puppy, now named Atlas, had taken up most of the intervening time. Rather surprisingly so, given the puppy was not yet old enough for any sort of extended training. His uncle had begun, but it was a matter of one command and a bit of reward, then letting Atlas scamper around.

Adam was fairly sure a small, fast-moving object that seemed to be growing as you looked at him was not the best combination with someone unsteady on his one good leg. But his uncle was happy, and that probably mattered more. And Mrs Whitmore seemed pleasantly amused. That was good, because if she'd thrown up her hands, he wasn't sure what they would have done.

Adam, himself, felt restless. He was penned in by the rain, and he couldn't focus on anything. His mind skittered off every time he tried. It was partly Thalia, herself. Now he'd got the idea in his head, he couldn't get it out. She was rather like a corvid. Not bright and flashy, like a blue jay, and not lurking like a raven or a crow. A rook, maybe, they chattered, but they could be incredibly social, hundreds of them claiming a grove of trees.

He wondered what she was like around other people. People who remembered how to have a conversation, for one thing. She seemed like - even with her friend - that conversation kept bursting out. Like a crocus in spring, barely there one day, then a riotous insistent pop of colour. He had barely known what to do with that before the War. Now he had no idea at all.

And there had been what she'd told him. That she'd been a VAD, which was not what he expected. They'd done real work, hard work. He'd known a few, when he'd been lightly injured, who'd tended to men much worse off. Infections, maggots, deep wounds, the lot.

And they'd done it with kindness, as Thalia had said. Sternness, a ruthless attention to their work that didn't leave time for much else. But they'd saved lives. And made the end of many a little bit better. Even if better was an odd word for that.

He wondered what Thalia had been like as a VAD. Mostly, was she always that fluttery? He'd seen in her walk a determination, a focus. And he was beginning to wonder if her chatter covered something else, like his own awkwardness. It had that feel to it, of a sleight of hand. Don't pay attention to all the ways you could hurt me if you chose to. Just look at the surface, what I'm making it easy to see.

Finally, when the weather cleared, he went off again with a cloak and a packed lunch and more tea. He needed to look at the apples, anyway, it was about time to get some help in and harvest the earliest to ripen. He needed to figure out how much help and how many ladders or wagons. It went back to the maths assignments he'd done at school. If you have ten apple trees with ripe apples, and two clear afternoons, how many hands do you need to harvest them, and what tools do you need to provide the workers?

He remembered Mistress Ford, who had taught that class, talking about the other things to include. Breaks, for one. Meals, and plenty of weak beer or cider to drink. Enough to keep their strength up. Not so much anyone would get drunk, at least not until the end of the day. She'd been very insistent on keeping the proper country traditions around harvest, and the reasons for that.

Adam had been in the orchard for about an hour when he heard a call from a fair bit away. Thalia, and her friend. They were both together, a few feet from the wall, waiting. Again, like he had permission to give or deny. He waved a hand. "Tree stump? Apple?"

"Apple, please! I was telling Hilaria about the Sops in Wine, if there's one? We can split it." Hilaria made a sharp contrast to Thalia, with dark hair and paler skin. She had the sort of dramatically stylish looks that turned up in the pages of women's magazines. She had long hair, that wasn't to the current mode, but of course magical women didn't. He assumed she was magical at any rate.

Thankfully, Thalia answered that promptly enough. "Hilaria Adams, Adam Walton. Oh, that's curious, isn't it? Hil was a couple of years behind me at school, so you know. We have rooms next to each other in London. And I told her about you."

Adam was desperately curious about what she'd said. Enough that he actually asked. "What did you say?"

He'd expected a hesitation, the sort of editing that everyone did, when asked about a past conversation where they'd been a sharp or judging or dismissive. There was none of that. Hilaria answered, smiling. "She told me she'd met you, and she wasn't at all sure about you at first, but that you turned out to be a real person and not an apparition. The apples were delicious, and you went to Snap. And I gather you put up fairly well with her conversational style when she meets people. Thal does go on, doesn't she?" It was confiding, even conspiratorial, for all Thalia was right there.

Thalia didn't seem upset by it. She settled down on the tree stump, and Hilaria claimed a nearby boulder, while Adam took his usual seat. "I don't know how I'm supposed to answer that." Adam admitted. To give himself something to do with his hands, he sliced an apple, then managed to muffle a swear as he nicked his hand. He immediately reached to let a drop of blood fall on the ground. It was instinct now, if he were injured somewhere that was his land, or near enough to it.

When he looked up, Thalia was standing. "May I?" She gestured at his hand.

Right. She'd been a VAD. She must have had at least an intermediate healing course, by the end of things, if not more than that. But it would mean touching her, or rather her touching him. She didn't seem concerned about it.

He looked down at his finger. It was a wider cut than he'd thought at first. Just the wrong angle, and on the pad of his index finger. Exactly where it would be most annoying to put a plaster. Where it would irritate him every time he used the walking stick or a cane, or wanted to turn the page of a book. He hesitated, looking up at her, and she just smiled back at him.

Now, she seemed serene, unhurried. Not like a rook, but a sheepdog. The sort of collie that was frantic and made all its own trouble until you gave it a proper job. She clearly knew her work and was better for having some. It was that which decided him. How she'd changed. He wanted to understand it better. He wanted, in short, more than he'd wanted anything for a decade, beyond wanting awfulness to be over. Which awfulness? He had a long list.

Here and now, he held out his hand. She stepped up to him, took it in hers, cupping her left hand under his, to hold things steady, then to peer at the cut. "I'd like to wash it out, and then heal it up. Just in case there's a splinter or bit of something in there."

Adam was fairly sure there wasn't, but he agreed that was a sensible way to go about things. He nodded, and a moment later her right hand was calling water. Not much, enough to just let it drip from the tips of her fingers and wash anything away. It didn't sting, though it made his finger ache a little, because it was cold.

Then she cast a second charm, running her finger just above his skin. He could feel the prickle of the magic, the brush of it, even though she never quite touched him. Not there, anyway. Her other hand was still holding his in place, steady as a table. She must have been rather skilled. A lot of the nurses he'd met had needed the direct touch on a wound or a sore or a boil. It made the whole thing a battle between the immediate promise of pain and waiting for it to heal on its own, with all the risk of infection. He'd always made himself hold still for the healing, but it had been a near thing a dozen times.

When she drew her hand back, she looked again, checking her work. His finger was fully healed, and Adam instinctively closed his hand. "You have a gentle touch with it."

That made her smile, suddenly. A warm smile, an intensely human smile, as if he'd said something she desperately needed to hear. Then she took a breath and released whatever it was. She was pleasant looking, as a rule, but something about that moment, she'd been beautiful. Alive, in a very specific moment, like a flower at its height of bloom. An apple, just before it was ready to be picked. Then she let her hand drop, and the moment was decidedly over.

He suspected she didn't think of herself as beautiful, and yet, there she was. But at the same time, it brought him sharply back to the way all beautiful things died. And that beauty was not for someone like him. Not anymore, certainly, he'd thrown all his chance of that away. He might aspire to temporary comfort or a moment of respite these days, but never transcendent beauty.

He covered his confusion as she went back to the tree stump to sit down again. "Pardon. Where were we?"

"Well, I was just about to ask what you knew about the house. Or the oddness." Hilaria was plain-spoken, clearly, though she was glancing at Thalia as if considering some new piece of information. Then she went on. "We discovered something odd, and we don't know what it means."

Thalia's chin came up. She seemed about to object when Hilaria just coughed, and Thalia subsided.

"What sort of odd?" Adam had no idea what to do with this.

"A diary. With some odd dates in it. Ones that don't make a lot of sense. Look, do you know, is there someone you know who knows more about the house? The history of it? I suppose it's apparently too much to find anyone who actually talks to my great-aunt." Thalia shook her head. "It's very confusing."

"A diary. You've read it?"

Thalia nodded. "The last two days. There aren't dates

on the entries, at least not readable ones? It looks like someone tried to blot them out. Easy enough to do with some drops of water or ink and some blotting paper. But there are references in the diary, to events. Some of them I can guess at, some I'd need a library? Maybe not the one here. That might be too obvious. And I might need something bigger."

"I need to be back in London by the beginning of next week, so I can go look if we can't sort it by then." Hilaria sounded like she was reminding Thalia of something already sorted out, thank you kindly.

Thalia nodded. "Just." She waved a hand at the hill. "It doesn't make sense. I can't describe it."

Adam glanced up at the house, then back at her. "That bothers you?"

"I'm - I'm a writer. If I can't describe things in words, words other people get sense out of, what good am I?" Adam expected she hadn't intended to reveal quite so much, or do so as plaintively. Her hand came up to her mouth at the end. "Oh."

He cleared his throat. "Some things there aren't words for." Then he considered. "Do you think it's magical, whatever it is? Is it causing problems?"

"Yes, probably magical. And I don't know what problems would look like. Feel like. It feels very static. Like it's always, I don't know. About the age I am now, early thirties. No longer an ingenue, still feeling like everyone else is far more adult and sophisticated and accomplished than I am."

CHAPTER 23
TUESDAY

Thalia wanted to burn up in embarrassment. Which would be rather a problem in an orchard, even with the ground as damp as it still was after days of rain. So, on the whole, it was good she couldn't actually go up in flames, and blow away as ash. But she wanted to.

She kept making a fool of herself. Adam kept looking at her, as if he weren't at all sure what to do with her. He probably wanted to pat her on the head, and soothe her and send her off to her room with cocoa. Father did that to Mother, sometimes. Not like that. The cocoa came later. And she knew Agamemnon did the same thing with Phoebe. Her sister went meekly when he gave her that look, that she was a disgrace to him.

Without thinking about it, she hugged herself tight, then realised that there were other people there. Watching her. Hilaria wouldn't mind, Hilaria understood, but Adam must be sure she was a fool. She was about to stand, to leave, to go anywhere else, when he stood, instead. He pulled the cloak off his shoulders and offered it, holding it out. "May I?"

Thalia gaped, not at all sure what to say. Hilaria said, helpfully, "That's terribly kind. She does get these chills from time to time."

It was a vapid sort of excuse, but it wasn't as if Thalia had anything better to say. She looked up, and Adam blinked down at her. He didn't try to put the thing around her shoulders. He waited until she nodded. It gave her several more minutes before she had to say anything, tucking it around her. The wool was soft and comfortable, and she was sure it was charmed against weather and moths. It had the feel of something well worn, not at all new, and much loved.

When she looked up again, he'd sat back down, and he was watching her. "Tea?" When she nodded, he poured some from the flask into the lid, and held that out to her. Even more time before she had to attempt to make sense. The tea itself was strong, bracingly so, and quite restorative.

Finally, she couldn't put it off any longer. She tugged the cloak a bit more around her. "This is wonderfully warm, thank you. And the tea." If nothing else, she could be polite. Thalia had been brought up to politeness before she could talk.

Adam smiled, a little quirk of his mouth, as if he weren't quite sure how that went. With her, anyway. She ducked her chin, not sure how to start up again after her last outburst.

"You said you thought it was magical. And that it seems, what was it, static?" Adam's voice was quieter now, as if he was also dragging himself out of thought.

Thalia nodded. Nodding was a lot simpler, honestly. She cleared her throat. "It's an odd point to be stuck in. I would understand, oh, the middle twenties? Especially." She swallowed. "I'm trying to figure out what it would have been like when Great-Aunt Avis was young."

"Which was when?" Adam leaned forward now, Thalia caught the shift, and looked up to meet his expression. He was interested. He seemed honestly interested, not just putting up with her. Hilaria, on the other hand, was suspiciously quiet.

"That's, well. We think Great-Aunt Avis was born in the 1820s, sometime. She'd have been in her mid-twenties in the early 1850s. Married around then, maybe?" Thalia thought it must sound ridiculous, and she could hear the pitch of her voice rise at the end.

Adam, though, seemed to take it seriously. He didn't laugh at her, didn't even smile. He glanced around at the trees, then back across the wall into the field. "Are there clocks up there? Do they run normally?"

Thalia was puzzled. "They tick. Time passes. But now you mention it, the one in the little dining room, it doesn't run down like it should. Whenever I look at it, it's only a quarter or so down. I've never seen Mrs Harley wind it, but that part doesn't mean anything. Why do you ask?"

Adam gestured at the orchard. "The apples here ripen more slowly than they should. I've seen birds, who nest closer to the house, younger than they should be this time of year, by a fair bit. What's it like, up at the house?"

Thalia hesitated. She wanted to ask him to come up and look, but she was fairly sure that wouldn't do. For one thing, he was a man. And a stranger. And from the village. Whatever was odd in the house, Mrs Harley didn't expect Hilaria to be troubled by it. Or Thalia. But you could be more open, less afraid, with someone who'd be out of your life, out of the county, in a few weeks or even months. It was quite another thing to let someone close who had ties nearby.

"Timeless, I suppose. It feels like spring, more than anything? The weather's brisk, same as it is down here, but it's, oh, a late April or early May? Chilly nights, but the beginning of the leaves coming out. I saw a description of it as the greening of the world. You know how when you come out one day, and all the trees are haloed in it?"

Adam smiled more broadly at it. "There you are. That's just the word for it. The halo. There's a shine to them, isn't there, like the light's dancing."

Thalia found herself smiling as well, on the edge of laughter suddenly, that he'd chosen that to compliment. It wasn't as if the idea was hers, but that he'd picked out something about words, how she used them, that gave her a bit of hope about writing something she could tolerate again. She let out a breath, slowly. "It's like the moment after the rain ends. Waiting? Not entirely patiently, but nothing is moving yet, nothing big, anyway."

Adam nodded again. "There must be gardens and plants up there?" he asked.

"Not many. It's mostly boxwoods and some holly and ivy. Evergreens. There's a row of rosebushes on this side of the wall, but the rest of that garden is just short grass." Thalia considered. "I got a brief look at the kitchen garden, but I don't think I know enough about what I saw. There was a greenhouse, something glassed in, and a number of herbs, but nothing much flowering."

"I don't suppose you could get a sketch, or even a photograph sometime?" Adam was still leaning forward.

Thalia shook her head. "Not unless both Mrs Harley and Bessy are out for a bit. I don't have a camera, but..."

Hilaria chimed in. "I can do sketches. You want to see how things are growing, what things are growing, then?"

"Exactly." Adam focused on her for a moment and then turned back to Thalia. "The shape of the leaves, the size of the plant, if there are any fruits or flowers. Have you done any botanical illustration before?"

"Some, but mostly in the form of a still life, which isn't the same thing at all." Hilaria wrinkled her nose up. "I wouldn't trust me with something incredibly detailed. I don't know enough about what to look for. Like those glorious glass flower examples, the ones out of Germany? Have you seen any of them?"

Adam gaped at her for a moment. "Glass flowers?"

"Botanical examples. Really quite useful, actually, for art, because you can see all the stages at once, if you have models for them. There's a massive collection of them being made for somewhere in America, quite famous, but people have made various smaller sets." Hilaria beamed. "At any rate. I can't do that, but I can do some tolerable sketches if we do get time."

Thalia hesitated. "Could we go at the problem the other way? Do you know, does your uncle know, anyone we could talk to? I mean, I don't even really know who the local Lord of the land is here."

"Lord Teague." Adam had the answer on the top of his tongue, apparently. She must have looked puzzled, because he waved a hand. "Useful to know to if there's a problem with the land magic. Or other sorts of problems. Snap sends out notices on a regular basis. Come from the stewards or the manor farm. Whoever can pass a note about the lord being at home or out of the country, or ailing."

"That's rather more useful gossip than what gets circulated where I can see it." Thalia admitted. Though she supposed that might be where the gossip columns got some of their material.

Adam smiled again. "A tad. I don't know the man, don't think I've ever met him. Uncle Benjamin hasn't grumbled too much about him, and I gather he didn't like the late Lord Teague much. But that's not the sort of thing he'd talk about with me."

Thalia tilted her head. "How long has your uncle lived here?"

"My grandparents, his parents, before him. They had a house in town, and the house here, for quiet, Grandmum said. Uncle Benjamin, it's his main home, but usually in the growing season, he's staying somewhere else, designing a garden and supervising the planting. Not truly local, as they see it, but agreeable." Adam had relaxed a bit, Thalia thought.

She wasn't at all sure how he was going to take the next bit, then. "Is there any chance I could meet him? Not to ask anything awkward, but just - perhaps. To get a better sense of what the land should be like? What he knows about the gardens, maybe?"

Adam considered, looking off toward the orchard, not at either Thalia or Hilaria. He spoke without looking back. "Both of you? How would I say I met you?"

Thalia shrugged. "He must be a bit curious about the place, surely? And the truth works as well as anything else here. I was walking along by the orchard, met you, introduced myself. You were agreeable when I wanted to learn more about the place."

Adam snorted. "Agreeable. He'll know that for a lie."

He didn't explain, and Thalia tilted her head. "You were quite pleasant to me. Given I barged into your orchard. And.

Well. Everything." She really had been rather presumptuous, looking back on it.

"I don't know what he'd do with it. He makes gardens for people like yours." Adam looked her up and down. "I..." He stopped and shook his head.

"You don't want him to feel put out in his own home. Or when he's supposed to be mending. Quite right, too. I really am not quite as scatterbrained as I look, honest. I can be quite controlled. Sometimes." Thalia considered. "It helps if I wear the right sort of clothes for it. The mood."

Adam raised an eyebrow. "And what would be right, here?"

Hilaria chimed in. "If you were writing it, Thalia, what would it be?" That was a challenge, right there, and Hilaria knew it.

Thalia straightened her shoulders and gave it her best. "Posit a woman in her early thirties, dressed in a wool skirt - the blue one, I think - and a cream blouse. That belted sweater I found at the second-hand store, do you think, the green one?"

"You look rather fine in that green. Approachable." Hilaria was no help at all, and they'd have to have a conversation about that later. "Sturdy shoes, if we have to walk down the hill, which we do."

"My low black boots, I think. And the blue cloche and the locket. Hair in a low roll at the base of my neck, to avoid the hat, and if it's brisk out, my coat as well. That's plain black, goes with everything, of course. It comes across as not too spinsterish. A woman of the professional class, which is what I am."

Adam sighed, "All right. I'll introduce you. When? Though Uncle Benjamin's not going out much, I suppose?"

"Saturday, and perhaps there could be a pub afterwards? For the three of us? I've not been to a pub in ages."

Adam nodded. "I'll - I'll do something about a message. Do you get post?"

"We do." Then there was a bell chiming from the town, and Adam glanced up.

"I should get back. Thursday, unless I write otherwise." He quickly gave them directions on how to find the house, and Hilaria had the sense to write them down.

CHAPTER 24
THURSDAY

"I'm only doing this because Mrs Whitmore is curious."

"You've said, Uncle. Several times. And I appreciate it. I'm curious about the place, and you must be too. And after all, she did have a question about the gardens."

Mrs Whitmore came in with a civilised small plate arranged with biscuits. Not too many biscuits, there were two each. Devon flats, he liked those. And Mrs Whitmore knew she made them well. He wasn't sure what the two women would make of them. He gathered it was the clotted cream that gave them a different taste than biscuits made with butter, but he was no kind of baker. An appreciative consumer.

They had rearranged the sitting room so his uncle could have his leg up, with chairs for the ladies and one for Adam. He had been sitting there, waiting, unable to focus on reading anything, until he heard a knock on the door. Mrs Whitmore went briskly over to open it.

"Good afternoon. I do hope this is the Walton home?"

There was a murmur. Adam couldn't quite hear what

Mrs Whitmore said, but then she came through. "Your guests, Magister Walton." She was pulling out the title, then, and making it clear she was magical as well.

The two women came through after her. Thalia was wearing almost exactly what she'd described. And the green did flatter her, rather a lot. It was a living green, with a depth to the colour that matched the blue skirt and hat, but also brought out her eyes. Adam hadn't thought her plain, precisely, before that moment where she'd healed his hand, but it was like a bird grown into her adult finery. Hilaria was wearing a skirt and sweater in a deep brown, more like a tree in an ancient wood.

"Magister Walton, a pleasure, and thank you for having us down. I do hope you're mending well? I'm afraid we couldn't bring anything unusually wonderful as a hosting gift. But Mrs Harley, she's the housekeeper at the house, she said this jar of the local honey would be appreciated."

Mrs Whitmore leaned over, peered, and nodded. "It is. Good hives, those."

Uncle Benjamin waved a hand. "Please, have a seat." He sounded a tad resigned, but Thalia was being pleasant and not fluttering. "Would one of you be mother, with the tea?" He didn't look at Adam as he said it, which only made it worse. Adam knew he couldn't pour tea smoothly most of the time, not with something delicate, anyway. Drawing attention to it, though, still smarted.

"Oh, of course." She hesitated for a moment, glancing at the tea set. "Cream or sugar?"

"Cream, thank you." It was by way of being something of a test. This was the good china, and it wouldn't crack with hot water added. Thalia busied herself pouring a cup, holding it carefully. She did the whole thing smoothly, without dripping, and Hilaria stood to bring it to his uncle. "Adam?"

"Cream, one sugar, please." When the tea was in his hands, he found he had to set it on the side table, or there would be rattling. He'd try again in a minute. While he was sorting that out, Hilaria silently claimed her own cup. Thalia didn't need to ask about that. Then, as Thalia poured her own, Uncle Benjamin spoke again.

"You've not been to Devon much before?"

"To visit Great-Aunt Avis, when I was rather young, eight or so. Oh, are those Devon flats? I remembered them from before, and Mrs Harley makes them, but everyone's got their own touch with biscuits, don't they?"

Uncle Benjamin grunted softly, but Adam was fairly sure he was warming to them at least a little. "Please, have a taste."

Thalia's response was delightful. She clearly enjoyed it. And she wasn't one of those women who ate like a bird and complained about the need for it. She had eaten the apples with the same easy pleasure, and it suddenly made Adam wonder what she'd be like in other moments. Music. Art. Literature. Even more physical pursuits. She didn't hide her joy, and that was beginning to puzzle him. She hid her pain, but that was just sensible, even if the contrast confused him.

Hilaria was a neat and tidy eater, and she was clearly deferring to Thalia here. Once everyone had complimented the biscuits, Thalia settled back. "Magister Walton, I do appreciate your time. I admit, I'm a bit baffled by the house and the grounds. And once Adam mentioned your work, I knew you were someone who might be able to help me understand."

Uncle Benjamin waved a hand. "Because I create gardens, yes?"

"Yes. I remembered your name, enough to place it finally. You did the gardens at Chetford, didn't you? And the townhouse gardens for, goodness. The Ellises, in Trellech. I was at a party there a couple of years ago, when they'd grown in. And I remember now, you consulted for something at the Temple of Healing during the War." She almost stopped in the middle of that, as if it might be too revealing.

His uncle nodded, considering her a little differently. "Do you remember enough about the Ellis garden, then?"

"I'm sure I don't know the proper language for it. But I remember - I was at school with her younger sister, and he'd just got that substantial promotion, hadn't he? Something at the Ministry, the sort of thing that comes with a desk and an office and someone like a guard dog just outside it. I remember it was something about picking out the colours from their heraldry, so there would always be some during the year, as things changed and bloomed and faded. Red and white - well, argent, in heraldry, isn't it? And gules for the red. Rather stark, I thought, but the deep greens made such a lovely contrast, the living plants."

Uncle Benjamin was nodding, looking pleased.

"It must be an interesting challenge to take that kind of thing on." Thalia leaned forward, her voice more conspiratorial. "But I'm sure they must have been a different kind of challenge to work for. She changed the flowers for her wedding a dozen times, I heard, and I can't imagine it went better with growing ones. Now, I know you can't say a thing against a client, of course you wouldn't. But I did rather like the way the holly was laid out against the grey stone of the house, so that in the winter, you'd see the red berries. And you didn't use an elder tree, where other people might have. I don't - I'm sure I don't know most of it. But that's a tree to treat with respect, and not one just to plant for show."

Uncle Benjamin's face cracked into a smile. "Ah, you're a danger to yourself, aren't you?" He nodded. "You've the right of it. The challenge of my work is finding something that suits the brief, while actually growing. When I was younger, I had to take all sorts of jobs, and do my best to talk them into something that would do what they wanted. These days it's easier, but some do get particular."

Thalia bobbed her head. It was working magic on Uncle Benjamin, who was clearly warming to her. "And you must get called in when a garden's not, well, being a garden properly. Some people just don't care for them. Restoring a garden, isn't that right?"

Benjamin nods. "I've done a bit of that. Some of the big houses, they've had gardens on the same spot for centuries, and that's murder on growing certain plants, unless you tend the earth properly. A bit of magic, a bit of alchemy, a bit of honest hard work."

"Oh, I'm sure." Thalia set her cup down, quietly indicating she was all business now, folding her hands in her lap. "I'll be honest. The house feels a trifle odd. And of course, Great-Aunt Avis isn't here to ask. So I - I mean, I do feel a responsibility. For letting my parents know if there's any indication that she needs more help or anything like that. Mrs Harley's grand, and her work is superb. I wouldn't say a word against her. But the gardens seemed awfully sparse, for the property, for one thing."

Uncle Benjamin considered, tapping a finger on the arm of the sofa. He looked like he wanted to get up and pace, and of course, that wasn't an option right now. "I've not had a chance to visit the gardens in years, Mistress," he pointed out.

"Oh, Hilaria did some sketches. She keeps going on about how she's not a botanical artist, of course she isn't, she does other sorts of art. But I do think she can draw an accurate tree. Or a rosebush, which there are a lot of. May we?" Thalia gestured artlessly at Hilaria, who produced a sketchbook, already folded to the proper page.

Uncle Benjamin held out a hand, and Adam helped pass it over without knocking any of the tea. "This was done recently?"

"Yesterday." Hilaria said. "It was cloudy, so I'm not entirely confident of some of the leaf colour."

"Just the roses, for flowers?" Uncle Benjamin traced his finger along.

"Mmhmm." Thalia said. "There are a few other things with flowers in the kitchen garden, I think, but not many. Not the sort of beds around the house I expected. The roses are just by the garden wall, coming down the hill."

Uncle Benjamin nodded. "Those are..." He peered at them, then fumbled for his glasses on the side table.

Hilaria coughed. "There's a detail of the roses on the next page."

"You were very thorough." Uncle Benjamin pushed the glasses on his nose, turned the page, and snorted. "Very deliberate. Do you know roses?"

Thalia shook her head. "Please assume I don't, other than liking them generally."

"These are Rosa chinensis Mutabilis. A hybrid introduced last century. It is a repeat bloomer, which means it will bloom several times from spring to around this point in the autumn. Nothing, erm. Very exciting, horticulturally. Reliable, but ordinary."

"What sort of plants would you be looking for, then? Thinking about?" That was Hilaria, sounding very interested now.

"Oh, a well-designed garden tells you about the interests of the owner. Some people wish to attract butterflies or honeybees, and they'll plant accordingly. Others want a visually radiant garden that will bloom and display bright colours changing through the seasons. Some want to use the plants for alchemical purposes, or ritual ones, and plant accordingly. Or for a personal stillroom, and they'll want medicinal plants, many of which are also rather lovely."

"I'm sure you think most plants are lovely." Thalia offered the compliment with a rather warm smile. Adam wanted that sort of smile turned on him, all of a sudden, and he fisted his hands in his lap.

His uncle clearly enjoyed the flattery. "Ah, now. You're kind. But right, too. I've rarely met a plant I don't like. Giant hogweed. Now, that's a hard plant to love. Nasty and huge. It can make your skin burn if you get the sap on you, and then you're in the sunlight. And nettles aren't a lot of fun in a garden, though I do like eating them, and they're proper useful."

Thalia dimpled, smiling back.

Uncle Benjamin considered, and tapped the sketch. "The roses are pretty enough, but there's no variety in this garden. Nothing for birds or bees or butterflies. Not even much for little woodland creatures. Roses make poor eating, though the hips are good for you. And there's a sameness to this, isn't there? It would look much the same, spring to autumn, no changes. But roses aren't always easy to tend, either. They can be fussy. Even established bushes."

"What does that mean, please?" Thalia asked, curious.

"It's a fussy sort of garden for someone who wanted the

same thing to look at. Why not more boxwood or yew hedges, cut them back when needed? Why not something easy to maintain that would show you different things? No, just these roses. And a bit standoffish." He looked up. "Not unlike your great-aunt, Mistress."

Thalia nodded. "I - well. I had something of the same impression. You needn't worry you've insulted me. And frankly, you haven't insulted Great-Aunt Avis, as far as I'm concerned, just accurately described how things are. Thank you, that's a grand help. Now, I'm sure there are much more fun things to talk about when it comes to the village. I was invited to that dance, Saturday night. We'll both be there. I'm sure you know a bit more about people in town."

Uncle Benjamin snorted. "Ah, for the gossip, we want Mrs Whitmore. Adam, be a help. Let her know we need her expert knowledge?"

Adam nodded. Once Mrs Whitmore was sure they wanted her gossip, she spent two hours telling the two women what to expect. Whose cakes to choose if they could, and a dozen other things. No one asked him if he was going, though Thalia made a point of including him in the conversation here or there. Mostly about what music he might like, or if he'd heard this song or that one. He never had, but he appreciated the thought.

CHAPTER 25
THURSDAY

Thalia thought the conversation was really going along quite well. Adam was quiet, but honestly, that seemed to be how Adam was, unless he had something specific to say. His uncle was a delight, relaxing into telling a host of stories. Thalia wondered if there was any way to get him to write them up. They'd make a charming memoir, or even a series of essays. If, at least, he could be persuaded to avoid talking about the foibles of some of the families he'd worked for.

He hadn't said anything too outre, at least. Certainly not outside the range of gossip among Thalia's family's circles. But he had unbent quite a bit, as if he'd not really had a chance to tell stories to anyone in some time. Or at least not anyone other than Adam. They seemed to get on well enough. Thalia had wondered if there was tension there, the way Adam hadn't exactly invited them.

When they were on the third round of tea, the puppy started yapping. Adam ducked his head. "I'll take him out, Uncle. I'll be fifteen minutes or so. We want him to get a run in, then I'll be back."

Thalia and Hilaria made polite noises. Hilaria offered to go help with the cleaning up, and the housekeeper seemed quite startled but pleased by that. It left Thalia sitting alone with Adam's uncle, in the quiet.

"He had a Bad War." Benjamin made the capital letters clear.

Thalia nodded. "I gathered." She hesitated. "I hope it's been good for you to have a hand here?"

"Truth is, I don't particularly need him here. But my brother thinks he needs to buck up."

That was a tricky thing to answer. Did Benjamin agree, or did he disagree? Thalia considered, then went for the obvious question. "And you?"

"I think he had a Bad War. The kind that will be a weight on him the rest of his life, one way or another. I'm certain my brother and his wife fussing aren't the thing. Clipping back the plant in the wrong season, that's how it is." Benjamin slapped his thigh with one hand, hard enough to make quite a loud sound. "What is he like in the orchard?"

That was an excellent question. "He pays attention to it. Adam explained the apple grafting to me. And other things." She frowned. "I'm not quite sure what you're asking."

Benjamin shrugged, shifting to face her better. "I do need a hand for a few months. But the question is what happens next. He's not talked to anyone much other than you. The library once. Something scared him, there."

"Not the librarian, I hope? The man's harmless. A bit persistent about the dance, but otherwise harmless."

Benjamin pounced on that, grinning. "I wondered how that came about. Well, you are a new face in town, of course all the men might have an interest."

"There are surely more women than men." It was the sad arithmetic of her generation, with all the papers decrying an age of spinsters.

"But they already know how the women here react to them. And you ..." Benjamin shrugged. "You're from London. That would get some interest, no matter what else. Even if no one here much wants to live there. Well, not most of them. That fellow with the garage has a thing about the moving pictures."

Thalia snorted. "Well, I'm glad someone does. I've been once or twice, of course, but I admit, I don't understand the idiom properly. How the stories get told. I always feel like I'm missing steps. Assumptions other people make about how the story goes."

"Some of it, I gather, is not so different from opera conventions."

"Blonde tenor hero, dark-haired bass the villain? Shrieky soprano somewhere around the eaves making complications?" Thalia had grown up not only with opera, but with all the catty comments about it.

"Just so. Narrative conventions. You write, Adam said?"

Thalia let out a breath. "Some. Not a lot published. Not nearly enough, anyway."

"Ah, I've known a few like that. The endless optimism that this time, people will notice, and the endless grind because they haven't yet. What do you write?"

"Literary stories, the sort of thing that - well, I had a rejection from *The Second Pan*, not long before I came down here." She hesitated. She didn't talk much about her stories with other people, not besides other people who knew her writing. "I don't care much for the moralistic fiction, and I don't think it's very literary. It's lecturing, isn't it? That doesn't take skill, it just takes volume."

"Both in amount and in loudness, yes." Benjamin nodded, approving of the phrase. "I have an idea of it." He waved a hand. "Words are not my art form. But you can't force a garden to grow against its nature. Perhaps your garden is something different." He added after a moment. "The editor at *The Second Pan* is Rhys Dormer, yes?"

"Yes?" Thalia replied cautiously.

"He skimps on his mulch and doesn't pay his people near enough for their skill. I can't imagine his literary response is any better."

Thalia blinked at him, then smiled. It was, to be honest, one of the kinder comments she'd got. "By those standards, who do you recommend, then?" It wasn't the way one was supposed to go about literary submissions, but to be honest, the recommended approach hadn't been doing her any good. Perhaps aiming at editors who treated their staff well would produce kinder rejection letters. Or at least more productive ones.

Benjamin considered. "Ralph Mackenzie, he does that sort of fabulist thing that could be a children's tale or something more fantastical for adults. Blast, I've forgotten the name of his rag. His house is a stunner, though, all sorts of murals on the walls, very Arts and Crafts, and the gardens were redone thirty years ago. I didn't change much at the core, just enhanced what was there."

"*The Respite*," Thalia said.

"And hmm. *Mackenzie's Formation*, that's the name. I know it doesn't sound like much from the title, but there are some quite good natural history and folklore pieces in there. And some fiction, though more of t'other. If you're enjoying the country air, you could make something out of that, possibly?"

"I am, rather. More than I thought I would. Not that the mysteries aren't - well. A bit mysterious."

"That's surely part of the whole theme. Genre. Being in the country, as it were. This isn't your native land. Where is that? Where are you from?"

"Kent. Not very far from London." Thalia said.

Benjamin nodded. "Good land, in Kent. At least these days. Mayhap it's the hops." Thalia smiled, agreeably, not sure what to say now, and Benjamin went on. "I'm glad Adam asked you round." He wasn't quite asking anything else, but Thalia could read the cue well enough.

"I enjoy talking to him. And if he's up for the dance, I'd be glad to see him there." Which was true enough.

Just about then, there was a commotion of happy barking from the door, and Hilaria opened it as she came past, to welcome a bouncing dog, and Adam. He looked a bit bemused. "It's getting dark out there, there are clouds coming in." He glanced from Hilaria to Thalia. "I could walk you up, bring a lantern?"

"Oh, that would be kind. If you're sure?"

That meant the next ten minutes were taken up with finding the lantern, and making their farewells to Benjamin and the housekeeper. She insisted on sending along a jar of jam. Thalia thought they'd impinged on the household quite enough, but this was apparently some mystery of country manners, or perhaps by way of a message of interest. So she would bring the jam back and let Mrs Harley sort out the proper interpretation.

Once they were finally back out on the street, Thalia glanced over at Adam. "It's a fair walk..."

"I'll manage." He seemed stubbornly insistent on it. But he had his walking stick. It was after all his uncle's lantern, and arguing about that sort of thing never ended well for anyone.

In the end, Hilaria hung back, distracted by various glimpses across the way, pausing to sketch some detail in the fading light. It meant she and Adam could talk. The problem, of course, was what to say. In the end, she swallowed her nerves, and said, "Your uncle was very kind, he gave me some new ideas. Do you think you'll come to the dance?"

Adam walked along quietly for a good twenty steps, just the thump of the walking stick on the packed dirt and the scuffing of their shoes. "Don't know much about dances."

"I'm fairly sure I don't know much about village dances. Artsy bohemian parties, yes, though honestly, at those I sit around and try the food and maybe people laugh at my jokes."

The self-deprecation at least made Adam smile for a moment. "If you're going." He glanced behind them. "And your friend."

"Hilaria will charm everyone. That's worth watching, actually. You and I can prop up a wall and let her do her thing."

That got a larger smile, which Thalia considered a victory. "And before then?"

"Mrs Harley mentioned she might need to do another day trip to Trellech. A problem with a tooth, I gather? I - I was wondering if you might come up and have a look at things. When she's out. I mean, it's not wrong for me to ask someone over, just." Just, she was terrified of the imposing housekeeper and her opinions. As well as what Mrs Harley might apparently pluck out of her head, based on past experience.

Adam chewed that over for a good thirty steps. Now

they were about to turn up the long drive to the house. "What do you think I'd see?"

"You know plants. And houses around here, a bit better than I do. And you've got fresh eyes." She swallowed. "Would you?"

He stopped walking for a moment, turning to look at her. "You honestly think I could help?" It was as if she'd unmoored something in him, some foundation of his being. Then he nodded. "I'm sure I can't, but I'll look."

"Good." Thalia beamed at him, then Hilaria bumped into her shoulder.

"Pardon. Wait, why did you stop? Is there something in the road?"

"No, no, Hilaria. We were just talking. I asked if Adam would come up and look at the house when Mrs Harley is out next."

"That's after the dance, isn't it?"

"It is. And you were thinking you needed to go back to London. But I was saying, you're fun to watch at a party. Adam said he'd come."

"She can't dance, you know." Hilaria said, conspiratori-ally. "She just wants someone to talk to when she won't."

"Not just that, you!" Thalia laughed. "Though, Adam, I do like a bit of company."

Adam hesitated, not sure what to make of the interplay between them. Then he coughed. "You both seem like the sort of people who like parties?"

"Yes. Just." Thalia shrugged. "There are different kinds of parties. I'm not as good at the dancing kind. I don't like lots of people up close near me, sometimes."

He blinked at her, and might have said something else, but Hilaria pointed. "There's the house. You can see the lights through the trees. I hope they're not worried."

"I did say we were going to be out for tea." Thalia nodded, but the mood had changed again, as quickly as the November winds. "I hope we'll see you in the orchard. Tomorrow, the day after?"

"It might be rain tomorrow." Adam glanced up at the sky.

"The next clear day, then, the afternoon." Thalia wanted to see him again. Moreover, she wanted him to know that. Not that she could come out and say it, in so many words. It would embarrass them both.

CHAPTER 26
FRIDAY

Adam took a breath and let it out. He'd had an idea, and once he'd got it, it hadn't let him go. Which is why he was standing in the street outside the library, waiting for it to open. He'd almost timed it right. He'd only had to wait a minute or two.

Promptly at one, the door opened, and Mr Dobbs poked his head out to hang the open sign on the door, then stopped as he saw Adam. "Do come in, please. Mr Walton, wasn't it?"

"Yes." Adam tried not to seem churlish.

"I have your card application here - if you want to fill out the last piece, I have the card all ready for you. Or nearly. Once I have the address. I could have filled it in, of course, it's not a large village."

Adam ducked his chin. He was trying to be civil. He certainly didn't want to be rude. But he barely remembered how to talk to people. Even if it had gone somewhat better with Thalia and Hilaria. "I, um. Yes. I appreciate that. I'm sorry I wasn't back."

Dobbs shrugged. Adam, in his mind, had assumed there

would be arrogance there, or dismissal, but this was somehow softer. "As I said, I don't care for loud noises either. I just know Mr Oswald is all roar and no risk. Here we go, here's the pencil." Dobbs paused. "Did you know there's a dance in the village hall? You'd be welcome."

Adam glanced up, startled. "Yes?" He managed, he thought, to get the sort of pitch in it that made a question.

"Tomorrow night, the village hall." He named the price. "Fundraiser for the hall, mostly, but if there's extra, it will come here, to add to the collection. Tickets at the door, there's a raffle."

Adam hesitated. "The young women, staying up at the house, they mentioned it. They had a question or two for my uncle yesterday."

"Oh, yes. Miss Morgan and her friend. I do hope they'll come. It's grand to have someone new. Yourself included, there." Dobbs indeed seemed very amiable. "The biscuits and cakes are usually excellent, too. And the punch."

Adam nodded. "I'm - it's been a long while since I've been at something of the kind." His apprenticeship, really. That had involved a lot of village socialising, though mostly among the magical folks. He suddenly realised he didn't really know the current standards for how to treat women in this sort of place. He knew the customs were different. Blast. He'd have to sort that out, and make sure the women did too. He wasn't sure if Thalia and Hilaria had considered that particular aspect.

"I'll, um. Yes. I'll see you there?" Adam felt that was amiable enough. He finished the last few lines on the card application and passed it back.

Dobbs smiled. "Grand. And here. Let me just make this note. Here you go." He passed the signed card back, of a size to be carried in a wallet. "May I help you find anything, or would you like to browse?"

"Um. Natural history writing? About the area, in particular, or folklore?"

"Ah, a number of those are out right now, but let me show you what we've got." Dobbs grabbed his cane and came around the counter again. "This way." That meant there were five minutes or so of Dobbs showing him the shelves and leaving Adam to putter through them. Twenty minutes later, he'd selected three books. A book of essays. His uncle had said he'd been talking about nature essays with Thalia last night, and Adam needed some middle of the night reading again. And then a book of folklore, and a volume by a local poet Dobbs had recommended. He brought them up to the counter.

"Here we go, then. Due back in a week, we can renew the loan if you bring them in." Dobbs stamped the cards and slips to go into the books. It made a satisfying thump, one that Adam had rather missed. "See you tomorrow, then. I'll keep a lookout."

Adam nodded and tipped his hat as he went out. He was still feeling in decent shape, and the weather was holding, so he went along to the orchard. He wasn't sure if he'd see Thalia there, or Hilaria, but it was worth a try. As he walked around, his mind got stuck on a particular phrase that had caught at him while he was browsing through the books.

It was the question of nostalgia, of holding on to what you could never get back. The time before the War, for him, as for so many other people. This village was near enough stuck in it, there were almost no automobiles. If you went further up on the moor, the accents were impenetrable. They hadn't changed for centuries.

The orchard was empty when he got there. But by the time he'd done a circuit of it and settled down for a bit from his flask of tea and an apple, he could see Thalia coming down the hill.

"No Hilaria?" Adam grimaced. "Pardon."

"It's a perfectly reasonable question, isn't it? And no, she's sketching something up at the house. A couple of the pictures caught her eye." She let out a breath. "Also, I think she's a bit squirrelly at the moment? About the house."

Adam let out a breath. "Not..." He thought about what to say here, and then his knee went weak, and he sat down again with a thump.

Thalia turned back toward him. She'd been looking down at the orchard for a moment, but she must have heard him land. "Are you all right?"

Adam waved a hand. Badly. He was fairly sure that was what the nurses had described as flailing in their notes. He dumped his hand back in his lap. "Fine." It came out as more of a grunt.

She tilted her head, opening her mouth and then closing it, before she claimed the tree stump she'd made her own. "Look, there's no reason you should tell me anything. Personal, I mean. Just. I'm not going to be awful about it. Or at least, if I am being awful, I really don't want to be."

He couldn't look at her all of a sudden. He stared down at the end of the orchard. The trees weren't going to do anything unexpected. Probably.

When he didn't say anything else, she coughed. "I was a VAD at the Temple of Healing. Most of the War. People who'd got brought in, the ones who most needed treatment. Before they got sent off to rest homes or specialist wards, or whatever."

"Including mental cases?" It came out of his mouth

before he could stop it. His tongue felt too quick and too sluggish, all at once. Like nothing quite fit together.

He could see her shoulder twitch. "Frankly, I think the ones who weren't horrified are the ones I'm worried about." He didn't move, and she glanced over at him. Something she saw made her go on. "They wouldn't let me go to France or Belgium. Not for my sort. And I didn't have proper nurse's training. Not the way they mean. But I saw..." Her voice caught, a rough burr like a splinter in a piece of wood. "I saw the people they'd given up on. Or near enough. Where they could patch up bodies, but had no idea what else to do."

Adam was having trouble with everything that was coming at him, the way she talked, the words she was saying. Especially the way her fingers were flicking out of nerves or pain or something he didn't know how to name. After a long pause, a silence that seemed to last for hours, he managed a sentence. "What did you do?"

"Not enough." Oh, that he heard and understood. The deep well of disgust and self-hatred she'd been hiding behind pleasantries and the stage dressing of cheerfulness. Not the resilient 'show must go on' attitude, exactly, but something where her sense of worth was built on not letting that awful sucking wound win. He knew it because he wrestled with it, nearly every night, and often a couple of times during the day.

He hadn't realised she had it too. That women might. People who'd never been near a trench or a battle, never had the explosions overhead and shaking the ground beneath their feet in an unending nightmare. He couldn't bring himself to reach out and offer her that small comfort, even if she might welcome it. He could barely get the words out. What he said, in the end, was a muffled, mumbled, "You do understand."

Her chin came up, her back arched, like it was a bolt of pain, lightning striking her and obliterating everything. Everything about her was still for far too long. When Adam felt that, he stopped breathing entirely for shockingly long. Then she sucked in a breath and her shoulders shuddered and she nodded once, before burying her face in her hands. It was the only place she had to hide.

Of course, he didn't do anything. Adam wasn't sure he could, honestly. His hands still felt like they belonged to someone else. He tucked them under his elbows for warmth and he waited. He wouldn't leave her alone out here with it.

Adam was beginning to regret that when she still hadn't moved, fifteen minutes later. He'd only been able to tell the passing of time by the echo of the bells from the church. Finally, carefully, he cleared his throat. The sort of noise that had a decent chance of not jarring him. By which he meant about one in three, but you did what you could with what you had.

She did startle, but not badly, he thought. Her eyes went wide, then she buried her face again.

"Hey." He tried again. "Tea?"

Thalia nodded slowly, as if she was sure the offer had something nasty behind it. By now, Adam could manage to pour it. But he just handed over the flask, to let her drink what she wanted, and for it not to cool in the pouring. She took a cautious sip, then several more, until she closed her eyes in something like relief. "Well. We're a pair, aren't we?"

Something in her voice made it easier for him. "Bloody

exhausting, isn't it?" He should have apologised for the language, but she shot him a sudden grin. A bit wild and feral, like she'd cast aside all the trappings of civilisation in the past few minutes. But it was honest. "Write about that." It came out of him before he could stop himself. She blinked at him, and seemed to be ready to recoil, but Adam pressed on. "It's real. Write about real things. What it feels like to you."

He heard his voice crack at the end, about the feeling. He certainly didn't let himself feel very often. It was awful when he did. Only, it had something honest, like he'd said. Something that mattered. Some pebble of value in the muck of the rest of his head and his soul.

Thalia didn't run, she didn't throw the flask back in his face; she didn't do anything but sit there and take one breath, then another.

"I don't think I can." Her voice trailed off to a bare whisper at the end. "Why would anyone care, anyway?"

"There's plenty of us no one listens to." She wasn't alone in that, either. "I just..." He shivered, now colder. "You were real, all of a sudden. All the way through." He didn't know how to explain it better than that.

The look in her eyes would haunt him. For days, for weeks, maybe to the end of his life, whenever that was. She made a wordless sound that might have been oh or no or a hum or a charm against evil for all he knew. Then she was standing, handing the flask back over to him, with a "Later." It was as if she had gathered all of her feathers up around her, shaken them into place, and was going to go far away now. Somewhere he had no hope of being.

CHAPTER 27
SATURDAY EVENING AT THE VILLAGE HALL

T halia had wanted to enjoy the dance. That was the point of a dance, surely. You went, you had refreshments, you had a good time. Or at least, if you didn't have an actually enjoyable time, you had an experience you could write about later. Everything was grist for the writer's mill. Wasn't that how it went?

Instead, she felt awful. It was a generalised sort of awful. Nothing she could pin down to illness or a bad batch of jam, or anything like that. Never mind that the food this afternoon had been excellent. Mrs Harley seemed to be making a point.

The housekeeper had clearly been a tad dubious about the two women attending the dance. The house didn't mingle with the village, after all. But at the same time, it wasn't a housekeeper's place to tell them they couldn't go. She simply handed over the latchkey. Whatever judging she did was done from the comfort of her own cottage. As it should be.

Now, though, Thalia had to navigate the complexities of

the dance. It was a mix of people, all ages, from those who'd just finished school or found jobs through to grannies. Some were clustered in the corners, gossiping. Some were dancing.

But of course, like almost everywhere else, a good quarter of the men who'd been of age during the War had some sort of visible injury. A limp, a missing hand or arm, scars on their faces. The fainter signs she'd learned to read just as easily, when a man didn't trust his feet would hold him up. Or that his balance or nerves wouldn't fail him. And of course, there were all those whose injuries didn't show on the skin you could see. And all the men who weren't there, who should have been.

Thalia had come to enjoy the various parties of the bohemian circles she moved in. But honestly, a good half of those were people commiserating - well, and sometimes whining - about how their artistic genius wasn't appreciated. It could be predictable and frustrating, but they were usually witty or clever or entertaining about it, somehow. And the rest of the time, it was food she didn't have to put together, and someone else's alcohol, and very few expectations.

Here, everyone seemed to assume her to be something she wasn't. Pulled together, maybe, or graceful. Certainly, they expected her to be gracious and charming. She had been smiling so much her cheeks were starting to ache, and she couldn't keep the endless names and commentaries straight.

Hilaria was having a better time. Hilaria generally had a good time at this sort of thing. She had a wicked gift for caricature in the right mood, and she considered all of this fodder for some cartoon. A practice piece, even if she never showed it to anyone besides a few chosen friends. And she had a gift for names, or at least a gift for avoiding people noticing she'd forgotten them. In between, she was cheerful and bubbly, the sort of person who drew you into conversation. It was why Thalia loved her and trusted her, but it wasn't helping tonight.

Thalia accepted a glass of watered down punch from an older man, who seemed about to leer at her when a woman his own age dragged him away. The other woman didn't look at Thalia, just resolutely forged ahead. Thalia took the moment to back up toward the side door of the village hall. It would have worked, only she bumped into someone. Taller, broad-shouldered, and he made a pained grunt. She didn't think she'd trodden on his foot.

When she turned, it was Adam. Thalia couldn't decide if that was better or worse than a stranger. Even just thinking about it made her head ache more. He frowned at her, and she half-turned away.

"Hey." He gestured. "Need some fresh air?" When she nodded, he opened the door, letting her out into a side street. She could hear some low-voiced conversation further down the lane behind the building. She supposed that might be where lovers snuck out to, or something of the kind, but the street itself seemed unoccupied. A moment later, Adam followed her, pulling the door largely closed behind him.

Thalia shivered, suddenly. Her wool coat was in the cloakroom, of course it was, and the wind had come up. Adam immediately shrugged out of his jacket, showing a sweater underneath. "Here. Please."

Once it was settled around her, she took a breath. It smelled like cedar and something else. Mint. A charm against moths, she thought. It did actually feel comforting, and certainly warmer than it had any right to be. She blinked up at him, owlish in the dimmer light.

"I get cold easily too." Adam waved a hand. "Designed for it." Charmed, he meant. His sweater at least had long sleeves. And she supposed she wasn't going to stand out here forever. "Are you all right? No, wait." He rubbed his face with his hand. "Can I help? Or was it all just a bit much?"

Thalia shrugged. "A bit much." She wasn't sure how to talk to him now. He'd seen things in her she hadn't wanted to show, had been terrified of showing, for so long.

"The noise? It's the noise that gets me. I can't sort out what's coming from where."

"Why did you come?" Thalia glanced up at him, to see a shift of expressions on his face.

"Good for me to get out. Buck up and do my bit, don't you know?" He made the phrase bitter. "It was easier to come than argue. At least if I made the attempt, they'd stop fussing for a bit. You?"

"I wanted...." Thalia had no idea how to put this into words. "I wanted to be normal. Do normal things."

That got a short barking laugh out of him, loud enough to disturb the fond nothings coming from the lane for a moment. Then he coughed. "And what's normal, then?"

Thalia shrugged. "This. Childhood sweethearts in their seventies having a dance. Nice little old ladies sharing their tea and special biscuits. Young married couples still coasting on the glow of the wedding and madly in love. A few kids peeking in the windows."

"And someone - more than one someone - drinking too much, and at least three fights. Several grudges getting their claws into each other. Rivalries from last summer's agricultural fair flaring up over the biscuits and punch." He contemplated the glass in her hand. "I don't suppose it's any good."

"Weak and watered down. So not likely to get too many people drunk very quickly. I suppose that's the point."

"People who want stronger drink go down the pub. There's a barrel of a wickedly hard cider in the back." He then shrugged. "So we're not normal."

Thalia turned to blink at him. "We're not?" Emphasis decidedly on the first word, there.

Adam shrugged a shoulder. "You've seen me. I've seen you. Enough to know you had a bad time of it, somehow." He held up his hands immediately. "I'm not asking you how. But enough like me I know what doesn't show." He almost went on, but then he stopped, as if wanting to see what she did with that.

Thalia felt her shoulder twitch. She couldn't deny it. Not when he put it like that. "I suspect people would say we're a bad influence on each other, then."

"We should be around proper-minded people, who are courageous and brave, and went through the War without it seeming to touch them?" Adam offered it smoothly, far too smoothly, and Thalia peered at him.

"You can't be serious?"

"Well, to be honest, I've always thought that sort just hid it better. In drink, maybe, or ..." He made a little gesture with his hands, indicating potions. Easier than worrying about if someone without magic might overhear and bring their oaths back to roost.

"Some people, it didn't seem to touch much." Thalia shrugged. "Or they weren't in places where it hit them the worst way."

"That, I'd believe. The last bit. I suppose we all have

tender bits." Adam hesitated, then dropped his voice almost to a whisper. "It wasn't exactly the trenches that did for me. It didn't help. But it was all the land being torn apart. Over and over again."

"You went to Snap." Putting the pieces together gave her something to focus on, and that helped with everything else, as it often did. She could feel her heartbeat settling down again now and she felt steadier on her feet. "You have..." Thalia considered, then gestured at the ground.

Adam shrugged slightly. "Did." He looked off, down the lane, in the direction of the orchard. "The orchard helps. I didn't think it would."

"Being out here. I don't know. Some of it's worse. Some of it's better. I don't know how to tell the difference." Thalia looked down at the ground.

"Here as in out of London, or here as in standing in the street right now?" Adam sounded very slightly amused.

It made her snort, almost despite herself. "London. I love London, just. There's so many people. So many unpredictable things. My block of flats is fine, it's mostly artists and writers. People don't make sudden loud noises often. They don't mind if you don't want to talk to anyone for days."

Adam was watching her when she looked up, as if she were some unusual species of flower. Or apple, she supposed. "What?" she asked, and she could hear the peevish note in her voice now. It wasn't attractive, it wasn't likeable. She needed to stop. She dug her fingers into her palm, hoping that would help. Sometimes it did.

A moment later, he was reaching out for her hand. "Hey." She couldn't look at him, no matter what, she felt trapped, now, but the sort of trapped where she couldn't move. He held her hand for a moment longer, then released it. He didn't drop the touch, or push her away. Adam was releasing her as gently as he could. Then his fingers caught on something and he grunted.

They stood there in silence, not looking at each other for a good minute, before he offered, quietly, "We're a pair, aren't we? But...." He swallowed, she could hear it. "I don't like you hurting yourself. I don't like anyone hurting themselves."

She wanted to ask him so much. Did he? Did he hate himself when he did, like she hated herself? Did he do other things, to make himself stop, when that kind of short small pain was the only thing that broke through the rush of everything else? Instead, she just stood there, stupid and quiet and bound up in herself.

In the quiet, he said, "Should I get Hilaria?"

Thalia shook her head. Hilaria was having a good time, and there wasn't much she could do to help. They'd have to make their way back up the hill, but they'd made arrangements for a pony cart for that. Toward the end of the dance, not now, in the middle. "Is there anywhere quieter?"

"Let me - let me ask Dobbs." Adam disappeared, half-stumbling, as if one of his feet wasn't quite behaving either, but he was only gone a minute or two. "There's a back room, quieter, some cards and chess and checkers. This way?" She nodded, uncertainly. "And I'll tell Hilaria where you are."

Thalia nodded. She worked on remembering how to walk like a normal person. An ordinary person who could manage to climb two small steps and go through a door, even though that felt very far away right now.

Adam offered his hand. "Do you - do you still want my help with the other thing?"

The house, right. Thalia nodded. Somehow, she

couldn't do anything else, like something was pulling on her. Something different, not just the old fears and terror and incompetence.

CHAPTER 28
MONDAY

Two days later, Adam walked up the drive to the house in broad daylight. He was increasingly sure it was a bad idea. Or, at least, a phenomenally complex and risky idea. Thalia had stopped by yesterday just long enough to let him know. But with his uncle and Mrs Whitmore nearby, he couldn't exactly ask how she was doing in any real detail. Not the kind that mattered.

Thus, here he was, with a walking stick in one hand and a basket in the other. He came round the last curve up to the house and blinked. It looked static, not even the wind blowing anything much near him. The plants, too, Uncle Benjamin had improved his eye for that. The roses were fading slowly, looking droopy. The ivy and the boxwood were unchanging, much the same now as they would be in winter or in the height of summer.

As he came up to the front door, Hilaria opened it, gesturing him in. "They're all gone. Even Bessy. For four hours, at least. Mrs Harley might not be back tonight, and Bessy's seeing her older sister for a birthday." It came out in a torrent, as Hilaria led him through to the library. Adam glanced around, getting a bare impression of the space as high-ceilinged and posh, but not very fancy for all that. There was no marble in evidence and precious little gilt, for one thing.

Thalia stood in the middle of the library space, turning around on the rug, then stopping when she spotted him. "Adam." She shoved her hands in her pockets, suddenly. "You came."

"You asked me." Adam pointed it out evenly. This was going to be awkward, clearly, but he didn't have to join in the awkwardness. Not necessarily yet, anyway. He was sure he would in time.

Hilaria snorted and flung herself on the couch, sprawling a bit in a puff of moving frock. "So what are we doing with our three certain hours?"

Thalia gestured. "There's three rooms I've not been allowed into. My great-aunt's suite - that door there, or there's one from the first floor landing. And then there's a room upstairs that makes odd noises. Or at least it did. I think." She shivered once, even though it was quite warm in here.

"What do you want me to do, then? I'm no good at lock-picking." It suddenly occurred to Adam that they should have discussed this rather earlier. He suddenly realised she might have been assuming he was competent at anything, despite evidence to the contrary.

Thalia turned again in a full circle, before she shrugged. "Hilaria can do locks. Though we've got the keyring." She shook her shoulders, like a horse settling. "Tell me I'm not going mad." She had a note in her voice now that made him worried she actually was. More than they both were already, by everyone else's standards. "Be a witness. I don't know. I just..." Her voice trailed off. "I think you should be here."

There were a dozen questions chasing through his head now. Why him? What did she think he could do if there was something wrong? Did she have particular reason to fear for her sanity, besides whatever had happened to her? Which might certainly be more than enough, of course. He swallowed. "You do know that I'm - that I'm not good for much?"

She shrugged, a sharp twitch of a movement. "And I am?" She waved her hand up at the door. "I just - you know things I don't."

Adam let out a long breath. "If you're sure. And this isn't a running sort of thing, I suppose."

"Very much hope not," Hilaria said. "I have blisters from the dance, still."

That broke the tension, and made Thalia giggle, before she looked up at Adam and shrugged. "See?"

Adam shook his head. "I'm not going to argue. Just - I don't know what you're expecting." Hilaria pushed herself upright at that, and said, "Well, if we're doing this, let's get on with it. Keys, doors, observations."

"Keys?" Adam asked.

"I figured out where the spare set live. Give me a moment, right?" Thalia walked past him, back into the hallway, toward what was probably a kitchen. If that was where you put a kitchen in a house like this. It wasn't just that it was big, it was that it fit oddly together, as if bits had been bodged on at different times. Which, to be fair, they probably had. Uncle Benjamin said there had been a house here at least since the Crusades, which was more than long enough for odd architectural angles to accumulate.

As soon as the library door closed behind Thalia, Hilaria

stood, planting her feet a foot from Adam. He took a step back. "Don't you hurt her."

Adam blinked. "I what?"

"I don't know what she's said to you. She talks all the time. Had you noticed that, and you have to piece together what she's not saying? She hasn't always been like that. It comes out better in her writing right now. But don't you hurt her."

All the fierceness was there, all the insistence. Adam wished, with the kind of desire that almost brought him to his knees with light-headedness, that he had a friend like that. Someone who'd threaten and insist and demand on his behalf. He closed his eyes so he could focus. "I'm glad she has you."

It wasn't what Hilaria expected. When Adam blinked and could look at her again, she was taking a step back. "What?"

"That you care about her that much. That someone does."

Hilaria huffed, but it was more good-natured now. "She - I don't know you. I don't know what she knows about you. But she wanted you here. So don't, don't do the wrong thing."

Adam was about to say that would be much easier if he had a clue what he was doing, but then Thalia was back. "This door or the other one?"

Hilaria considered. "The other. Then we can try the second floor if we need to?" She got a glare from Thalia and amended it to "When we have a look."

Thalia nodded, and turned sharply on her heel, off toward the main staircase. Hilaria gestured for Adam to follow as she brought up the rear. Adam made it up the stairs well enough. The handrail was sturdy. Thalia had taken a sharp left, bringing her to a door set into the side of the landing, and now she was rummaging through the keys, picking one out.

When she got the door open, it gave them a good look at the room. "Hil, get a lantern?" There were, of course, no lamps lit. Adam certainly didn't want to go into the room without a better idea of what was there. All of them were quiet while Hilaria went to her room and came back with a lantern. Nothing stirred. No sound of anything.

Once Thalia was holding the lantern, she shook her shoulders. It was a bit like a horse bracing for a coming race, all the coiled need to run bundled up and restrained. Then she walked forward. Adam had seen that face too many times. His men going over the top, resolute, even in the middle of their terror. He reached one hand out, closing his fist on air, rather than her clothing. Too late to stop her, like he was always too late.

He could feel Hilaria brush by him while he stood with his eyes closed, trying to find the will to move. Adam was still standing there what felt like forever later, watching the scenes replay in his mind while he leaned against the wall. He could barely tell it was panelled wood, not the board keeping a trench from utter collapse into mud and muck.

Adam heard it before anything else. "May I take your hand?"

That, of all things, didn't fit into his memories at all. It was as if they couldn't make space for it. Either that was wrong, or the memory was wrong. It wasn't possible for both things to fit at the same time. He took a shaky breath, then managed a little jerky nod. If the voice was different, and then someone touched him, maybe he wasn't in the middle of France again.

A moment later, he felt fingers under his. Smaller,

slighter. Cold at the tips, but the way someone who was good at pastry had cold hands. The odd thought made him snort and then gasp to catch his breath as he almost inhaled wrong. It took him several more breaths to sort himself out. When he got his eyes open again finally, Thalia was right there. "Ready?"

He nodded, and she tugged him forward, to the centre of a room. It was like stepping into late springtime. The walls were painted green, the green right before summer took over. Panels had flowers painted, and other parts of the walls were hung with photographs and prints, bird after bird, dozens or hundreds of them, all sizes.

Some part of him could name all the flowers, all the birds. It wasn't just what he'd learned at school; it was something more than that. Sitting with Uncle Benjamin, hearing his stories. There was a cuckoo there, and swallows and swifts and a photograph there of a nightingale. Others, half a dozen other species at least, that he couldn't identify at first glance, he'd need a guidebook.

But other than that, the rooms looked normal enough. Not what Adam would choose, not what anyone in Adam's family would choose. But it was arguably what a widow in Thalia's family might prefer. Maybe. If she had a particular fondness for birds. Only there'd been that bit of folklore, too, hadn't there been? Mistress of Birds.

Thalia spotted it, the same way. "There's so many birds. There's a story in one of Great-Aunt Avis's books, more than one of them. About a woman - a witch, a queen, one of the Fatae, maybe - who could command the birds to go or stay. Who could steal their power, whatever it was. Some birds brought wisdom, or skilled hunting, some came and went with the seasons, some held magic, or led to treasure.

Thalia shrugged. "I thought it was just a story, but now I can't help wondering."

Thalia dropped his hand and turned around in place, then took out a notebook and started making notes. "Do you know what the birds are? Or the plants?" She asked Adam like he was ordinary, like he hadn't just frozen up less than five minutes ago.

He coughed. "Most of them." He listed off the names, the ones he knew, pointing them out. "Migratory birds, I think, all of them. These ones I don't know. Can you sketch the head and colouring?"

"Sketching's what I'm here for." Hilaria came up beside him, and as Thalia pointed out the ones of particular interest, Hilaria went around with a pencil, making quick little scratching noises. The whole thing took them a bit. While they were working, Adam circled around where they weren't currently standing and looked at the details. Overall, it was much of a muchness, but he called out a few new things he'd spotted. Even a puffin tucked into a corner, those weren't remotely local at all.

"Any you recognise from around here?" Adam asked the question without really thinking about it.

Thalia froze. "Birds?"

"Birds." There was that queer note in her voice again, an echo that shouldn't be there.

"Nothing closer than your orchard. It's - I thought it was just very quiet. I'm used to the birds in London, how they're always making noise right by your window when you want to sleep in. None of that here. I don't think I've even seen one, not close."

Adam frowned. "There was a hawk. Too young for the season, down by the orchard. Not yet fully fledged, which was - that's very wrong." He could feel the wrongness edge closer, lurking now.

He didn't know how long it took, because it felt like time moved oddly. More oddly than it usually did for him, rather. Adam and time were not on the best terms this decade, truth be told. When he finally thought to take his pocket watch out, it had only been about forty minutes. Thalia caught the movement. "Time?"

"Half-past two. Do we ..." He nodded back toward the door.

"Let me go through to the bedroom." Thalia did, while he and Hilaria waited at the doorway. This room was simpler, almost like Adam had imagined a nun's cell to be. A bed, a washbasin and pitcher, a chair with a reading lamp and a small bookshelf, and a dresser. There must be a wardrobe somewhere nearby.

"Upstairs?"

Adam nodded, and they went out, Thalia looking around one more time before she carefully relocked the door. They went upstairs, and she fumbled twice with the keys before finding the one that worked. This time, Hilaria held the lantern up high.

When Thalia opened the door, there was a shiver of light, like the world cracking open. Then the room resolved, somehow, into a seemingly ordinary space. A huge iron cage stood in the middle of the room, as tall as the ceiling, like a massive pillar. A bird, small and brown, hopped from perch to perch, then let out the unmistakable sound of a cuckoo, two long hoots.

The sound hit them all. It wasn't just the sound, it was like a wave of muck, pouring out toward him. That's what Adam felt, like he was back in the trenches, surrounded by death and destruction, knowing more was coming.

Knowing it was something broken in the world, fundamentally and absolutely. It pulled at him, the same way, that both made it impossible to move and critical to flee.

Adam had the bare presence of mind, somehow, to grab at both women, tugging them back. Thalia somehow grabbed at the door, pulling it closed. Leaving whatever that was on the other side. Both the women were pale white, and Hilaria was half-reciting something under her breath, before she was bolting downstairs like a darting hare.

CHAPTER 29
MONDAY

Thalia had the presence of mind - or perhaps, just practise keeping going in the face of panic - to lock the door. She felt the key twist and latch, and said, "It's locked" as she tested the door. It wasn't just in her head, she'd done this, it wasn't a lie her own mind was telling her.

She didn't have words for what she'd felt, and that was, perhaps, the right way to put it. It had something of the Silence in it, the idea that she'd lost all her words, all the ways she could communicate. The worst thing she could imagine, and then some.

She heard a scuffling sound behind her, and when she managed to look back, Hilaria was pressed up against the wall by the stairs. "You, I..." Hilaria spun. "I can't stay." She spun around and dashed down the stairs, and Thalia just caught the flip of her skirts as she took a sharp turn toward her room.

Adam was standing at the top of the stairs. He looked all right at first, then she could see how his fingers were gripping the bannister until they went white. His shoulders were hitching slightly as he breathed.

Thalia glanced at the locked door, then took a step towards him, and another, looking back at the locked door again and again. He blinked at her, his pupils wide. "Take a breath. And another one. You - can you come downstairs?" She waited while he peeled his fingers off the railing. He leaned on the walking stick with one hand, and the railing with the other, making his way cautiously down.

Thalia waited until he was halfway down, then cautiously edged down sideways, watching the door as she went. It didn't move; it didn't shake. She didn't hear any startled noises or threatening ones. And yet, there was that unsettling feeling of wrongness. It wasn't doom. Thalia knew what doom felt like, down to her core. She knew how despair grabbed at you with claws. Anxiety scrambled along, grabbing and clinging and sliding off everything in its path, leaving chaos behind it.

By the time she was at the bottom of the stairs, Adam had moved over to the wall between Thalia and Hilaria's rooms. Thalia could see Hilaria flinging things into a suitcase, grabbing books and setting them in place. Finally she put her drawing case on top, before she latched the luggage and turned around defiantly. It must have taken longer to get downstairs than Thalia realised.

She'd lost time somehow. Again. Worse than usual. There was just a blankness in her head, where she didn't know how she'd got downstairs. Hilaria was nearly all packed, and even at the speed she was going, that must have taken time. Five minutes, ten, fifteen. And all Thalia had in her head was emptiness. It made her shiver hard.

"Don't say it. I won't. I can't. I don't know how you can." Hilaria's hands were on her hips. "If I go now, there's a train tonight, isn't there? Say I got an urgent message, someone at home is sick, I need to take care of them. Whatever you like. If I forgot anything, mail it on." She grabbed the suitcase by the handle. "This place is..." She glanced up at the far corner of the house. "Wrong. More wrong than I thought."

Thalia held up her hands. "I -" She couldn't argue. She didn't have it in her, for one thing. There was something wild in Hilaria now, something Thalia hadn't seen since the end of the War. "I - we'll - walk you to the station. Do you have everything? Need me to make up a sandwich." She felt the old habits slide into place. There was a crisis, the time for panic was later. Later wasn't now.

Five minutes later, they were walking out the door, with a sandwich from lunch wrapped up in some spare paper. Hilaria had a tight grip on her suitcase, though Adam had made only a faint gesture at carrying it. He was walking, at least, but he hadn't said a thing since the top of the stairs, and he was walking stiffly, leaning more on the walking stick. Thalia suspected he hadn't realised how much of that was showing.

They got halfway down the long drive when Hilaria turned around. "Have your nails grown while you've been here?" It was a completely out-of-the-blue question. Thalia blinked at her. Hilaria waved fingers in front of her face. "Mine haven't. Has your hair grown?"

"I hadn't noticed?" It sounded feeble as soon as the words were out of her mouth. Thalia thought through it, then tugged her hair down from the knot at the back of her head, pulling the hairpins out deftly enough despite everything that had happened. She tugged the curled end down, then frowned. "It should be a good inch longer." Her hair grew fast, and she'd been here long enough.

"Nails. Hair. Did you notice, your great-aunt's rooms, it was like time didn't exist? No clocks. No recent photographs at all. The birds, all the birds, those awful staring birds like they're watching you, wanting something. But no people."

Adam cleared his throat. She'd almost forgot he was there, he'd been so quiet. Maybe because he was scared whatever it was, in that room, would hear him, which would only be sensible. "Photos show age. The ones that are out, they're all..." He shrugged. "Rather timeless. Nothing that really shows the date clearly. Are there?"

Thalia shook her head. "I've been baffled by it. I mean, even my father looks - he could be twenty or forty or sixty like he actually is, and I don't think I could tell, the way the photos are. But— he dyes his hair." She hesitated, but she was pretty sure neither of the others would name it. "In that room?" She let her voice trail off as she saw Hilaria's face.

"Not this close." Hilaria turned and resolutely started down the drive again. It wasn't until they reached the main road, such as it was, that she stopped. "We're off your property now?"

"Not mine, but yes." Thalia crossed the road for good measure. "Here."

"That bird. It's wrong. It's made of wrong." The words tumbled out of Hilaria now. "I don't know why, I don't know how. I don't know how I didn't feel it more, sooner? But it's made of wrong."

Hilaria had feelings about things, though rarely this strongly. The worst of it - or the best, Thalia didn't even know anymore - was that Hilaria was right. There was something deeply wrong. Not exactly an evil and good wrongness. She'd been near enough to that. Been far too near the middle of it, once.

Thalia wasn't the sort of person who made oaths to the Silence very often. But it felt like that, something huge and overwhelming, like an ocean or a war, that pulled everything into its grasp. A massive whirlpool, the kind that swallowed ships and never let go. She'd had all the lectures at school about what it meant to break one of those oaths, the way fear would seize an oathbreaker, how if they tried to keep going, their fear could destroy them. This was what they'd meant. How the world felt broken, with a shattered piece that let her see exactly how much, sharp enough to pierce flesh.

She sucked in a breath. "What kind of wrong?"

Hilaria gave that a bit of consideration. Adam had taken up a spot leaning against the fence, his eyes half-closed as if he were thinking for his life. While Hilaria was thinking, Thalia coughed. "Adam? Are you all right?"

"Trying to 'member something." It came out as a mumble. She could barely make out the words. She nodded and turned her attention back to Hilaria while keeping an eye on him. Hilaria was frowning at her.

"What?" It came out a touch peevish.

"You're going to be a mess when I'm gone. Tonight." Hilaria waved a hand. "Stay in the village. Somewhere. They've got to have an inn."

"That's admitting that there's something wrong. Bessy would guess. Or Mrs Harley, for sure."

"That's the other thing. You're thinking you're fine now, and you're going to fall apart in a few hours, when you think it's over. But that thing in there, it's not over. And you can't live like that, not again."

Thalia flinched away, even when Hilaria reached out. Perhaps especially because she reached out. "You're right to go. I can't. So." She shrugged. She'd keep going, like she knew how to do, even in the worst moments.

Hilaria let out a long sigh, one dramatic enough to let Thalia know they'd be having words about this, eventually. Whenever, sometime in the distant future, Thalia went back to London. About how Thalia didn't have enough sense to keep a mouse, to come in from the cold, to flee from wrongness. On the other hand, it meant Hilaria was recovering enough.

"Come on. Train." She glanced. "Adam?"

He pushed himself away from the fence, taking up his walking stick again. They walked down in silence, accompanied only by the scuff of their shoes on the dirt road, the thump of Adam's stick, and the muffled bump of the suitcase against Hilaria's leg. The train station, thankfully, wasn't busy. After twenty minutes, Hilaria said, "Just. Go where you're going. I'll be fine. You need... you need to figure out what you're doing."

It was about the room, and it was about everything else, and they both knew it. Even if Adam didn't get all the undercurrents. He'd gone very quiet, like he was afraid to take up space. But once Thalia hugged Hilaria, and promised to write in the journals with whatever update, he picked up a steady pace beside her. She expected him to slow as they went back past his uncle's house, but when she paused, he gestured. "I'll..." He didn't finish the words, but the gesture made it clear he expected to come with her.

They walked up the hill. Halfway up to the turn up to the house, Thalia looked up and frowned, then held out her hand, feeling the first raindrop. "You should go back."

He shook his head. "Won't. I'll wait outside if I have to."

There were dozens of things she wanted to say to that. That she was worried enough about herself. That she wasn't sure what help he'd be. Thalia was a grown woman, she didn't need a sheepdog. They were both a mess, and likely to make things worse. The list went on and on in her head. In the end, she bit back all the sharpness and awfulness. "Why?"

"Have an idea." He let out a long breath. "And you shouldn't be alone with it. Especially if there's a storm." The wind was picking up, a curious twist to it that didn't bode well for anything out in it.

She turned sideways. "And you won't tell me."

Adam shrugged. "I'm not telling you things. You're not telling me things."

"Different things!" This came out pitched and sharp and harsh in her ears, never mind his. "What things?"

"About you. Not so much about the house. I'm - you've been honest about the house." Other men would have made an arch question out of it, an assumption that was what she was lying about. Or at least not talking about. Adam was just stating a truth, laying it out like you'd cut up an apple. Straight and solid and somehow specific.

She closed her eyes, just standing there in the road. He gave her a moment. "You need anything right now?"

That, too, was so specific. He knew how everything had come down to one moment. How her head was replaying turning the key in the lock, over and over again. How the metal felt in her hand.

"Tea. If we're going back up there."

"Seems that we are." He didn't seem thrilled by the idea, but Adam wasn't trying to talk her out of it. "Is there somewhere, not in the house, we can talk?"

Thalia considered. Something with a roof, and preferably walls. "There's a shed. Out down past the house. It has a roof. Probably also mice, and I don't know what else."

"We'll give that a try. I've sat in worse." Thalia supposed there was that about the War, in the trenches. If no one was actively trying to kill you at the moment and you weren't drowning in mud, everything else might be manageable.

"All right. I'll see about flasks of tea or something. Get my journal." She shivered. She'd have to go up to her room for that.

Adam hesitated, then touched her arm. "I'm not much, but I'll be with you."

CHAPTER 30
MONDAY EVENING

By the time they made it back up the drive - and the hill that was the drive - Adam's legs were aching. He missed the ordinary sort of ache after climbing a hill. This was the curious and frustrating hollow twitch that meant he'd be a great deal more likely to fall down soon if he weren't very careful.

It was bad enough he almost invited himself in to sit, but he knew if he sat, he'd never stand up again. Thalia seemed more than a bit twitchy. They both were, and it was as if they both knew that starting to talk about it before they were sitting somewhere quiet would end badly.

So instead Adam leaned against the wall while Thalia ducked into the kitchen and then upstairs to her room to bring down her journal and some books. That trip was very fast. She went dashing up the steps two at a time, and almost skidded as she came down.

She flipped through her journal, frowning. "There's a note in the journal saying that Bessy won't be back tonight, a storm is blowing up, and that Mrs Harley can't get back either. Asking if I can make myself a sandwich and make sure everything's shuttered." She looked up, a bit baffled. "Well, on one hand, we have time to do whatever we're going to do?"

"On the other hand, we're alone with the house." They were not in the house.

It did decide Thalia on something. "Look, let's see if their cottage is unlocked. I don't mean to pry or anything, but - there must be a room we could sit in that isn't very personal? Better than the shed?"

Adam considered that. "Warmer than the shed." He cursed, suddenly, under his breath. "How bad a storm? The apples."

"I don't know exactly. I wish we'd got a paper in the village, but maybe there wouldn't be anything in the paper. Do you need to let your uncle know?"

Adam nodded and let out a long breath. "All right. Cottage, if it's open. We can always say we were making sure it was set for the storm. And you write to Mrs Harley, and I'll write to Uncle Benjamin, and I guess we'll..." It felt overwhelming, but he knew the only thing to do was take it one step at a time.

Mercifully, the cottage door was just on the latch, and it opened easily when Thalia tried it. There was a string to turn on the charm light above, and it lit up agreeably, illuminating a simple sitting room. There was nothing terribly personal there. One chair seemed obviously Mrs Harley's, with a book and some knitting beside it, and by mutual agreement, Thalia and Adam took the ends of the small couch. Thalia brought out what she'd packed up, and then her journal.

Adam focused on his own, saying that he'd walked Thalia back up, and didn't want to leave her alone in the house with the storm coming up. It sounded queer to his ears. Surely his uncle would suspect something, if not Mrs Whitmore. For a man who'd been near enough a hermit to volunteer to be in a strange place overnight with someone he admittedly barely knew, it was a tremendous stretch.

It felt like less of one. Oh, his legs ached, and his heart did too, at what was locked away up in that corner bedroom. But being with Thalia, that didn't feel nearly as odd or wrong or sharp-edged as he'd thought it should. For all her own nerves, there was something he could rely on there. Maybe he had always been more afraid of people's reactions than anything else.

Thalia was taking longer to write whatever she was writing. Rather than dig into the sandwiches she'd brought out, he considered thinking about something that had caught his attention again on the way up the drive. He was still deep in thought when she cleared her throat cautiously and he realised she was done writing.

"Penny for them?"

"My thoughts?" He tried to corral them again into some sort of order. Thankfully, she wasn't sitting there staring at him. She laid out a linen napkin on the table for tidiness, and then set out two sandwiches, solid ham and cheddar and strong mustard he could smell from here.

"Is that all right? I realised I didn't ask what you'd like. Not that there's a lot of choice right now."

"You like the mustard?" It wasn't, he thought, the sort of taste you associated with well-bred women. Too strong, too potent, too not-their-cup-of-tea, somehow.

Thalia glanced at it, as if the mustard had somehow personally betrayed her. Then carefully, she said, "It makes me sure I'm feeling something." She couldn't look at him while she spoke, focusing instead on a spot somewhere over the sandwiches, over by the hearth.

"Mmm." He tried to choose among all the things someone might say there, and settled finally on, "Glad to have company in that."

He hadn't been sure until that moment that it would be the right thing, but she lit up with it. She'd clearly expected some sort of disapproval or misunderstanding or something worse, and. Well. Adam wanted to ask about that, but he knew how awful it was when people asked him. Instead, he said, "Your penny gets me going on about the plantings. The ivy and the roses and the boxwood."

"And the holly." She nodded. "What about them?"

"You must know some of the references, in poetry?" Thalia read things, she swam in the literary river. "What do they have in common?"

She frowned, furrowing up her forehead, her hand hovering over her sandwich as it sat on the table. "The greenery?" She then blinked. "They're much the same in winter, aren't they? But that doesn't explain the roses."

"The roses are - well. No, it doesn't. The roses should have gone to rosehips long ago. It..." He gestured. "There's no obvious sign of the season from the planting, except for that. And roses, especially those, can bloom repeatedly. For months."

"So where you'd normally expect a procession of flowers and herbs and plants and all that, instead what we have is...." She tapped her fingers on the table, thinking. "Roses. And greenery."

"And a cuckoo. I think it's a cuckoo. It sounded like one." Adam took in a deep breath and let it out slowly. "You have the books?"

Thalia nodded, then her hand darted forward, and she took the sandwich. He nodded. "Let's eat, first. We're here, we're inside, it's not too cold. We can take our time figuring out what to do next." Adam gestured. "Are you sure Hilaria will be all right?"

"Oh, I'm sure. She knows where the portal is. She can get back to London from there. I'd worry if she were taking the train all the way back in a bad storm, but she didn't have to go far."

"She - you." He didn't know how to ask if it had broken their friendship, broken something irreplaceable. Something of it must have come out in his voice, because she glanced sideways at him. "I - you are good friends? I hope this doesn't, I don't know. Spoil things."

"Hilaria's very sensitive to some things. I'm sensitive to different things. If we hadn't learned how to give each other space, we wouldn't be such good friends. And to be fair, it was not at all what either of us expected when I invited her here. I mean, I was expecting something more like a first wife in the attic, or something out of a Bluebeard legend?"

Adam blinked several times, rapidly. "I believe those would be rather worse. Comparatively speaking. Though I'm not at all sure how you measure that sort of thing, now I've said it."

"Not a proper measurement system, I suppose. Does one have milli-Bluebeards?"

"Let us posit a unit of one Bluebeard meaning running for our lives." Though he had to admit the locked door was evocative. Secret locked doors had that quality about them, of the dangerous and forbidden, even if they only held a storage cupboard for a perfectly harmless broom and bucket.

"So, I don't know. At the moment, we're somewhere around three hundred milli-Bluebeards?" Thalia wriggled her hand. "I mean, I am … worried, and scared? But it also didn't directly come after us."

"To be fair, it's in a cage." Adam pointed out. "Behind a locked door."

Thalia frowned. "True." She let out a long breath and focused on eating a few more bites of her sandwich, then washed it down with tea. When she'd done that, she looked up again. "What do we do now?"

Adam considered. "May I ask you a difficult question? A personal one. You don't need to answer, but…" This had been pressing on him, the more he thought about going back up those stairs with her.

"Possibly." Thalia sounded wary now.

"We both admit we're going to go back up there." Adam said. "You know I'm a coward. But I do know that, well. You need to know the measure of the men going into battle with you."

"You keep saying you're a coward." Thalia said. "But you've been rather clearly not running away. Even when given the chance to make a polite excuse and disappear." She gestured back toward the house. "I expected to be on my own with this. Whatever it is. Even when I got here, I expected something was odd."

Adam tried to find a way to argue with that and needed more time to give a reason she wouldn't immediately logic away. "Why do you know about the mustard? And the being terrified? You weren't near the Front, were you?"

Thalia sucked in a breath, the sudden instinct. She shook her head. "No. Only." She glanced away, over at the fireplace. "Why do you want to know?"

"You're like me. And I don't know why. I mean. My reasons are fairly obvious. Banal, cowardly, lazy, good-for-nothing, but obvious."

Thalia lifted her chin at that, suddenly staring him down with the intensity of a cat about to pounce on something. "Don't you talk about yourself like that." Her voice hitched. "Or me. If we're alike, don't talk about us like that. I can't bear it." Her voice went sharp and hollow, like she was on the edge of tears all of a sudden.

Adam knew he'd ruined it. Everything. He shook his hand out, bumping hers in the process, and suddenly she grabbed onto it. "Are we alike?" she asked, demanding to know.

His vision was swimming again, and at least he was sitting down. He closed his eyes to make that better. Or at least, much easier to ignore the problems he was having. Adam leaned back to feel the back of the sofa. "Enough." It came out as a hoarse whisper, like he'd been shouting for hours, his throat tight.

Adam couldn't run. He couldn't even stand up right now, nor reclaim his hand. He felt pinned there by the relentless weight of something beyond his ken. He'd thought of it, back at the Gospatricks, like a massive lion pinning him down. A great cat deciding how much it was going to play with its food, or something of the kind. It was a nebulous, uneasy stasis.

CHAPTER 31
MONDAY EVENING

Thalia took a breath. Perhaps some part of her had known it would come to this, if she kept talking to Adam. He'd had plenty of chances to walk away, to turn his back, to go back to his own life. But so had she, and she'd kept wanting to talk to him.

"It's complicated." That sounded bad, to her ears.

"Mine was simple. It was a war. I was a coward. I broke, in the face of the enemy. I left my men alone." His voice was quiet, but like an undertow, dragging everything along and down with it.

"You were an officer, you said."

"I was. A temporary gentleman. You know the term?" Adam didn't really look at her, just sideways.

Thalia nodded. "That must have meant you - they saw something in you."

It got her a hollow laugh. "I volunteered nearly as soon as I could. 1914. I'd been apprenticing with an uncle, but he had sons coming up. He didn't need me." He turned his hand over, palm up. "And I wanted to do something that mattered. I did well, they promoted me. And then they offered to make me a temporary gentleman in 1916. I hadn't gone to the right sort of school, my family's in trade, but I guess by then someone had translated what Snap meant to the Army. Enough. They knew I could read and write and figure well, they knew I'd had training. I wasn't just some country bumpkin."

Thalia leaned back. "And then things went wrong?"

"That's a way to put it. Not in the midst, for me. I - I didn't let my men down like that. But we were down to a third of the men I'd started with. Some injured, a lot killed, or next thing to it." He rubbed his hand over his face. "Over and over again. If it had just been once or twice, or a few weeks, I'd have managed. Did manage. Only it didn't stop. Cycling in, up to the front for a few days, then back again, over and over, never any real break. When we did get a day or three behind the lines, it was all laundry and getting - our feet were awful. Any bit of skin that got wet stayed wet."

Thalia nodded. "I saw some of that. What happened. And heard the stories. Bad socks, bad boots. Could you use charms at all?"

That made him look up, his eyes a bit wide. "I did. And I hated myself for it. Because why should I have feet that didn't rot when they did? I did what I could. Bending down during inspection. But I couldn't do that to everyone."

"And a great many boots. Even if they'd all been lined up, neat and tidy in front of you, you might not have managed all of them in one go. Or over and over again."

His jaw dropped. She'd never seen anything quite like it. Then he thought through it, the implications, and buried his face in his hands again. "Oh." She knew then, he'd been blaming himself for that too, for not being good enough at something he'd never been trained for, might never have had the raw power for. Along with everything else he blamed himself for.

Without looking up, he went on, his voice a bit muffled now. "We were behind the lines, and I just couldn't. Couldn't walk, couldn't stand, couldn't talk for weeks. Just sat there and shook and froze. They tried..." He hesitated.

"1917." Her voice came out briskly. "They'd have been trying any sort of pain stimulus they could. To get you to respond." She'd heard about it, though of course they didn't do that kind of thing in the Temple of Healing. She'd seen the aftermath, though. Scars and small burns and caustics, all the ways men tortured each other in the name of science and virtue.

Adam nodded, a tiny movement, like he'd got frozen again. "Not for long. Sent me to a hospital in Bristol. Then to Scotland, Craiglockhart, that wasn't as awful. Then home, then a rest home, back and forth. Some time with the Gospatricks. That helped a bit. My parents didn't know what to do with me." It was coming out of him in short, clipped words now, tumbling over each other. As if he'd stop forever if he tried to slow down.

"And no one understood. Even the places that weren't as awful."

That made him look up at her, focus on her, and he shook his head. "You know."

Thalia nodded carefully, feeling like any movement would shatter her balance and leave her in a heap. "I do." She swallowed. "Never told anyone all of this straight out. Hilaria was around for half of it." And had figured out enough of the rest that Thalia could nod or shake her head.

Adam hesitated, and then he reached out one hand, leaving it palm up on the sofa between them. She looked at it, like it was some small bird that would fly away as soon as she moved. Then, carefully, she put her hand in his. She couldn't close her fingers, and he didn't, but the touch was enough to remind her there was someone she was talking to.

"I had an older brother. He was killed in 1917. Passchendaele." Not the same bit of War, not the same trenches. But near enough.

"I'm sorry." Adam's voice was soft now.

Thalia shook her head. "Plenty of people lost someone. It wasn't just that. Though I'd looked up to him. He didn't think my stories were foolish. He - he was kind. Included me. My sister's eight years older. It might as well be twenty years. She thinks I won't grow up."

Adam's fingers curled briefly against the side of her hand, but he didn't say anything.

"Pierus - he'd been an officer for a year by then. Seasoned, he knew what he was doing, more or less. He wasn't - he didn't train for war, but he'd listened to all the stories. He used to have hordes of little tin soldiers he'd move around, studying the battle plans. Waterloo and all that. Some of the Boer War, my parents knew people who'd fought there and come home, and he couldn't get enough of the stories."

Adam's hand shifted slightly. "Boar House?" He clearly knew the Schola houses well enough to guess at that. Bravery and a certain amount of stubborn pig-headedness, as people usually put it. Not necessarily much in the way of brains.

Thalia snorted. "Yes. My parents didn't know what to do with it. They'd talk about how he took initiative, how handsome he looked in uniform, how charming he was. And that was true, but they didn't understand it."

Adam hesitated before asking, "And you? Which house?"

"Seal." It came out of her in a murmur. "They - they have no idea what to do with that."

"All right." He took a slow breath. "Please, go on?"

It seemed insurmountable, still, but Thalia was sure now if she didn't say this now, she never would. And she'd already spent a decade with it hollowing her out from the inside, with jagged edges. Telling someone probably wouldn't help, nothing else had, but it was at least different. A new angle on the problem. And maybe Hilaria was right, after all.

"Pierus, they were to get a new officer. Young, just out of training, just old enough to be there. And he came and reported, and he stood up too straight."

She could feel Adam's reaction, more than she saw it, she couldn't make her eyes focus now. He shifted his hand to hold hers, slightly better, though loosely enough she could pull away if she wanted. If she'd been able to move.

"Pierus - tried to get him down. And then there was a shot, and." She shrugged, cutting the words off abruptly. "You know."

There was the sort of silence that Thalia had when there were too many words and hurts crowding around her head to let any of them out. Then Adam cleared his throat. "I do. Too many." He stopped again, as if weighing something. "That wasn't all of it." He didn't make it a question. He didn't press her to go on. But he was right, and he knew it.

"No." She took a deep breath, the sort that was on the edge of sobbing hysteria that lasted half an hour. "I was in the Temple of Healing, one of the wards. Not enough private rooms, even for officers. And another twenty men get brought in, fresh from coming across the Channel. I recognised one of the names. They'd sent a letter, eventually, with a bit more detail than the telegram. The circumstances. In case it made any of us feel better to know he'd saved another life."

Adam stayed silent, but she could see his chin come up.

"Same man. Boy. Foolish boy. He'd - he'd done something else. Risked other people. Two more had died. And he'd - he lingered. For a week. Dying by inches. They tried to save him. Needed..." Now her breath was coming too fast and too hard. "I'd learned to lend my magic by that point. I wasn't good enough for other nursing, not beyond small wounds, but I could do that part. And they - drained me, over and over, trying to keep him alive. And it didn't help. Three others died in that week. But..."

"But you gave everything you could to save someone who'd got your brother killed. Through carelessness, if nothing else. And who'd..." Adam's voice got an edge to it. "They talk about triage. Saving who you can. But we know some people get more chances than others."

Thalia shivered, suddenly. "That." The part she'd never been able to soothe away. That maybe they could have saved one of the others, if they'd tried. If they'd had space or a chance to breathe and think it through. Anything other than the frantic endless race to do anything they could, when they'd already given everything they could for months. Years.

They sat in complete silence for a long time. Minutes, certainly, maybe longer. "How long did you keep nursing?"

"The end of the War." She heard his gasp, the way it hit him. "They needed every hand. I couldn't stop. They gave me a fortnight off, some country house with other nurses, all the starch gone out of us. Then back to work. A different ward. Eventually one of the long-term care homes, when I wasn't good for anything. For a long time, I was too tired to hurt with it."

Adam squeezed her hand then. "I got to stop. I can't imagine..." She could feel him, now, the tension in his fingers. "And after?"

"Moved to a flat in London. My parents didn't, they thought." Thalia had no idea how to put that into words. "Mother got tangled up with spiritualists, and not the helpful kind. Father was always distant. Phoebe got married. She says she's happy." Thalia wasn't sure what happy looked like on anyone anymore, but she was even less certain about her sister than most people.

Adam was quiet again, though now his thumb stroked once, then twice, against the side of her hand. It was as if he wanted to reassure himself she was there. "Do you use magic much?"

"I didn't for a long time. Not beyond a light charm. Cheaper to do it myself." Cheaper and exhausting sometimes, but cheaper won out.

"And I'm sure you haven't seen a Healer. I mean, I haven't either. They had their chance at me. I'm not giving them another."

The way that came out made Thalia snort, finally breaking some of the immobility she felt. "No. Besides, they just tell me to sleep and eat well. And who can sleep, right?"

That got her a raw laugh. "I read. In the middle of the night, two or three or four in the morning. For hours. I don't know what I'd do without books."

CHAPTER 32
MONDAY EVENING

Adam looked down, where he was still holding Thalia's hand. He hadn't realised when he took her hand how deep that was going to go. How much they'd betrayed her, in so many of the same ways they'd betrayed him. And now, he didn't want to let go. He certainly didn't want her to face what was in the house alone. Especially since she'd as good as admitted her magic hadn't recovered.

Maybe the Gospatricks could help her, where they had only been able to do so much for him. It was an unexpected thought, wanting to help someone. He'd spent so long coiled in on himself, where every attempt to open up had brought jagged uncertainty. People treated him the wrong way, even though he could never explain what was wrong. Even the people who meant well.

Except Thalia. Hilaria, a bit, as well, but he hadn't spent any time with just her. Adam could see why Thalia liked her, though, and more to the point, why Thalia trusted her. There was none of the false kindness, the kind that laid a pit trap under your feet. No coddling, but also a comfortable acceptance of where the limits were for her friend.

"You said Pierus liked your stories." His mind was circling around something else, and he held up his free hand. "I'm thinking about the house too. Give me a minute or three."

"And in the meantime, we talk about my writing." Thalia's voice had that echo back now, but she took a breath and let it out. As if she were about to walk across a narrow shaking wooden bridge, and she was not at all sure it would bear her weight. "He did. I was writing. Oh, everything was different before the War."

"Of course it was." Adam shrugged. "I don't understand - certainly don't trust - the people who pretend it isn't. Why wouldn't that change your writing?"

She looked at him, suddenly wide-eyed, as if she hadn't expected to hear that said straight out. Certainly not as he'd said it. "You - no one's ..."

Adam tilted his head. "You spend your time with artists and writers. I don't know them well, but I read. People work through things in their writing. Some of them are obvious. I mean, look at *Principles of Conviviality* and - what was it, came out three months ago, *Perseverance*. Something like that."

"*Perseveration*." Thalia blinked at him, a bit startled. "You do read widely. And order widely, unless you have a very good library at home?"

Adam shrugged. "Bit of both." He watched her carefully. "You don't think someone like me reads things like that?"

"Given that last I heard Maurice complaining, he'd only sold three hundred copies, and knew where over a hundred of them were. I think we can say not a lot of people read that sort of thing. Good reviews, not exactly a great reach."

Adam snorted. "I'm not sure I'd say it's good. But it was interesting." He considered. "And not the sort of thing you write. Or wrote?"

"It's certainly not a sort of thing I can sell." She let out her breath in a frustrated puff, and tightened her fingers against his hand without apparently realising she was doing it. "Your uncle suggested I try something else. Nature writing. Children's stories. He doesn't think much of the editor for the magazine that gave me my last rejection. Skimps on the mulch, apparently."

Adam snorted, relaxing again. "Uncle Benjamin has extensive opinions about mulch, and I'm not going to argue with them. But he does have a point about people's consistencies, doesn't he?"

"Maybe he does." Thalia shrugged. "What I've been doing doesn't work. It's making me miserable. And worse than that. I mean, misery's a friend to writers and artists, the right sort of misery."

"I've always wondered about that. It seems an awful way to choose to live." Adam paused to choose his words exceedingly carefully here. "You and I don't have a choice about parts of our misery. But I wonder about people who stay somewhere like that, when they have a choice. Mentally, I mean."

Thalia furrowed her eyebrows, tilting her head as she watched him. "Some of them have reasons, too. Like..." Her voice hitched. "Like ours." As if she was still coming to terms with talking about it.

"Of course." Adam had thought about that, late into the night. "But you know the people like that better. Not all of them."

Thalia looked down at the floor. "Not all of them. Certainly not all the same way. Some people like to, it's like bragging, isn't it? How miserable they are, as if it's a race anyone would want to win."

Adam nodded. "It happens with veterans, too. I know for me, sometimes it's been justifying why I can't do anything worth doing anymore. But I admit, I..." He waved a hand. "It was good for me to come out here. More because it got me away from Mother and Father's expectations and disapproval."

"That's the thing, isn't it? I could go back to my parents, get them to marry me off to someone probably not awful. Take up being a society wife in Trellech or London or maybe somewhere else. And yet I won't. All the expectations and the disapproval, and I'm still stuck."

"Do you want any of that?" Adam shifted his hand, pulling hers a little closer to him, changing the angle. He hadn't quite meant to, but she looked up when he moved, with the little half-smile that reassured him.

"No. Only. I don't know what I do want. I thought I wanted to write proper short fiction. The sort of thing that gets published in literary magazines, that people talk about it."

Adam couldn't help smiling. "A small number of people, mostly in bohemian parties with good food, better drink, and a lot of smoke?" He waved his free hand. "They're not the only people who read."

"You mean look for something else." Thalia considered. "I know a couple of people who do that sort of thing. Not exactly children's stories. But a sense of wonder, of seeing what's around the next corner. I don't - " She ducked her chin suddenly, "I don't think I have that in me anymore."

"I know you do." It came out of him, certain, in a way that surprised Adam himself.

"You can't possibly." Thalia hadn't looked up, but she didn't pull her hand away.

"Remember where we are? We're sitting in someone else's sitting room, working up the nerve to go up a staircase in a house with a mystery. I know we're going to do that. I'm not sure I'm brave enough, but I know you are. You've been looking around that next corner since you got here."

She closed her eyes and he watched her face. It was a great iceberg calving off, the slow weight and power of a landslide, or a wave breaking and pulling back. It changed the landscape in startling ways. Her hand shifted urgently, until she was threading her fingers through his, her thumb brushing his palm. It tickled, and he didn't care.

They sat like that, with her barely breathing, as if time had stopped. Finally, after what felt like hours. She blinked and then squeezed his hand once. "You're here too."

"I am." It was a different kind of admission, not the momentous self-realisation she's just had. As if her image of herself had cracked open like an egg, revealing something entirely unexpected. He ducked his chin. "It's - I don't have words for it." He fumbled, and then added, "I'm not the writer here."

That made her laugh, a little half-hysterical giggle, but it also made her smile after that. Adam liked her smile, the more he got to see it. When she was unguarded, it had charm to it and a deep heart.

"You have more experience with planning. And probably with birds."

"Domesticated birds." Her smile was, in fact, a bit contagious. "Give me a chicken, a duck, a quail. I can muddle through with pheasants."

She gestured back toward the house. "What do we

think, then?" He held up his hand, and she said, "Let me lay it out."

"I was going to say. I want to hear what you think." Adam swallowed. "Tea, first? Fortification."

Finally, she let go of his hand, long enough to reach for the flask and bring it to where she could drink some. After he did the same from his own, she set it back down, and then held out her hand again. This time it was deliberate, choosing.

"This isn't just about tonight, is it?" Adam glanced at her hand, and then back up at her face. Her hair was coming down in a few wisps from the bun at the back of her head. There was something unguarded and open now that she'd let him in. Like he was seeing all the walls she'd lived inside from the other side. Everything in order, on the surface, full of bright light and flowers, and with a sense of everything that might lurk tucked away neatly into cupboards and desk drawers.

"Not unless you want it to be just about tonight." Thalia hesitated. "Cart in front of the horse, I suppose? But I think I'd feel better knowing that we're going to keep whatever this is. That we're not just here because of what's in that house."

"More later, then." Adam agreed. "One complexity at a time. That's something they teach us at Snap. Sometimes you really do have half a dozen emergencies at once. A flood, a leak in a roof, a calf coming the wrong way round, something wrong with your feed, all that. But most of the time, some of those can wait, just a little."

Thalia snorted. "Triage." She didn't sound bitter about it now, though, or like it had cut her in passing.

"You brought the books. You said you'd read a fair bit."

"There's a lot of lore about birds, and I don't know

what's true. Only. There was a story about a mistress of birds, using them like bits of materia, to control the magic." She let out a puff of breath. "There's lore about cuckoos. That they bring the spring, besides the part about laying eggs in other birds' nests."

Adam thought about that slowly, rolling it around in his mind. "Hilaria said her nails haven't grown. The plants around here, they don't show the season properly. Nothing that blooms and fades, just the greenery and the roses."

"The apples." Thalia offered it cautiously. "If there's a radius of effect. I don't remember how you measure that sort of thing, not without looking it up, or consulting someone? But I remember there are magical effects that get weaker as they go out. Some of the protections on Schola are like that."

"So if the effect begins here..." Adam thought about the geography. "There's not much west of here, as you go up onto the moor. Nothing where it would show. Or north. Just down to the east and the orchards."

"Unless it went quite far, your orchards are the only place where it shows. And your uncle likes the orchards, but he's not very fussed about them. So long as there's cider, eventually. Not like a farmer relying on a crop to be harvested for sale would be."

"It would explain why they're slower to ripen. I think you might be on to something." Adam nodded. "What do we do about it?"

Thalia closed her eyes, as if girding herself to go over the top. It was that certainty, twined with fatalism, that he'd seen so many times before. "We open up the cage and let it go."

CHAPTER 33
MONDAY EVENING

Thalia said the words, and they rolled around in her head, like marbles coming to rest, glinting with colour and shine. Open the cage and let the cuckoo go. If it was actually a cuckoo. For all they knew, it was some sort of strange creature of the Fatae, just shaped like a bird. Something that shouldn't be here, certainly shouldn't be captive here, not since the Pact.

Adam blinked at her several times. "You're sure."

She hadn't been until she said it, but Thalia nodded. "I am." That felt strange to say, but right, as if she'd hit on the proper wish in a story, the one that fixed everything at the end.

"I'm not saying no." Adam hesitated. "But tell me, what am I saying yes to?" He hesitated, then squeezed her hand again. "Please?"

It was the 'please' that got her, the one word, the way he was trusting her. Somehow, someone trusted her to make a decision. But then, he knew what that cost was. More than most people, he knew what he was asking. To be honest, people hadn't put much weight on her, not since she'd broken down into pieces. She'd fluttered along, never quite touching the ground. If you flew and flew, they couldn't put more weight on your shoulders. It made her think of the captive bird, how it couldn't fly now, maybe not ever again.

The realisation, the image, had her pulling her hand away, scrambling for a stub of pencil and a scrap of paper. She managed to write down the notion before she lost it. Thalia made a few notes, read them, added another, about the distance to be travelled, then she tucked the paper safely into the cover of her journal. "Story idea."

Adam blinked again, then smiled, shyly. "Something I said?"

Thalia considered him, cocking her head. "Something you are. That's even better." The words, or maybe her tone, made him flush and look pleased with himself. As if there were some flower blooming, promising fruit to come, if that was the metaphor she wanted. She swallowed. "What you're saying yes to...."

He leaned forward. "I'm not arguing, not really. Just. We need to know we're doing the same. Preferably, for the same reason."

The pitch of his voice, the hint of hope in it, that they had the same reason, amused her. "Alright. We have a theory that - somehow, time is bound up here. Arguably, because sometime in the unspecified past, my great-aunt kept a cuckoo, or something of the kind."

"Assuming it's not some avian member of the Fatae, or some illusion, or I don't know what else."

"It is bird shaped and in a cage. We are going to treat it like a bird. It can sort out its own metaphor." Thalia found she was rather insistent about this point. If they went too far down the rabbit hole of whether it was or was not actually a bird, they'd never do anything.

"Fair enough. How do we do that?"

Thalia considered. "There's a window. The cage was, I think, on wheels. We could wheel it over to the window, pull the curtains around it to shape it, so it doesn't fly into the room, and let it go?"

"Into the storm?" There was a gust of wind rattling the windows.

Thalia let out a breath. "We have to try. And I don't think." She hesitated. "I haven't trusted my intuition, not really, since - since back then. But I think if I don't now, I'm never going to."

Adam shifted, taking her hand again, and looking her straight on. He didn't do that terribly often, she'd noticed, but now he just watched her. "All right. I can - there are some tricks I know. Hardening the air. It's handy with domesticated birds. Or sheep. Sheep are exceptionally stupid sometimes. They'll put a leg or a head through anything. I don't think I can force it out of the cage, but I can make sure it doesn't get stuck in the room, panicked."

"All right. So. I open the door. The bird stares at us." That seemed like it needed to go on the list of things that would happen. "Do we have gloves, maybe, if it tries to peck? I don't know how moving the cage might go."

"There should be gardening gloves or something of the kind. I've got a thin leather pair. A good thick tea towel would do, honestly. Barring it turning into a raptor."

Thalia shivered at that. She'd been close to falcons a few times, and even the smaller of the type had terrifying talons. "Please, no." She nods. "We'll look for gardening gloves by the kitchen door, then. All right." She considered.

"Open the door to the room. Open the window next. Move the cage, and you do your thing with the air. And then..."

Adam nodded. "I don't think we can plan past that point. Open the cage, though."

There was silence, both of them sitting with what could happen, what might happen. "Does everything plunge into November, immediately? Does it - does it hurt Great-Aunt Avis?" Thalia frowned. "Do we have a right?"

Adam hesitated. "She left you here. She wanted someone here. And she went away. She chose to. Do you think it trapped her, somehow? One of those twists of magic, or whatever it is?"

Thalia closed her eyes, thinking. "I -" She stopped. "You might be right. She had all sorts of choices. Maybe she couldn't let it go, but she could let someone else be here who could? It's hard to think around the - stagnation here?"

"Stasis. Hibernation. Estivation. Only it's always summer, not winter."

Thalia shivered. "Ugh. All right. Assuming it's actually a bird, it has a right to make its own choice. If it's a bird-shaped something else, that doesn't change. We open the cage and the window and we see what happens. If this does hurt Great-Aunt Avis, she had some hand in it. She's been alive a very long time, and also it's just wrong. Whatever's going on. I don't exactly feel wonderful about this analysis, but it's still better than how I made decisions for at least three years, so I suppose that's what we're going with?"

It came out of her in a rush, all the things she'd thought and never put together into words, especially to anyone else. Even Hilaria. Adam gaped at her, then he smiled, another of those illuminating smiles. "That's honest, isn't it?" He let out a long sigh. "I don't think I know how to make decisions either. Not like I used to."

"And this?" Thalia leaned forward, now a bit hopeful.

"I think we go and do this. Thinking about it's not going to change anything for the better. What we have to go on is wisps of lore and our own feelings, and we can't be logical about either of those. So, we need gloves, the keys. Whatever we want to bring back to the house."

Thalia turned, dropping his hand to pack up the remains of the sandwiches, tucking everything into her bag. When she looked up, he was standing, and he offered her his hand. "We'll do it together, whatever we do. Does that help?"

She considered, really thinking through it. "It does. And then there will be an after." She was beginning to think she might like peering around the corner at what came after, too. She stood, and then together they went out the door, carefully turning out the light before going back across the courtyard in an increasingly driving rain, to the side door.

There, Adam did spot a pair of gardening gloves, while Thalia went into the kitchen to find the extra key set and another lantern. Finally, there was no way to put it off. Either they were going to do this thing, or they weren't.

They stood in the front hall for a moment. "The storm's quieting down a bit." he said. "And it's only just dusk. If we're going to do this..."

Thalia nodded, and they carefully climbed the stairs, each of them claiming their own spot on the railing for steadiness. Up one flight, then the second, until they were standing outside the room. Thalia held the keys out, her hand shaking. "Do I?"

"You. It's your great-aunt's house. I'll be - I'll be right behind you."

Thalia took a breath, and then one more just in case. She forced herself to put one foot in front of the other, and to fit the key into the lock. She could have sworn she heard something, but she couldn't make out the sound. She twisted her hand and felt the lock give just before the door swung open. Automatically, she reached for the charm light switch, and they turned on, despite everything. It set the room alight, everything visible.

She could see the great cage, painted a pale and incongruous green, sitting in the middle of the floor. There were wheels on it, thankfully, and what looked like handles. She managed to get a good look at them before she was transfixed by the bird. It was perched, facing her, as if it had known they were coming.

Before she could panic and flee, there was a hand on her back, between her shoulders. Adam spoke up from just behind her. "We'd like to help."

The bird didn't move, but something in the repressive, cloaking, lurking feel of the room shifted the smallest bit. Thalia sucked in a breath, and then forced herself to take a step and another, until she was a foot from the cage. She could feel Adam brush by her until he opened the window.

"You've been here a very long time, haven't you?" Talking directly to the bird made no sense at all, and every bit of sense. "We're going to open your cage and give you the choice. It's windy out there, and raining."

It let out the two pitches, hoo-hoo, dropping down the third musically, cocked its head, and did it again. That awful feeling, the pressure of the Silence, though, that wasn't there. It was an ordinarily creepy room, if that were the right way to put it, full of shadows and wrongness, but with enough space they could think and move.

Thalia shrugged the gloves on, and then, when she was sure Adam had the window, carefully pushed the cage closer, hearing it squeak as it rolled across the wood floor. It took a moment to get any momentum, to fight against inertia. But she was aiming for Adam. There he was, he was waiting for her.

Somehow, amazingly, that gave her enough to keep moving. Almost before she knew it, they were there. Adam had got the window open and had done something that made it feel like the cage bumped up against a rubberised cushion. Thalia glanced at him, but didn't want to take her focus off the bird.

Adam hesitated, then reached carefully, slowly, as if he were pushing through thick jelly, and then managed to unlatch the cage and pull the door open toward him.

Nothing happened. Thalia could hear her heart beat, once, twice, a dozen times. Then, the bird hopped once, along the perch, to one closer to the door. Thalia didn't move, she could barely breathe. Adam didn't shift at all, though he'd drawn back his hand.

The bird hopped again, the long tail arching up to counterbalance. Then one more hop, before it leapt out of the cage, beat its wings twice, and zoomed out of the window. Its wings spread out, the magic of the flight taking Thalia's words away.

She blinked, and it was as if they were in a different room. Nothing had changed visibly, but everything had. Gravity felt different, light felt different. It was like Newton must have felt, in all his complex research, or one of the other great scientists.

CHAPTER 34
MONDAY EVENING

A dam could see the cuckoo swooping once or twice, and then darting off. Southward, which he supposed made some degree of sense. He blinked after it, trying and failing to get his eyes to focus properly. Once he was well and truly sure the bird was gone, he closed the window carefully. It clunked slightly at the bottom, a sound he felt more than heard.

Adam hesitated, thinking about locking it, but it had been unlocked, hadn't it? And it was a second floor window, with no one around. He didn't trust himself to reach that far, or even to move that much.

It left them alone, together, in a room that now felt hollowed out. Adam felt himself leaning heavily on the wall next to the window and twisted to peer at Thalia. He felt hollow much of the time, and especially right now. He was sure, looking at her, Thalia did too.

It took all his effort, but he pushed away from the wall, towards her. She was still standing with her hands resting on the heavy metal curves of the cage, as if she didn't know how to let go. Her feet were braced slightly apart. He was sure her knees were bent just a little.

Adam walked toward her, not sure his legs would obey him. He'd left his stick downstairs. Thalia, though, looked worse off. He glanced out the window. "The rain's stopped. Let's go outside."

She blinked at him, as if she couldn't focus, and he held out a hand to her. "Here we go. Can you open your fingers?" He went finger by finger, talking her through it. It sounded like nonsense to him, it did when other people tried. And yet, it seemed to help her. Giving her something to do, specific steps, maybe. Maybe that was why the Gospatricks had taught him that way.

All of a sudden, he was holding both of her hands and she was staring at him. Thalia seemed to be seeing him for the first time, as she took a step forward and hesitated, looking for something specific. Adam wasn't at all sure what she wanted, to touch him, to take his arm, but he shifted, and then she was hugging him. Holding onto him, as well, as if he were the trellis and she were the rose.

"Hey." It wasn't unpleasant, having someone this close. He'd thought it would be. He could barely stand people near him. Instead, she was warm, and she was trusting he'd be there, and he refused to let her down. He'd done that enough, over and over. Perhaps this time, he might do something different.

They stood like that for what seemed like hours before he cleared his throat. "Outside? I'd like some fresh air."

"Oh. Oh. Pardon." She swallowed, looking up at him, then finally she released him, shifting her hand to take his arm. They weren't much - both of them were walking unsteadily. Drunkenly, except that it had been ages, a decade and more, since he'd been able to drink to drunkenness. He suspected the same thing for her, honestly. The lights were still on, though. The house hadn't seemed to change. Down one flight of stairs, then down the next. At the bottom, outside the kitchen, Thalia gestured at the door. "There are bottles of cider."

"More sandwiches and cider?" She nodded and gestured for him to follow her into the kitchen. It felt like he was invading, but he certainly didn't want to be standing alone in the hallway. She brought out the bread again. Then she gathered up the mustard and ham and cheese from the keep-cold box, making the sandwiches with brisk move-ments. Or at least, they were brisk until she stopped, after spreading the mustard, and leaned on the counter.

"Are you all right?" It sounded feeble. Of course they weren't all right. Neither of them had been all right for a long time. And tonight, well, that was new and different, but that didn't make it better.

She lifted her chin, as if she were going to stubborn through it. The way he did. And then she ducked her head again, leaning harder on the counter.

Adam froze, not sure what to do. He wasn't at all sure what was all right to do, for one. And then he wasn't sure he was up for doing anything. His legs felt wooden again, locked in place. He closed his eyes, trying not to stumble over the words, "I'm not."

She didn't move, at least not that he could hear. And he thought he'd be able to hear her, on a hardwood floor, this close. The way he could hear the clock ticking at the far end of the room, and the wind against the shutters.

Adam tried again. Words were what he could offer. "Here's what I think. We give ourselves as much time as we need to get our hands and our knees working. We take those sandwiches and some cider outside. We sit, and we eat, and we stop. No one expects us anywhere. No one will be coming here, not until tomorrow. And then. I'll sleep where you like. Down here. Hilaria's room." He hesitated and tried cautiously for a joke. "Well. Not on the second floor."

That did get a noise out of her, a stifled gasp, then a sucked in breath and an uneven, "No. Wouldn't make you."

"Right. Take your time. I'd help, but pretty sure a knife in my hands wouldn't do much good."

As he managed to get his eyes open and more or less focusing again, he saw her nod. "Sandwiches. Right. Mustard. Cheese. Ham. There might be apples on the table?" She moved slowly, as if through a fog, but she picked up the cheese, laying it out.

Adam glanced at the table, and made himself take one step, then a second, until he could reach the apples. They were a yellowish green, well-ripened, and he thought they might be Lucomb's Pine. Not from his uncle's orchard, and not from anywhere closer, either. They ripened in October, but stored well until sometime in February. It must have come from the market or the grocer. He gathered up two, and then folded them into a linen napkin to take outside.

By the time he'd managed that, Thalia had done the same with the sandwiches, tucking them into a basket. She trailed her hand along the counter, as if wanting to make sure of the support, as she walked to the far end of the kitchen. She came back with two bottles, then found a bottle opener.

Finally, they made it back out into the hallway, then out to the front door. Thalia hesitated, then grabbed a cloak and what looked like a wool blanket from the bench by the door. Adam stepped outside to give her space, and then stopped.

It felt like it had his last spring at Snap. He'd had lambing duty, but he'd been sent back off to bed at three in the morning, after the last of the ewes had settled down. The night had been cool, with a crispness he associated with fall more than spring, but the sky above him had been glorious. It was black, dotted with stars that shone and danced, the arch of the Milky Way threading through it. It had been a night where everything was possible. He'd helped a lamb be born, and he'd been treated like a man who knew his worth. And then he'd been set free to take joy in the stars and the fields and everything in between.

This felt like that. Adam hadn't expected that at all. Nothing was different about the landscape. The land had not shifted into late autumn. The trees he could see had leaves, though admittedly, anything deciduous remotely near the house was shrouded in mist. It wasn't as if he'd see the colours at night, anyway.

The sky above reminded him of the proper season, and he wondered, all of a sudden, if that had been different here, too. If even the stars had appeared to slow and stand still. It seemed unlikely. Perhaps people just never looked up, or never thought about it. That was a more typical sort of twist of magic. Not noticing held up a lot of things in the world.

Thalia made her way carefully over to the garden wall, as if feeling the ground before she moved her weight. She sat, then twisted, swinging her legs over to the far side, with the house behind her, looking down the fields toward his uncle's orchard. She set the basket down next to her, and then worked on unfolding the cloak and the blanket, twisting to offer it to him, and peer up at the house.

Adam took a long look at it and then copied her movements on the other side of the basket. He let his legs hang over the edge, tucking the blanket around him as she settled the cloak. "A bit of air," he agreed. It seemed banal to say, but he needed this space, this quiet.

She didn't press him. That was what he found most refreshing about her, most comfortable. She chattered, or at least she could, but she also knew when it was too much. He wondered, now, what was going on in her head. But he was glad to accept a sandwich, a bottle, and not rush the moment when they had to make any other decisions.

It was a good while later when she finally spoke. Ten minutes, fifteen. He'd heard three different owls, a few other birds, the rustle of something in the underbrush at the edge of the field by the drive. The birds were new, from what she'd said, and he could hear them very clearly now. "Did we do the right thing?"

Adam gestured. "I think we did. It feels different. Open. I don't know what changed, maybe we won't ever know. But it's different."

She nodded and looked off into the distance again. "What do we do now?"

Adam felt his breath catch. "When we're ready, we go back, and we settle ourselves for the night. And we face the morning when we get there."

Thalia went quiet again, finishing her sandwich. "You meant it about the couch?"

"You don't want to be alone either, then?" He hadn't quite meant to say that, it had slipped out before he could stop himself.

"No." She said so immediately, then she ducked her chin. "I - what's all right with you?"

"The sofa. I could sit up in your bedroom, if you wanted. I don't expect I'll sleep much."

She considered that. "Normally, I'd say the same.

Tonight? I don't know. It - I feel heavy now. Like everything is effort. More than - well. More than usual."

"You told me some difficult things. We did something I couldn't have imagined, even this morning. There's some reason to be tired." Adam tried to keep his tone light, but she blinked at him.

"You're not what I expected." She glanced down so she could pick up the bottle and drain it. "You let me do things."

Adam shrugged. "You seem quite competent at doing things, honestly. On the whole. And we don't have the sort of whatever, where I have any right to tell you what to do."

Thalia opened her mouth, then closed it, and nodded sharply. "No. We don't." In someone else, it might have been cutting, pushing him away. Here, he wondered what she was thinking. It felt like she needed the space, to think, to get her balance back. He could give her that.

"I'm ready when you are. Your room, build up the fire, put the back of the chair under the door to keep it closed, and hole up for the night."

Thalia let out a long slow breath, as if she were measuring it out, then she nodded, and swivelled around to climb down from the wall.

CHAPTER 35
TUESDAY

When Thalia woke, it was morning. Visibly morning. She could see the sunlight pouring in the window, and she heard annoyingly cheerful birds. That brought her awake immediately, with a start, but it wasn't a cuckoo. Something small and chirping.

Her movement was stalled by weight on top of the blankets, and then Adam jerked awake. He didn't quite hit her in the nose with his elbow, but it was a near thing. She went quiet and small, curling up again on her side and hoping that helped.

Something in her movement caught his attention, and Thalia saw him take a breath, then another, before he managed words. "Pardon. I should..."

Thalia shook her head. "Stay. I mean." She nodded toward the door, which still had the back of the desk chair wedged under it, to prevent the door opening. It took her a moment to find more words. "We should figure out what we're doing."

Adam took another breath and let it out, to steady himself, then he shifted to lean on one elbow, looking at her. She couldn't make sense of it, the way he was looking, the quality of it. She certainly didn't have words for it. Some writer she was. But there was openness, there. Kindness and gentleness, certainly. But it wasn't the sort of condescending kindness she'd seen in far too many people. Oh, poor girl, had a hard time, unspecified. Oh, she lost her brother, well, that's a shame. He was always the golden child.

This was something curious, something that was paying attention to her, in specific. Then he caught himself doing it, and asked, "How are you?"

"Shouldn't I ask you that?" Thalia pushed up on an elbow. "I had an odd dream or two. And..." She hesitated. "I liked you being there." It slipped out before she had time to guard herself.

"You did?" Adam looked down, away from them, then back at her. "I'm glad you wanted me to stay." They hadn't talked much last night. Thalia had drifted off to the sound of his voice, reading aloud quietly from an elderly translation of Homer's *Odyssey* she'd had lying around.

The bookmark had been in just where Odysseus bested the suitors, in a feat of strength and surety. Penelope had kept herself far safer than Thalia ever had, in so many ways, but she'd been running to the end of her resources by herself. And Odysseus, well, he had had a long and many-turning path to find his way home.

Thalia nodded. "It's..." She gestured at where he'd put the book down, properly closed with a bookmark in, which was more than she managed a good third of the time. "I woke up in the night, just - lying here." Lying there, listening to him breathe, had been incredibly soothing. Knowing she wasn't alone. However short a time that lasted. It was as comfortable as having Hilaria in bed with her. Not just the way she'd been with her very rare lovers. All two of them.

Adam just kept watching her, not saying anything. Thalia took a breath. "The house feels different. The same scope of change as Odysseus coming home."

He didn't move. It could have been uncomfortable, that stillness, but instead it was like he was letting her see him, not covering anything. "What does that mean?"

"I - well. I don't know. I suppose I should write to my parents, see if anything changed." She shivered once. "I hope it didn't mean bad things for Great-Aunt Avis. Even if we did a right thing too."

"I would like very much for her to explain what was going on. I don't know if I'm going to get that wish, but if you find a psammead, that's mine."

Thalia blinked up at him. "You read it?" She'd thought he'd brushed off the childhood book.

"Uncle Benjamin had a copy. It does make very good reading at three in the morning. Everything works out. I like that part." Adam shrugged. "I like mystery novels for the same reason. They bring order into the world? But I can't always deal with the murders or the people who are suspected and all that."

Thalia was considering that, and then heard the journal on her desk make a noise. It made Adam jump, certainly, wheeling around to peer at it. It wasn't anything like a bird, only it had the same high pitch, but more like a bell.

"Your journal? May I?" He was certainly closer. And she'd have an awkward time wriggling out of bed if he didn't move. When she nodded, he pushed himself upright carefully, as if making sure his head and balance had time to catch up. Then he stood, before turning to reach and offer her the dressing gown draped over the end of the bedframe.

Once she had the journal in her hands, she thumbed through to the current page, and then frowned at it. There were half a dozen messages from her parents that had come in last night and this morning, they'd slept through them, somehow. The actual content was straightforward, however. "Great-Aunt Avis is insisting on coming home. Sometime..." She looked down at the times. "Tomorrow, I guess. They have to get over the Channel."

Adam rocked back slightly, then settled on the end of the bed. "So what do we do?"

Thalia swallowed. "I don't much want to be alone. I suppose. I suppose we should go through the house. And see if there's any damage near the storm? Check with your uncle? Be responsible adults. And I suppose Bessy and Mrs Harley will be back sometime today." She brought her hand to her mouth. "I'll have to figure out what to tell them."

"One thing at a time." Adam considered. "Look, let's do a check through the house. It's only about half nine. Then we can wash up, and see about some breakfast, walk through the grounds, down through the orchard, and back by Uncle Benjamin's. I can pick up some clothes and things, and stay up here another night if you like. If you think the housekeeper won't throw a fit."

Thalia grimaced. She could easily imagine the expression. Hilaria gone, and a young man here instead. On the other hand, did she care what the housekeeper thought? Quite possibly not. "Are we up for that much walking?" she asked. It was we, after all. She wasn't sure about her own knees. Or her ankles.

Adam snorted, amused. "Well. Start with the house." He then stood and said, "That first?"

Thalia nodded, and when she had space to stand, she stuck her feet into her slippers, pulling the dressing gown around her. Adam had slept in shirtsleeves and trousers. She'd shrugged off her dress to her cami-bloomers, while he had turned his back. She tugged the dressing gown a little closer. They did a circuit of the downstairs first, and all was as it should be. Then the first floor, including peering into Great-Aunt Avis's rooms from the door. Nothing appeared to have changed. Finally, they checked the second floor, leaving the room where the cuckoo had been for last.

Nothing had moved since they'd been there. The window was still closed; the cage was still by the window. Without talking to each other, they circled back to the kitchen. Thalia made up eggs and toast, with Adam offering a few comments so they came out rather less overcooked than usual. They ate in silence at the kitchen table. "What do we do now?"

"Wash up, and see where our feet take us?" Adam offered it again. Thalia nodded. An hour later, they were setting out down the fields, after making sure the storm hadn't done any damage to the greenhouse in the back or any other buildings. The orchard had had a few branches break off, but not too many, and not too much damage to the apples. They did look more like ripening than they had last time Thalia had been there a few days ago, but it could be a trick of the light.

Adam's uncle had welcomed them in. While Adam was packing up a bag to bring up, he looked Thalia up and down. "All well, then?" She couldn't tell if he was approving or warning her off. She wasn't sure if he knew himself, honestly.

"Adam was a great help last night. And I'm glad of the

company, if you can manage for a day? I gather my great-aunt wants to come home, so I don't know beyond that."

Benjamin waved a hand. "I'm getting around better. Still need him to see to the apples, mind. But we won't be doing that today or tomorrow, most like. There're trees down on a couple of roads need to be cleared first."

By three, they were back up at the house. Mrs Harley must have seen them coming, because she opened the door for them.

"Mrs Harley, I hope your tooth is better? And that Bessy - oh, hello, Bessy. You got the note that Great-Aunt Avis wants to come home?" The housekeeper nodded, but Thalia barrelled on. If she stopped now, she'd trip over her own words. "This is Adam. He stayed last night to help make sure everything was sorted. Is it all right if he stays up here tonight? Hilaria had to go back to London, poor thing. Can he have her room? I can make up the bed. You must both be busy getting things cleared after the storm."

Five minutes later, they were in Hilaria's former room, and Adam was helping her change the sheets. With the door closed. Once they had the bed sorted, Adam sat on it, and Thalia joined him. "You handled that well." Adam sounded amused. Then she felt a brush of fingers on hers. "Look, can we talk?"

"I had to get through it, or I'd - well. But we're good now. I mean, supper, and then we can read in the library or something. They won't come up here? I don't think? Though I'm sure Mrs Harley must have seen upstairs by now."

"She didn't say anything." Adam considered. "Well. Housekeepers. She might to your great-aunt. And about you being scandalous."

"We're not, though. Are we?" Thalia wasn't sure.

"Alone in a room with a man you're not at least betrothed to? Wouldn't your parents have words?" Adam sounded so desperately unsure. Thalia squeezed his hands.

"My parents have no idea what I get up to, about that or anything else. I've - a couple of men, not more than a couple of nights. It was after the War and they didn't..." She shrugged. "Neither of them fought. They were safe behind the lines. And they didn't understand why startling me was a bad idea. For them, as well as me. You'd think self-preservation would have been an incentive."

She didn't come out and say what had happened, but she watched the realisation of what must have happened dawn on his face. "Knee them, did you?"

"Entirely accidentally. They woke me up the wrong way. Well, one of the wrong ways, there are quite a few. Turns out."

Adam chortled softly. He muffled his mouth with his other hand, but she could hear him, and then see how his eyes crinkled all the way. "You didn't. Goodness. Who, do I know them?"

"I don't know who you know." Thalia considered. "Neptune Collins - isn't that an uneuphonious name? Is that the word I want? And James Hazel."

"I know Hazel. Couldn't have happened to a better man. He's got a reputation. However did you end up with him?"

It did rather reflect on her taste. "Someone brought him to a party. He was charming. I was all nerves, and - I wanted to see if I could do the thing, you know? I wanted to know if I'd lost that too."

"Oh." Adam hesitated. "And?"

Thalia let out a long breath. "Look, are we having that conversation as friends who understand each other enough, or - um. With more specific purpose behind it?"

Adam was quiet for a good minute. "It's not you, but I need to think about it some. Could we - it's awkward. Could we talk about it after supper? When they've gone to bed?"

Thalia nodded. It was a sensible enough request. And honestly, she wasn't sure what she thought either.

CHAPTER 36
TUESDAY EVENING

There was supper. Then there was reading in the library, as Mrs Harley and Bessy finished up for the night. Curiously, Mrs Harley had warmed a bit to Adam himself, though he was sure she must have known the rumours from the village. Mind, Adam had been careful to compliment the cooking. Not that that was a challenge. The food was excellent, a bit of chicken and roast vegetables, with spoonfuls of gravy.

If she'd noticed anything different about the house, she wasn't saying anything. She wasn't even peering disapprovingly in the corners, like Adam's mother would have. It wasn't as if they could change anything now, and they weren't going to get answers until Great-Aunt Avis came home, if then.

It left Adam more time to think than he'd entirely wanted. He kept circling around two very clear points, and he wasn't at all sure how to explain the one without breaking off any chance at the other. Finally, the house was quiet for the night and they retreated upstairs. "My room or yours?" he asked, pausing with his hand on his doorknob.

"Mine." Thalia gestured. "The fireplace draws better. Change or - um. Whatever you think makes sense?"

Adam did change into pyjamas and his dressing gown. He left the walking stick, since he knew he could manage from here to there well enough. When he knocked on her door five minutes later, Thalia called out, "Come in?" She was settled on the sofa, a blanket over her lap, feet sticking out from under the hem in fuzzy slippers. Her hair was in a braid down her back, loosening around her face.

"Hey." He glanced over at her. "Where would you like me to sit?"

She blinked up at him. "Here? It's nice and warm. Not too warm? Does that bother you like it bothers me? It feels like my skin gets all wrong. Itchy and tight." Thalia shivered, then, and stopped talking abruptly.

"Hey." Adam tried it again. "We're just talking, all right? Together. Being awkward about it together."

That got a smile from her, as he'd hoped. "I think I can manage awkward." She looked away from him, off to the fire. He had to admit that was a good reason to sit here. The fire meant they had somewhere to focus besides each other. "I'm not entirely sure where to start. It's like either end of a seesaw. All one way or the other, very little middle."

Thalia smiled, suddenly relaxing. "Oh. You too?" She shifted then, and after a moment, offered her hand, palm up. He looked down at it, seeing the callouses on her fingers from writing, from other things too, and he set his hand in hers.

"Me too." Adam let out a long breath. "I feel quiet with you." That part, he was utterly clear on. "I don't feel I'm a failure."

Thalia opened her mouth, then closed it, before she squeezed his hand. "You feel like you are a lot?"

He shrugged. "Look at my life. No work, my family can't stand me around, I mope, I sleep far too late, I can't even harvest apples." He tried to make the last into something of a joke, and it fell flat.

Thalia considered. "And I write things no one wants to read. Or at least, no one wants to buy for other people to read. I'm not married, I'm not doing the things women are supposed to do. Any of them. And frankly..." She stopped, as if she were admitting something she'd never admitted out loud before. "I'm not sure I want children."

Adam was caught by that. "Is that why you won't go back to your parents? One of the reasons, I mean. You clearly have a list."

The way he put it made her smile. And oh, Adam loved that part. He twisted a little, then hesitated. "May I?" He gestured with his other hand, his left. She nodded, unsure what he was going to do. When he reached to brush a bit of hair back behind her ear, she looked at him, wide-eyed. He asked again, "May I?" before leaning in slowly.

He could feel his body gathering itself. Not the way it had before the War, before all the signals went wrong. He'd felt this a few times before. The moments when his own hand and some fragment of his imagination were enough to work him up to a proper sort of arousal, not just a mechanical release. He didn't care, and he leaned in to kiss her. Gently, at first. He barely remembered how this went.

By the time he pulled back, he was breathing shallowly, trying to get his bearings. She shifted, settling a hand on his shoulder. She must have felt something there, the way he was quivering. Or perhaps, more obviously, the way he had his eyes closed. "Hey." She said it back to him, gently, and then offered. "Have a shoulder?"

She was shorter than he was, but more of his height

was in his legs. Sitting, it didn't feel overwhelming to lean against her, to feel the strength of her shoulders and arms. More than he'd expected, honestly, in her tidy frocks. He didn't lean against her hard, just enough to not feel so alone.

When he'd finally relaxed again, he felt her shift slightly. "That happen a lot?"

He shrugged his other shoulder, trusting she'd get the sense of it. "I wasn't sure." Adam grimaced. "That was the other thing. I don't know what I'm good for. When it comes to - bed things."

"Well, clearly, we're not going to win any prizes for sleeping. Though we did all right last night?" She was more tentative about that.

"I woke up for a bit. Around two, maybe. You?"

"Around four. Apparently, we were courteously leaving three in the morning for each other?" The thought clearly amused her, enough that she laughed softly.

Adam felt himself smile. "Well. All right. Do we want to try that again tonight?"

"The sleeping? Or the kissing?" She squeezed his hand again. "Both? I'd like both."

"Both." Adam let out a long breath. "Do you feel like that? When it's too much, and your body won't even let you have that much?"

Thalia was quiet for a good minute, both of them watching the fire. "My body's different from yours. That way, as well as others? But yeah. I feel a rush of something, and then it's a one in two chance that things don't go well. And I don't want to be with someone who doesn't care again."

"Oh." The realisation of what she meant came out of

286

him in a rush. "Can I hit them on the nose? Or in more sensitive parts? Both of them?"

There was a quivering stillness, then she murmured. "That's how I know it's one in two. James Hazel didn't care much about what I was feeling. He didn't stop to ask, you know? Thought I was overwhelmed by his manly whatever."

"I hope you left bruises." Adam grumbled, feeling very fierce now. It was protective, certainly, though Thalia was clearly quite capable of taking care of herself in a number of situations. But he didn't like the idea of her being in that position. His mind skittered off to other thoughts about positions, then. He tried to bring himself back. "I don't feel I'm much of a man, honestly."

He wasn't sure what he'd expected her to do with that. She twisted so she could look at him, reaching first to cup his cheek and encourage him to meet her gaze. "May I touch you?"

She didn't say where, but it didn't change his answer. "Yes." Then he braced himself, for whatever was coming next, the way he braced himself to stand, to go down a step, to walk on rough ground.

Thalia gave him a few breaths to gather himself. She didn't rush him. But then she dropped her hand, drawing it down the centre of his body like a dance. Like she was crafting some illusion with her fingers, before she brought it to rest just there. Where she could feel his wanting, as complicated as it was, undeniably there. She didn't dive into teasing, just held her hand there, a firm pressure that didn't shift.

"What makes a man?" She let out a long breath. "If you couldn't, here." Thalia didn't move her hand, but he knew exactly what she meant. "You have hands. A mouth. A mind. I like your mind. We can work the rest out in time. I think, anyway."

Adam closed his eyes, wanting to float here forever. It was warm, it was soft, nothing hurt, and there was an incredible intimacy of letting her be so close. Knowing she was. They sat like that, tight together, for what seemed like ages.

He didn't realise he hadn't spoken until she cleared her throat. "What do you dream of? Alone?"

"Fantasies, you mean?" Adam turned his free hand palm up. "Besides the obvious?"

"A body that does what you tell it, a reliable amount of the time? A mind that doesn't get caught and confused and tangled up on the small stupid things?" There was a shift of her shoulders. "Take that as a given, you."

It made him smile again. Not to have to explain it was such a relief. Oh, he was sure they had differences in what they felt, how it took them. But to have it be an orchard they both knew, scars and downed branches and all.

"The simple one? Being able to take time. To pause, and just - like this. Being. No one's given me that, in, well. When I was younger, I was all hasty. Since, well. Before." He considered. "That's not much of a fantasy, no. I'm not given much to telling stories about it, exactly, but the idea of being someone else, different. That appeals. Maybe I'd like to try that out, with someone good at stories."

"Huh." She made a quiet noise, chewing on it. Her hand hadn't shifted. He liked the steadiness more than he could say. "I liked - before - the physicality of it. I don't know if I would now, the sort of thing that leaves you breathless and worn down to nothing."

"We've both been there far too often to seek it out." he agreed. "But touch, perhaps? Oils or scents or whatever?"

"Is that something you know about?" Her voice had a note now, a little spark of curiosity she couldn't repress. Was choosing not to, with him.

"Snap teaches about all things made from what we harvest. Not fussy alchemy, but good, honest apothecary and stillroom work. I'm not sure I'd trust myself with some of it, hot oils and waxes, but I might find a way."

"You know what's good, though." Something in what he'd said had given that note of interest a solid anchor. "I - positions are complicated, aren't they? When you don't trust your knees."

"Or your wrists, or your breath, or your anything." he agreed. "But we can lie down, see how we go with it. Not tonight, though?" He made it a question.

"Not for that. I mean. This house. And who knows about Great-Aunt Avis. But." She let out a breath. "My flat's got someone in it. But you're welcome when we've sorted that out. Wherever I'm living."

Adam nodded slowly. "There's a lot to sort there. But." This felt like the huge thing. Larger than opening the window to the world last night. It was as if the stars were moving in their places. "But together."

"Together. I'd like that. I don't know who I am anymore. What I'm good for. But I - you." She shrugged and then shifted to lean her head on his shoulder again. "You said I make it quiet. You make it steady. For me, anyway. I can see where I'm going better."

Adam nuzzled against her hair. "Shall we, may we, migrate to your bed?" He chose the word deliberately, as if facing the word here would make the rest of it flow, releasing something that had been caged up for far too long. "And stretch out and be together."

Thalia looked up into his eyes. "Oh, I'd like that. And we might both sleep as well as we're going to."

CHAPTER 37
WEDNESDAY AFTERNOON

T he next morning was a flurry of waiting, it turned out. Adam had snuck out her room around dawn, so he could properly emerge from his own bedroom. Mrs Harley disappeared shortly after breakfast to go meet Great-Aunt Avis at the train, following her trips by ferry and portal.

It meant they were stuck, sitting around and waiting, for most of the day, until near three in the afternoon. Finally, Thalia heard the pony cart pull up in front of the house. Just the one old woman getting out, Thalia's parents were nowhere in sight. Ten minutes later, Mrs Harley came through. "The mistress would like you to join her upstairs after supper, when she's rested."

"My parents?" Thalia hesitated.

"Gone back to London, mistress. Mistress Morgan's orders." Mrs Harley went around, giving the library one more good dusting. "Go have a walk, please?"

It was the 'please' that got Thalia. "Of course." They had gone out, down to the orchard, and back up again. The apples were definitely ripening. "I'll need to be spending some time down here this week. Sorting out the..." Adam waved at it. "You?"

"I can't think past this evening." Thalia said. "But we'll see. Something." She softened her uncertainty, the way it made him suddenly wary, with a kiss. She took her time. They'd learned last night there was no reason for either of them to rush, it went badly. And plenty of reason to take their time and linger in the moment, too.

After supper, Mrs Harley showed them up to Great-Aunt Avis's room. "Please let me know if she needs anything." Thalia caught the note of worry there. Mrs Harley wasn't sure how to read what was going on, that was suddenly clear, and she did care for Great-Aunt Avis.

Each of them took up a seat on the sofa, facing Great-Aunt Avis's chair. She wielded the space like a weapon, as if she were laying everything out to her specification. Thalia hadn't seen her before she left. She couldn't measure the difference, whatever it was. But there was a twinkle in the old woman's eyes that made Thalia the tiniest bit less nervous.

"You are Thalia." It wasn't a question. "And you are?"

"Adam Walton, ma'am. A friend of Thalia's, my uncle lives in the village."

That got a regal incline of the head. "And are you also responsible for the events of two nights ago?" She left the implications there, dangling. On one hand, Thalia was impressed by her control, her deftness, her self-possession. On the other hand, what was one supposed to say to something like that?

Adam cleared his throat. "It has been my pleasure to assist Thalia in tending to the needs of the house and land."

Great-Aunt Avis laughed. It was a rusty laugh, like she hadn't permitted herself that kind of freedom in far too long. But you could see and hear in it what she'd been like in her prime, her twenties or thirties, whenever they were. It wasn't flappers and Bright Young Things, then, but Thalia supposed every generation had those who lived for the flow of the moment. "Well said." She leaned forward, hands resting on the cane that had been propped by her knee. "You let her go. The cuckoo."

Thalia froze, but then she made herself nod. She certainly couldn't make herself speak, all the words had got clumped in her throat.

"Good. Thank you." Great-Aunt Avis bestowed it as a blessing, then leaned back, looking suddenly like she was a marionette whose strings had been cut. They sat like that, the three of them, for ages. At least five minutes, once Thalia started counting the ticks of the clock, up over three hundred, three-fifty.

"You have questions." Great-Aunt Avis pushed herself upright again. "Would you pour, dear? Spare my hands?" There was a tea tray set out on the side table, and Thalia nodded. "Cream and two sugar, please."

Fussing with the tea took another several minutes, and it was only when Thalia sat down again, barely risking a glance at Adam, that her great-aunt went on.

"I was young and foolish once. Young, foolish, beautiful, and desperate. It's an old house, and Father had been a spendthrift about money. Mother, too. More corvid than sense. Not that corvids aren't sharp birds, mind, but they do like the shine of a thing. But they'd set my dowry aside, in a trust with the Scali even they couldn't touch."

Thalia couldn't argue with that at all. Great-Aunt Avis went on without a pause. "And then there was Franklin Morgan. From an excellent family, and much deeper roots. I'd lived in the house when I was little, and I wanted to stay in it. We needed money to do that. And so I married him. It was supposed to be a mutual benefit. Money, land, property."

Her lips pursed. "He wasn't as awful as might be. But Franklin had expectations. Standards. The least sign of age had to be sanded away, brushed out of existence, as soon as it appeared. He dyed his hair from the day he turned twenty-one and spotted a single silver strand amongst the black. Hours, given over to his toilette every day. It makes for a small mind, I've found, to my sorrow."

Thalia was not entirely sure what to make of the implications there. Adam saved her from asking. "Did he expect the same from you, ma'am?"

"Oh, oh yes." She considered. "Your - what was he to you, dear?"

Thalia cleared her throat. "My father's uncle, Great-Aunt Avis. Papa's the only son of his generation."

Great-Aunt Avis nodded. "He expected the best, and that included me. And he chipped away at me, about my looks. Always bringing me advertisements for a cold creme. Or leaving some issue of *The Englishwoman's Domestic Magazine* for me to read about the latest way to tend my skin or my corset." She grimaced. "He approved of tight-lacing, too. You're very lucky not to need to do that, dear."

Thalia couldn't help snorting. "Mother still wears one. Lighter than those, but she insists it improves the posture."

Great-Aunt Avis waved a hand. "You've a fine upright figure, and you've got lovely shoulders, if you show them off a little. Now, what was I saying?" She took a sip of her tea and went on. "We made a proper show of it, but time went on, and I was older. And I hadn't given him a child, as I should have. Mind, that was mostly his fault. I was some-thing of an innocent when we married. But even I knew that a man had to come to his wife's bed more than once in six months to have much hope of a babe."

"Great-Uncle Franklin was a man of unshakeable opinions, then?" She could see how that ran in the family, though her parents had obviously been more successful at the bedding part of the marriage than that.

Great-Aunt Avis laughed one of those sharp laughs again, beaming at her. "You are clever, aren't you? And clear-tongued. That's even better. At any rate, I wasn't measuring up, and I got rather desperate. It was my house, of course, or so you'd have thought, my dowry, but the laws were rather a mess, then. It wasn't like we were landed, with a proper line of descent that ran through magic. There would have been all sorts of fuss. So I set about doing what I could to keep him."

Thalia decidedly didn't like the sound of that. "Keep him, Great-Aunt Avis?"

"Oh, yes." The old woman shrugged. "Cosmetics go only so far. Charms, a bit further, and proper clothing, shaped to suit. But I needed more than that. I happened to hear, in passing, a bit of folklore, that cuckoos bring the spring. If they bring the spring, then, well. They take it away again when they leave in the fall, don't they? Like the tales of Persephone? That's what I called her, you know. The cuckoo."

The weight of it hit Thalia. It was falling into some awful story, the reverse of the myth. One where instead of endless winter and barren lands with Demeter's grief, it was a perpetual static spring where nothing grew properly, nothing turned round to harvest. You could starve as easily on the few spring greens as in a brown and dead field.

If she had any sense, she'd leave now. Something had got broken for Great-Aunt Avis a long time ago. And it was at least part Great-Uncle Franklin's fault, Thalia was very clear about that. But despite all that, despite the wrong-ness, Thalia wanted to understand what had happened. She had to have the whole story in her hands.

"Where did you find it?"

Great-Aunt Avis shrugged. "Oh, I've long since forgotten now. That was near enough eighty years ago, dear. Do you remember what you did eight months ago?"

Thalia grimaced. She did, yes, but only because it was the exhaustive drumbeat of all the things she'd done wrong that month. The monologue that played out in her head when she wanted to do anything else. Adam, thankfully, spoke up. "We've different sorts of memories than you do, ma'am, I'm sure. May I ask, um, perhaps the context?"

"Oh, that? I found old books, not from before the Pact, but old enough to have some real magic in them, old magic, before everything got split apart. It had a recipe for a lure, for good hunting, for birds, and I made that up. I'm not much in a stillroom, but I could do that much, and I made some of my own creams and bath oils and such. I had a proper stillroom, then. And I caught up the cuckoo, and brought her up in a wicker cage, and made her a nice comfortable home."

Then she frowned. "Only, well. She stayed. Stayed and stayed and stayed. I could open the cage, to clean it, to feed her. I felt a pull to, no matter what else I wanted to do with my day. A compulsion, that's the word." She chattered along, as if she had just ignored all the implications, the encompassing magic.

"Did you manage it all by yourself?" Thalia was just as compelled, now, to stay and find out what had happened.

"Oh, not entirely. Mrs Harley came and found me. Dear Florentia, she's been so very loyal. She'd help me tend

Persephone, make sure all the windows and doors were closed, the curtains shut, the charms redone every day so Franklin wouldn't hear a thing."

"And you never wanted to let the cuckoo go?" Adam spoke again, navigating the way through, rather like a tugboat in harbour must be, fierce and strong and determined.

"Want and action are two different things entirely, young man." The response was immediate, sharp, and quelling. Then Great-Aunt Avis shook her head. "I couldn't. I thought about it, many nights, in my bed, and I couldn't make my hands move to even the smallest piece of it. Nothing that would free me from my choice."

Thalia considered, working through it in her head. Keeping the cuckoo was a great wrong. But if Great-Aunt Avis was telling the truth, she'd had little choice, since. On the other hand, there was no reason to assume she was entirely truthful now. She'd spent most of her life lying about almost everything, at least by omission, as far as Thalia could see.

It left Thalia utterly unsure what to do here. Should she feel sympathy, or should she blame? Should she scold or reassure that all that was over now? Great-Aunt Avis was a stranger, in all the ways that mattered, not even a blood relation. Whatever real empathy Thalia had for awful circumstances had run out long ago, sometime during the War, with her magic.

CHAPTER 38
WEDNESDAY EVENING

Adam let Avis talk on. He was beginning to think of her as Great-Aunt Avis himself, safer to stick to ma'am. He had no idea how she'd take that sort of thing. When the conversation stopped again, he cleared his throat. "Did you realise the effect on the house?"

"The house was just fine, young man. Better than fine, actually, we've had much less maintenance. The gardens." She shrugged. "Tending to that, the plans for it, that was my role. Franklin didn't bother. And he was often up in town, anyway." It wasn't clear from her tone whether she meant Trellech or London, and it might well have been both. Avis leaned forward and added conspiratorially. "I'm sure he had mistresses. Well, at least three that I know of, and likely more."

Adam had no idea what to say to that, so he nodded cautiously. "And the gardens, ma'am?"

"Oh, I arranged to plant things where it wouldn't be so noticeable. Things that bloom over and over again, given the right conditions. The greenhouse helped, but the rest of the garden has always been a trial. We've got most of our produce from the village."

"And you haven't gone down there?" Adam was sure about this part.

"Goodness, no. I mean, they'd notice, wouldn't they? We didn't socialise with the village much when I was younger. The other manor house nearby isn't magical, and - well, there are standards, aren't there?" Avis was, fundamentally, Victorian in outlook, with all that implied, Adam felt. A steadfastness to ideas and ways of being in the world that wouldn't budge for anyone.

And the village would have noticed. Anyone sensible would have noticed when she didn't age for decades. "And Mrs Harley didn't comment? Or, I believe Thalia mentioned you saw the doctor regularly?"

Avis blinked at him. "Why should she? Florentia is a dear, mind you. Always thinking about things. And taking such good care of me." She snorted. "As to the doctor, he'd come up every month or two, we'd play a game of chess, and he'd go away. I wouldn't dream of an examination or any such thing. Often in dim light, too."

"Did you like how it was?" Adam felt there was something he was missing. That he and Thalia might be missing, though it wasn't like he could stop and consult her. They certainly hadn't known each other long enough yet to do it subtly. And for all Avis had been out of society for a long time, he didn't want to assume she'd miss the more obvious signs and gestures. She struck him as very sharp, really, considering everything.

The question did make her stop and think. "I liked being young. Until it got very tiring to keep up. Thinning, and not in the way that leads to better lines for one's frocks."

Thalia cleared her throat. "So what changed here, Great-Aunt Avis? I mean, here we are."

"Well." Avis shrugged. "I couldn't open the cage. I've never asked Florentia. I mean, how would you start that conversation, goodness? But she never did either. I couldn't make plans to leave on my own. Somehow, they always fell through? But your father and mother have a certain stubbornness of purpose, and once they insisted on my leaving, came and packed me up, I could, well. Let them." She spread out her hands. "And the hotel in France really was quite lovely."

Thalia pursed her lips. "And you - did you wonder if we'd find out?"

"Oh, yes. I'm glad it was you, dear. Not your sister. Your brother might have done the right thing, but only if you put it to him as a battle strategy."

Thalia froze for a moment, then her hand went to her mouth. Before she could do anything else, Adam shifted on the sofa. To be close enough she could turn into his shoulder. Avis was honest, more or less, but it was a brutal sort of self-centred honesty. Adam didn't much like it. Thalia leaned against him at least, rather than pulling away, and Adam went on to spare her trying to figure out what words were too quickly. "So when the opportunity presented itself, you took advantage."

"Oh, yes. And I really was rather badly off, I gather. There was a pleasant doctor in France. A British one, but very sensible. A woman, if you'd believe it." She shrugged. "At any rate, she prescribed rest and good food, which was easy enough to do. And staying in a warmer climate for a while. Until I felt like returning."

Adam nodded. "And then, two nights ago?"

"Oh, I'd drifted off. The timelessness gets one, and it

turns out that was the same there as here. What does one do after supper if one no longer dances or charms men?"

"Ma'am, you are still quite aware how to charm, surely." Adam could at least attempt gallantry here. It made her dimple and beam.

"At any rate, I felt when it happened. When the bird was gone. And I knew I could and should come home. The question, of course, is what one does now."

Thalia had somewhat recovered by this point. "I'm sure my parents were rather put out to be sent off again, Great-Aunt Avis."

Avis giggled like a schoolgirl. "And how! Your father has always had a sour expression from the time he was young, I've thought. But they would rather be home with their comforts and not needing to appear to fuss over me." She looked Thalia up and down. "Now, you, you have spirit. Like I was, when I was young."

Thalia mustered enough coherence to say, "That's not how I'd describe myself, Great-Aunt." But she did look a bit pleased at the comment. The sort of thing Adam now suspected she'd be chewing on for a good while.

"You should stay. Do you need to go back to, where was it, London? Not even Trellech, my. Very unusual for a girl."

"I've been on my own for a decade, Great-Aunt Avis. But someone else is using my flat. And of course..." She glanced at Adam. "I'm clear Adam's not made to live in town. Not enough apples."

Adam felt himself flushing at that. It was all true, but it wasn't just the words themselves, but how she'd said them. Fondly affectionate, a warmth he hadn't felt directed toward him in a decade. She'd shown it last night, in their quiet conversation and touch, but this was even more so. Saying it in front of someone else made it more real.

"There is no reason you shouldn't stay." Avis shook her head and got a thoughtful look. She then picked up her cane and thumped it on the floor three times. Then she settled into contented silence. Not long after, they all heard steps on the staircase, and then a knock on the door.

"Come, come." Mrs Harley came in, leaving the door ajar behind her.

"Florentia, dear. First, as I'm sure you're aware, Persephone is no longer at home. Thanks to these two young people." Avis's voice was brisk, clear, as precise as Adam's father's in the middle of a business exchange. "Thalia will be staying on for the time being. Would you make sure she has all she needs for her comfort? I expect we will also be seeing Master Walton around regularly. Make sure a room is made up for him as needed."

Mrs Harley glanced from one to the other. "Yes, ma'am. Of course." She didn't comment about the cuckoo, but of course, what could she possibly have said to that?

Avis sailed on. "Arrange an appointment with my solicitor, amending my will, please. As soon as possible. And my man of business." She eyed Adam. "Do you think your uncle would take on a planning commission here? To set out a proper kitchen garden, and whatever else the estate needs?"

Adam considered. To be honest, his uncle was going more than a bit batty with boredom. They could arrange a cart up here easily enough, and chairs for his planning. "I would be glad to ask him, ma'am. He might well enjoy the challenge." How Adam was going to explain the state of the garden and the landscaping to Uncle Benjamin would at least give him something to think about at four this morning.

"There. Please consult Thalia as well about meals. I'm sure the young have different preferences."

"The food has been excellent, Great-Aunt Avis." Thalia tried to get a comment in, but Avis swept on.

"There, now, I need my rest. It has been a long day. I will see you tomorrow, Thalia. Florentia, half an hour and then I'll want your help to change for bed."

Mrs Harley nodded, and stood back, waiting for Thalia and Adam to stand up. She closed the door behind them. Without a word, Thalia gestured downstairs and Adam nodded. Mrs Harley stopped at the bottom. She murmured "Thank you, mistress, master." Then she promptly disappeared through the kitchen door into her own realm.

Five minutes later, once they were well away from the house, Thalia finally spoke up. "Stay tonight, would you? If it's not a bother for your uncle?"

"I was about to ask if you wanted me to stay." Adam shook his head. "How I'm going to explain the garden..."

"Tell him the truth." Adam gaped at Thalia, blinking. Thalia went on. "Not all of it. Just say there was some magic affecting how time worked. He's seen the apples. I expect he'd like the challenge of putting it right."

"I can't imagine what it's done to the soil quality. Probably either fabulous, nothing grown in it for ages, or it's horrendous. He'll have fun with the testing, and we can start that now." Adam shook his head. "I expect he'll recruit me to do all the moving around bits. Maybe we can get a class round from Snap, to do the testing." That would be a great deal of work, tramping over the entire property, and Adam certainly wasn't up to it.

"I can help. Besides writing. I mean."

"Of course you'd be writing. I don't want to get in the way of that." Adam turned and took her hands, facing her.

"I want you to figure out what that's like for you now. If you want."

She stood on tiptoe, to kiss his lips once, gently. Not the sort of kiss that would push either of them to breathlessness, just enough to remind them they had that, too. "Thank you. For being curious about what might come out of it. It helps. Thinking someone's interested?"

Adam snorted. "Don't I know it. You be interested in the gardens and the apples. I'll be interested in your words. That works out well."

Thalia nodded and then leaned her head on his shoulder. "I don't think Great-Aunt Avis is entirely sane, you know?"

"Do you think the cuckoo was something that broke the Pact? It can't be, though. Or she'd not be here. But close to it." He swallowed. "How it felt, when we first looked." He was, perhaps, a little surprised to be brave enough to say it so directly, to make that gesture at the Silence.

"Not broke it. Bent it. Like breaking the spine of a book, and the pages coming loose when they get brittle."

Adam shivered at that metaphor. "Rather." He let out a long, slow breath. "You don't feel unsafe here? As if Great-Aunt Avis might do something else?"

Thalia was quiet, just resting her head and breathing for a good minute. "No. Not anymore. And you saw her. I don't think she's going to go out catching more birds. Whatever was lurking is gone. It will be better with more house cleaning and sprucing up, and more plants and, I don't know. Being very adamant about seasonal decorations for a bit?"

"Well, there's Christmas coming up. We can get in lots of evergreens and mistletoe and holly, and go on from there."

"Pussywillows in the spring." Thalia said promptly. "I love how they feel. And there's all sorts of spring flowers."

"Overflowing summer bouquets. Gourds and apples in the fall. You could talk to Mrs Harley about playing that up in the menu, too."

"She was - she was so relieved, wasn't she?" Thalia shook her head. "Maybe sometime she'll tell me what it was like for her?" They both heard the owl, then a long hoot, and Thalia smiled. "We don't need to sort all of that out now. Plenty of time for that later."

EPILOGUE

DECEMBER 1928

Thalia glanced out the window. The dusting of snow that had fallen overnight was still there, at least on the grass, and being tremendously scenic. She'd heard the pony cart a few minutes ago, but had been so focused she hadn't managed to look up as Adam drove it up toward the restored stables.

Now, though, she heard the soft sound of the bell behind her, charmed to be muffled just the right amount. It was loud enough she'd hear it if she wasn't deeply focused, but deep and quiet enough not to startle her. None of that shrill sound. "Come in?"

"Tea?" Adam had a mug in each hand, good hearty country ceramic, from that summer's fair. "Mrs Beeton is just putting things away in the kitchen, but I said we could manage fine with soup and sandwiches tonight. Let them settle and get warm."

"Oh, that's fine, of course. Long day for them. And you. Sit, sit." She gestured, and Adam settled into the chair by her desk they kept for these moments. She'd taken over the old office for her own, painting the bookshelves in shades of bright teal and golden yellow and accents of a deep glowing red. It was terribly outre. Her parents didn't approve at all, but it harkened back to an older time in the house, she thought.

"There's a letter from the Gospatricks, you'll want a look at that, but they asked if we'd go round sometime in the new year, Elen has another idea about something. Mrs Harley wrote back. Checking in how we were doing now it's winter." It made her reflect back. Great-Aunt Avis had seen one more winter, one more early spring, it turned out. But she'd died peacefully in her sleep, two days before anyone saw a cuckoo in the area. Mrs Harley had given her notice once the funeral was over, saying she'd be glad to help find someone suitable. She felt if Mrs Harley had also wanted to keep an eye out, just in case her great-aunt had some other exceedingly poor idea, just as Thalia and Adam had. The funeral had liberated her from that particular burden, however it had come about that she was carrying it.

It had been a shock, somehow, to find that Great-Aunt Avis had left Thalia the house. And yet, who else would she leave it to? Her father obviously thought he was the only candidate. But no, the house and enough money they could live comfortably for a good long while. Those were Thalia's. Enough money she could figure out what she wanted to write, without needing to rely on it for her rent or food. To have a breathing space.

Adam had plans to make the farmland pay for itself and more. He'd installed a useful breed of sheep. There was a small dairy with a reasonable supply of milk for the house and some to sell in the village. As well as the apples, always the apples. His uncle had turned the orchards over to him this year entirely, and there were bottles and bottles of cider, fermenting away in the sheds now.

All of that brought in a bit extra, beyond what they ate and drank. In time, they had space for cheese-making, or perhaps some other crafting. That was all well and good, but what she really loved was seeing him out on the land, learning all the ways it shifted from day to day and week to week.

They'd knocked together a set of rooms to be properly theirs, with a spare bed tucked away for when one of them had a particularly bad night. Thalia's sister was now on about when they were going to have little ones. Where Thalia might have argued once, she let it flow over her. Probably never. Children made unpredictably loud noises. They couldn't understand when they were very young, why a parent couldn't do a thing.

Perhaps eventually they'd look at adopting someone old enough to understand that neither Thalia nor Adam were quite as other people were. And probably wouldn't ever be. They'd always need a bit more quiet, a bit more of a stick to lean on, a bit more time than others.

Or perhaps Thalia and Adam would instead be a quiet, restful space for a series of artists and crafters who needed a sturdy roof and a good meal. Along with some time to come to grips with what they'd been through, in bigger ways and in smaller ones. That would be a fine thing too. To be a space where people could find their sea legs in the world after some personal disaster.

She'd clearly missed something Adam had said. He was leaning back with his hands cupped around the mug, grinning at her. "Get lost in your head again?"

"In the good way. Thinking about what had changed. No, I told Mrs Harley we've been loving Mrs Beeton's soups, and Mr Beeton's done wonders getting the fireplaces to draw properly, and they both seem to be very happy. I hope they're happy?" They'd both been in service before they were married. They'd taken other work while they raised a family, but this sort of position suited them both well, it turned out.

"They're very happy. She was saying on the way up it was just the right amount going on. Our meals, the farmhands when they're up here. The maid." They had another girl from the orphanage, who had a room up at the top of the house. It made for comfortable sounds in the evening, not unsettling ones. He flicked a finger at the desk. "How's that? Oh, wait!" He rummaged in the inner pockets of his jacket. "I said I'd bring the evening mail up, spare the postman. Here."

He handed over a long envelope. Thalia recognised the address. It was a thin letter, too thin to mean much, surely? She reached for the letter and slit it open, then read it. And then read it again.

"Thal?" Adam leaned in. "You all right?"

"They're not buying it. Not exactly? But they'd like me to write up half a dozen like it, and see if they can make a series out of the idea. A proper serial." She'd written up a story that was half legend, half fancy, about magic and the moor, both the wilder magics and the tamer domestic ones. And she'd had so many ideas for a series.

The first story had been fine, she supposed, but it hadn't been quite right. Broad enough. The idea she could branch out, that they'd be interested in seeing that. It wasn't a sale, not yet, but it was the promise of, just maybe, something much better.

Thalia set her mug down. "Walk before supper? Or are you worn out?"

Adam smiled. "Walk."

IF YOU ENJOYED *BOOK* and would like to read more of this series, please sign up for my mailing list to get all the latest news and fun extras.

Your reviews (on whatever review site you use) are much appreciated, too!

Read on for more historical details about this book and more about the world of Albion.

AUTHOR'S NOTE

Thank you so much for joining me for Thalia and Adam's story. My thanks as always go to my editor, Kiya Nicoll, to my early readers, and to a couple of others who kindly shared their thoughts on the impact of some of the more physical symptoms of PTSD on the body. This book is also much better for me attending a panel on Gothic fiction at this year's *Flights of Foundry* virtual convention.

Today's author notes start with a few general notes about the book, then talk in a bit more detail about shell shock and PTSD. (If you'd rather not read about that, skip to the third section starting with "Anna and Una" for the notes on the rest of the book.)

Overall, I'd wanted to try a more Gothic romance feel for a book, and a remote house on the edge of Dartmoor was just the thing. Of course, the context of Albion gave me a little more scope for spookiness than some of the classics in the genre. The key idea came when I was reading about British seasonal folklore and the animals, plants, and birds associated with different aspects. As soon as I read about there being lore about people trying to capture a cuckoo to maintain an eternal spring, I knew I had a story. Normally, they arrive in April, bringing the warmer months with them, and return to Africa in August and signal the coming autumn.

As Thalia comments during the book, there is a radius effect. Adam's uncle's orchards are on the edge of it, so time moves oddly but isn't in stasis, and the house is far enough away that other parts of the village aren't affected. (I have a map with a radius drawn on it, to make sure.) The effects are a bit varied - many body processes continue reasonably normally, because someone's inherent physicality and magic overwhelms the stasis, but others like nails or hair growing slow way down. Similarly, plants stay alive, but they don't change much with the seasons.

The **roses** are Rosa chinensis 'Mutabilis', a repeat bloomer introduced to Europe in the 19th century. That means they'll keep blooming through the summer.

I originally wrote a version of **chapters 11 and 12** where Adam and Thalia realised they were both magical. It's fairly rare for me to go back and rewrite an entire chapter, but when I got through chapter 12, I slept on it, and decided to try it the other way. As that's what ended up in the book, you know I found it more interesting for that to be ambiguous for them both much longer.

Before I get into the other details, I want to touch on a sizeable part of this book, namely Adam's **shell shock** (which we'd now call post-traumatic stress disorder), and Thalia's own PTSD, which was not particularly recognised by anyone in her life. While there were cases of it earlier in military history, mostly related to infantry and exposure to explosions and shelling, it became a much larger concern during and after the Great War.

The treatments (as briefly mentioned in chapter 31) were often brutal, an attempt to get a response to stiumuli by any means available. For a time, even using the term shell shock was censored and banned, and it was only in the last year of the War and the later aftermath that any real progress was made on offering caring and supportive treatment that allowed many of the men with shell shock to return to their lives in some form. Craiglockhart was one of the best known institutions treating men with shell shock. The Gospatricks, mentioned in several places, appear in *Carry On*, as well as briefly in *Casting Nasturtiums* (collected in my *Winter's Charms* anthology).

That didn't help everyone. PTSD and other similar trauma can have a huge effect not only on someone's mental health (including depression, anxiety, insomnia, and other concerns), but also on the mind and body. A number of people experience the kinds of physical impact that Adam does - dropping things, not being able to trust where his feet are. Some people have systemic issues like challenges in regulating blood pressure that make it tricky to stand up. And of course, people may also have flashbacks, memories, disassociation, or other experiences.

A number of my characters have these experiences to some degree, but Adam had a much worse experience in a number of ways, and the impact has been much more serious for him. A decade later, the symptoms themselves have settled down, but he's not able to handle many kinds of work or living situations with anything like equilibrium. Thalia has a different set of challenges, where she's constantly vigilant and anxious, torn between wanting to be around the artistic friends she's made, but finding the noise and chaos of the city to be difficult.

I wanted to give these two people a space where they could have a good life. And because it's a romance, to have that together, with someone who understands all the ways the mind and body can be complicated and frustrating.

Anna and Una, mentioned briefly in chapter 1, appear in "A Dog's Chance", which was written for the *Her Magical Pet* charity anthology. It's also available as an extra if you sign up for my newsletter. (Sign up, and every email has a link to all the treats. It's fine to subscribe and then unsubscribe if the ongoing newsletter is not your thing.)

The Second Pan is a magical literary journal, riffing on the many literary journals of the period.

Apples took so much research. I have a deep appreciation for the lovely people who build and maintain databases of apple varieties. I spent quite a long time narrowing down apples that were known to be in Devon, and which were old enough varieties to have been growing in that orchard for a bit. And then, of course, sorting them by when they ripen, figuring out what they look like in detail. All the apple varieties are real, I didn't make any up. The customs Adam follows, about greeting the "Old Man" of the orchard (the oldest tree), are common to a number of places.

Pete Brown's book *The Apple Orchard: The Story of Our Most English Fruit* was also a great help.

Snap is one of the Five Schools, and not one I've had cause to spend any time with before this book. Adam, of course, attended. It's the school which focuses on agricultural magics in all their varieties, and students who attend come away with a wide range of skills and magical approaches to keeping livestock thriving, tending their fields and orchards, preventing and mitigating blights, and much more.

The Snap tie is green and tan. They're rather likely colours for an agricultural focus, but when I started looking at other ties that might be unremarkable in the area, I realised that the Devonshire regimental tie was a very close match. Of course, if you only know one or the other, they're easy to mistake for each other. (And Thalia is more used to looking for the pendant or other piece of jewellery with a set stone that's used by most people who attended Schola.)

Thalia's musings on the word **forest** have to do with the fact that originally in English, a forest was a legal designation, a piece of land set aside for hunting, by the King or a designated lord. Think of it as a hunting preserve that often happens to have trees, rather than the trees being inherent in the definition.

Eve's pudding and **Devon flats** are both baked goods (as I hope is clear from context). Eve's pudding involves apples being baked in a batter, often served with a thick egg and cream based custard. Devon flats are a classic biscuit (or in American, cookie) which use clotted cream where other recipes might use butter and/or cream.

The **Hairy Hands of Dartmoor** are a real story, what we'd think of as an urban legend these days. There are several reports of hairy hands reaching and yanking steering wheels of cars into the retaining wall along that stretch. Theories on what was happening vary.

The **hare** legends throughout the book all come from local sources.

On that note, **Sabine Baring-Gould** was a rector who wrote an astonishing number of books about Dartmoor (his beloved home) and many other topics, including a great deal about folklore. The pieces Thalia quotes are all from his *A Book of Dartmoor* which is available on Project Gutenberg and a number of other sites, since it is now in the public domain. I first became aware of Baring-Gould thanks to Laurie R. King's *The Moor,* one of the books in her Russell and Holmes series. (Yes, that Holmes.)

I'm normally very careful about checking what words were in use in whatever year I'm writing, but one of my early readers spotted me trying to use the word tsunami, when Thalia is thinking about flooding. (My early readers are the best at this sort of thing.)

The song and story about the sisters and the harp is known as **Twa Sisters** most commonly. Not the most useful title, I know! It has a long history, with more than twenty versions in English, dating back to before 1656. You may also find it called "Minnorie" or "Binnorie" or the "Cruel Sister" or "The Wind and the Rain" among other titles. It involves one of the sisters getting jealous of the other, drowning her, and then someone making a harp from the drowned sister's bones, which then sings of the murder. Murder ballads are consistently themselves, here.

The glass flowers are a real thing, and they are utterly gorgeous. I'm familiar with them because of the extensive collection of glass flowers in the Harvard Natural History Museum, a collection of over 4,000 models made by father and son (Leopold and Rudolph Blaschka) between 1886 and 1936. If you search on "glass flowers", you should get a number of wonderful photos and explanations. While this was the largest and most varied collection, glass flowers were made for study and university use in the period by other people. They're stunningly beautiful works of art, every detail perfectly tinted for learning.

Lord Teague, mentioned briefly, is indeed Mabyn Teague's son. (She appears primarily in *The Hare and the Oak*.) She regrets the state of her relationship with him at that point, but he is doing reasonably well by his land.

Giant Hogweed is a real plant, growing to huge sizes, invasive in Britain, western Europe, and North America. It can grow to between 2 and 5 metres (6 to 15 feet), and the sap is phototoxic, raising blisters and scars on exposed skin.

Finally, this book touches on the way the War damaged the **landsense** of so many men (and some women), and how listening to the people who went to Snap might be a help here. If you're interested in the land magic aspect, the *Land Mysteries* series (coming out starting in November 2022) deal with this aspect of Albion in much more depth. They're set in and around the Second World War, featuring characters who've appeared in my other books.

Again, thank you for reading! The best way to know what I'm up to is to sign up for my newsletter, but I also share book releases on my social media sites. Signing up for the newsletter will also get you extras.